Copyright © 2024 by Melody Tyden

All rights reserved.

Cover design by: GetCovers

HONOUR AMONG ROGUES

MELODY TYDEN

CONTENTS

CHAPTER ONE

~Savannah~

The two-lane highway stretched straight ahead of us as far as I could see, mountains to our left and open fields to our right as our trio of werewolves headed north towards the Canadian border in Felix's comfortable truck.

I'd never been over the border before. Hell, I'd only been out of Montana once, and that had been to visit my mother when she retired to Arizona. In fact, I'd barely been off pack land since my overprotective older brother took over as Alpha of our werewolf pack from my equally overprotective father.

"If a wolf's not your mate, he only wants one thing," Vaughan growled at me the last time I brought it up, when I simply asked for permission to make a trip into the nearest human city with some wolves from a neighbouring pack.

My brother and I shared the same curly hair, the deep shade of brown matching our eyes, but he had more than half a foot's advantage on me in height and considerably more bulk, which he tried to use to intimidate me when he wanted to get his way.

"Trust me, Sav. They're pigs."

"Well, maybe I'm in the mood for some bacon," I retorted. "Or some nice, juicy pork chops I can really sink my teeth into."

Licking my lips for good measure, I placed a hand on my hip, jutting it out to draw attention to my figure, leaving him in no doubt that I had fully grown up, no matter what he would like to believe.

Vaughan groaned, his eyes closing as if he were in pain. "Really, Sav? I'm your brother."

"Then stop trying to clam-jam me!"

A laugh echoed from behind me where Felix, my brother's Beta and best friend, had walked into the Alpha's office. Slightly shorter than my brother but just as well-built, blond-haired and blue-eyed, I'd had a pretty big crush on him growing up but he'd never given me the least bit of encouragement. Probably because my brother would have cut off his balls if he so much as looked at me without us being mates.

"I'm not sure what I'm interrupting, but it sounds a hell of a lot more interesting than last month's utility bills," Felix said with a grin.

My brother gratefully ushered him in. "You're not interrupting anything. Savannah, my answer is final. You can have these other wolves over here if you want a girls' night but you're not going off our territory."

Only two months had passed since that argument, but the tables had completely turned. My moody, sometimes-loner of a brother finally found his mate, but in the mess that accompanied their meeting, he found himself in debt to the Alpha of the Ravenstone pack up in Alberta. To satisfy his obligation, the Alpha asked that Vaughan send me up to meet with the ranking members of his pack to see if I'd like to take any of them to be my mate.

It sounded like Vaughan's worst nightmare and my wildest dream come true: a bunch of virile male wolves all eager to please while I got my pick of the bunch. In my mind, I pictured a werewolf version of the Bachelorette where the contestants would have to not only impress me but fight each other to prove their worth.

Preferably while naked.

The idea that Vaughan would actually agree seemed impossible, and yet, he did. He must have felt really guilty about breaking the treaty he'd signed to mate with the Alpha's daughter, Amanda. When he met his true fated mate, that contract went out the window, despite the fact that the other woman had already arrived at our pack, ready to take up her new position.

She sat beside me in the truck as we crossed the last few miles of highway leading up to the border, her pretty, soft, dark-brown hair hanging down over her face, obscuring it from view as she looked out the window to her side. Amanda had hardly said more than a few words on the trip so far, obviously not looking forward to returning to her pack cloaked in failure.

Behind the wheel on my other side, Felix acted as escort for the both of us, per Vaughan's orders. He'd been instructed to stay with me until I decided which of the men of the Ravenstone pack I would bless with my mating oath. Of course, I might not choose any of them. Vaughan had made that clear to both me and the Ravenstone Alpha: the choice would be entirely mine, even if my choice was to decline them all and go back home.

It seemed risk-free, and guaranteed far more excitement than a typical night in the Crimsontooth pack, especially now that my brother and his new mate would be spending every free moment alone together.

Finally, my life was about to get interesting.

"What can you tell me about the single men in the pack, Amanda?" I blurted out, unable to keep my questions in any longer. Felix shot me a warning look, but I'd managed to wait a couple of hours before asking, which should have earned me a prize for restraint. I'd been thinking of little else.

Thankfully, she didn't seem offended by the question. Rousing herself as if her mind had been far away, Amanda straightened in her seat. "I can't say I ever thought of them in mating terms. Most of the leadership team are older than me, which makes them much older than you."

Irritation tugged at the corners of my mouth. I wasn't *that* much younger than her, and at twenty-two, I was tired of everyone treating me like a child.

"And there are that many who aren't mated?" Felix asked, even though he just gave me a hard time for my curiosity.

"Some have lost their mates, some have stayed single by choice."

"By choice?" I repeated. "What if they find their fated mates?"

She simply shrugged. "In our pack, the mate bond is considered optional. You can accept it if you want to, but there's no expectation that you will. For those in power, the expectation is often the opposite, especially if the fated mate doesn't enhance your own position."

That sounded rather cold. I'd been raised to view the mate bond as a precious gift, though it didn't always work out. Sometimes, people didn't find their mates, or didn't find them soon enough. Vaughan almost didn't. And sometimes, a mate wasn't a good match.

More often than not, though, a fated mate was considered the ultimate goal, so it surprised me to hear her pack didn't agree.

"They'll consider Sav a good catch because of her connections?" Felix guessed, and Amanda nodded.

"With my father's approval, she'll be seen as a desirable mate. You really will have your pick."

Those last words were directed at me with a smile, but a touch of unhappiness lurked behind it. Did that stem from her recently-thwarted mating pact with my brother, or did it have another meaning?

To be honest, I didn't love the idea that the men would only be interested in me because of my position as the Crimsontooth Alpha's sister. I wanted to be mated with someone so passionate about me that he'd stop at nothing to have me, no matter my status. I wanted someone who wanted *me* for exactly who I was, warts and all.

My friends teased me for having impossibly high standards, but I didn't see the problem. If we were just having fun, a delectable body would suffice, but the guy I promised to spend my life with? He was going to have to have a lot more than that going for him.

What she said about the mate bond being optional still intrigued me, so I returned to that. "There must be a lot of rejections in your pack, then."

"There are," she agreed mildly. "Or sometimes, there's no rejection, but they carry on as if the bond never happened until they meet someone else."

"Seriously?" Felix sounded just as surprised about that as I felt, his eyes darting from the straight road in front of us to Amanda on the far side of the truck. "That must be torture. Doesn't the need for your mate get stronger the longer the bond goes unclaimed or unrejected?"

"It does. I think some of the wolves are masochists. Or maybe sadists. They want the pain, or they want the other person to feel it."

"That's terrible!" I exclaimed in horror, realizing perhaps for the first time that the trip might not be the entirely pleasurable experience I'd been anticipating if the men up there behaved that way.

Amanda must have seen the concern in my expression because her tone immediately turned more conciliatory. "That's not going to happen to you. I'm sorry, I didn't mean to scare you. It's not actually that common that they leave the bond unbroken. I know which ones you need to watch out for. Once you meet them and pick out any that are interesting to you. I'll give you all the gossip."

That sounded better, but my heart continued to beat a little faster than it had before as we pulled up to the border crossing.

"Where are you folks heading today?" the woman in the booth asked, flipping through our passports that Felix handed over.

"We're taking our friend back home and staying for a few days to visit her family." Felix's answer contained no lies, though it left out quite a few details.

"Any weapons in the vehicle?" she asked.

"No."

That *was* a lie, I'd seen Felix pack his favourite knife before we left, the one he used when he went out to track down other supernatural creatures as part of his hobby, and I didn't know why he'd lie about it. If they caught us in a lie, that would be a lot worse for us than simply declaring it.

Unless... he didn't want Amanda to know he had it?

He lied so smoothly, nothing about him betraying any kind of nerves, that I had to admit I was impressed. The border guard didn't suspect a thing as she handed our passports back and wished us a pleasant stay.

I hoped for a good stay too, but already, things were starting to feel a bit more complicated than I initially thought they would be.

Chapter Two

~Savannah~**

On the other side of the border, things looked mostly the same. The distance signs were in kilometres rather than miles, but the mountains on one side of us and prairie on the other carried on, unbothered by the man-made lines to separate one country from another. Our werewolf ancestors wouldn't have recognized the distinction; their only concept of borders was the ones that marked one pack's territory from another and those ones were taken very seriously, both then and now.

"The turn-off is coming up on the left," Amanda warned us when we were getting close. "The road's going to get a lot bumpier."

Vaughan had told me the pack was remote, but I assumed he meant like ours, hidden away in the forest but still within an hour of the nearest human town. However, as we turned off the highway onto a dirt road with massive potholes that Felix had to swerve to miss or risk blowing a tire, I realized his definition of 'remote' might have been a little more extreme than mine.

The ground quickly rose up beneath us as we entered the foothills of the Rocky Mountains and the forest pressed in, covering the world around us in shadow. We drove for miles - or kilometres, I supposed - and didn't see another vehicle or any sign of life.

"There's a sharp right coming up," Amanda directed. "Miss it, and we'll end up in the lake."

Felix took the corner slowly as a breathtaking vista opened up to our left, a crystal-blue lake tucked between the trees, with a few vehicles parked down by its shore. The mountains suddenly seemed a lot closer.

"Are those humans?" I asked in surprise, noticing a couple standing near one of the trucks. "People actually come out here?"

"They come this far," Amanda confirmed. "But they usually stop there before the road gets worse."

Worse?

Right on cue, Felix caught the edge of a pothole, sending me bouncing off my seat with only the seatbelt stopping me from hitting my head. Thankfully, I wasn't prone to motion sickness, but my stomach still heaved a little bit anyway.

"Fuck, sorry," he muttered, his grip on the steering wheel tightening. I couldn't be sure if he meant to direct the apology to us or to his truck. "How much farther?"

"Not too far. It'll turn into a trail just ahead."

She wasn't kidding. The dirt road beneath us gradually gave way to two tire tracks cutting deeper into the heavy forest for several more miles until at last, a small cabin appeared with a small parking area in front of us.

"This is the border of our territory," Amanda explained as Felix parked the truck and gave the dashboard a grateful pat. "From here, we go on foot."

I glanced in the back where all our bags were piled up, and Amanda smiled, understanding my thought process without me saying a word.

"We have a system to transport everything. Don't worry about that."

They certainly seemed to have it all sorted out, and when two large men came out of the cabin to clear us for entry, I immediately perked up. Now we were talking. Tall and broad, and around my age, they looked like they would definitely know what to do with me, at least for one night.

Neither of them paid any attention to me as we climbed out of the truck, though. Both of them bowed their heads to Amanda instead.

"Welcome home, Lota."

The use of the archaic title for the daughter of an Alpha surprised me. We didn't use it in our own pack and I didn't know any other packs that did. The werewolf version of 'princess', it felt outdated and a bit condescending, at least to me, but Amanda accepted it graciously, not giving any indication that returning to the pack hadn't been her choice.

"Thank you. Felix and Savannah are my guests and I'll be escorting them to the pack house, per my father's wishes. Will you make sure our luggage is brought to us as soon as possible?"

"Of course."

The men had still barely glanced at me, but I'd lost interest in them anyway. The wind had carried a new scent to me while they'd been talking, something sinfully sweet that I couldn't quite place. Like roasted marshmallows, almost, but better. More like the whole damn s'more.

Yum, my wolf hummed in my head. *Where is that coming from?*

You tell me, Tala. You're the one with the tracking nose. Though I looked in the direction the wind blew from, I couldn't see anything other than the same trees that surrounded us on all sides.

"Is there a candy factory around here?" I blurted out.

That got the men's attention, finally, as they turned to look at me in confusion, as if I had said something truly ridiculous.

"Are you hungry?" Felix teased me. "I guess it has been a while since breakfast."

It had, but I didn't think that explained it. "Don't you smell that?"

He took a deep sniff. "I don't smell anything but the forest. Clean and fresh."

He meant that as a compliment to our hosts and they took it as such, giving him a nod of approval before returning to their duties. "The women can undress and shift inside the cabin."

Following Amanda's lead, I headed inside where she gave me a small satchel to put my clothes in. Once we'd both shifted to our wolf forms, the men returned and attached my satchel around Tala's chest. Felix waited for us outside, but as soon as I stepped back through the door, the smell hit me even stronger than before, so strong I could nearly drown in it.

You really don't smell that? I asked Felix through our pack mind-link. Members of the same pack could communicate with each other telepathically, which came in handy in our wolf forms when we couldn't speak.

He sniffed again, his eyes widening as he did. *Actually, I do smell something. It almost smells like...*

He didn't get to finish his thought. A loud growl echoed from the trees to our left, from the direction the smell had been coming from, and the Ravenstone men immediately sprang into action. "Rogue!" one of them called out, pressing a button on the side of the cabin that must have connected to some kind of pack-wide security system.

"Go!" the other one shouted at me, Amanda and Felix. "We'll chase him off."

A flare of excitement bubbled up inside me. Rogue attacks were few and far between in our territory. Most wolves lived in packs, but rogues were wolves that had been kicked out of their pack for one reason or another. They were dangerous and unpredictable, and I found that... well, a little bit sexy, to be honest.

I'd also heard they usually smelled awful, rather like rotting flesh, but this one smelled amazing, if he was indeed the source of the smell that almost had Tala drooling.

Unfortunately, I didn't get a chance to find out anything more about the interloper. Amanda and Felix both obeyed the instruction we were given to run, and with no choice but to follow them, I took off into the Ravenstone territory as the border guards shifted behind us, ready to defend us and their pack from the rogue wolf, whatever he was after.

Already, this had been more exciting than anything that had happened to me at the Crimsontooth pack for months, and we hadn't even made it to the pack house yet. There, the real excitement awaited, and all my earlier nerves disappeared as anticipation filled my wolf's body.

My adventure was about to begin.

Chapter Three

~Jasper~

Coming out of the haze always left me nauseous. It felt disorienting, like the world had spun around but left me behind, and I wobbled unsteady on my feet as I blinked in the cool afternoon sunshine.

As always, when I regained consciousness, I was in my wolf form.

You okay, Sterling? I asked my wolf, checking in with him like I did every time we awoke. We had the routine down to a science, though I couldn't even be sure how long we'd been going through it.

I'm hungry, he growled grumpily. *And tired.*

I was tired too. Whatever we did in the haze always seemed to take a lot of energy, but we wouldn't be able to sleep until we figured out where we were and whether we were safe from danger. And until we had something to eat. Since the haze always took more out of Sterling than it did for me, I would have to keep control of our body until he felt strong enough to take over again.

Shifting to our human form would be pretty much pointless. I could barely even remember the last time I'd been human.

A sniff of the air and a quick look at the terrain placed me just outside the Ravenstone territory. What was I doing so close to the border? My old packmates wouldn't hesitate to destroy me if I inadvertently crossed over their pack boundary. Wolves I'd once considered friends had become bitter enemies, and the worst part was that I had no idea why.

Just as I decided to put some distance between me and the border, my ears pricked up at the sound of a vehicle. Not many cars came down that road, and never without a good reason. The pack must have been getting visitors, and even though I knew it would be better to disappear before they arrived, my curiosity got the better of me.

My mom always used to say that it would get me into trouble one day.

Keeping low to the ground and moving slowly so I didn't attract any attention, I crept forward until I could see the wooden cabin that housed the border patrol officers. As I suspected, a big truck had pulled up outside, the engine turning off right as it came into my view. The cabin door opened and two pack members came out, though from that distance and only being able to see their backs, I couldn't tell for sure who they were. One pair of broad shoulders looked a lot like another.

From the driver's side of the truck, a tall, blond man I'd never seen before got out, and from the passenger side, I recognized Amanda, Alpha Warren's daughter. She wouldn't recognize *me*, I felt quite certain, especially not in my wolf form. I'd never been important enough to be part of the Alpha's inner circle, but even so, I bent down even lower to the ground just to be sure I wouldn't be seen.

When the last person climbed out of the truck, though, my heart nearly stopped in my chest. Her curly brown hair bounced as she hopped down onto the ground, her skinny jeans and fleece jacket showing off the curvy, hourglass shape of her body perfectly. Tall for a female wolf, effortlessly beautiful and full of confidence, she seemed like something straight out of a dream, a dream I'd long since forgotten. I couldn't take my eyes off her.

Mate?

Sterling said the word in my head with such uncertainty that I had to ask him to repeat himself. *What?*

I... I think she's our mate.

For a stunned moment, I could only blink in surprise. Could that actually be true, or were we both a bit delusional from all the time spent on our own? It had been weeks since I'd even seen another werewolf, so it might be a hallucination. Inhaling as deeply as I could, I tried to catch the scent that would confirm it for me, but the wind blew in the wrong direction, carrying her scent away from me.

Even without that confirmation, though, as soon as Sterling put the thought in my head, it felt like it had to be true. My fatigue vanished, replaced with a new kind of energy that raced through my body, making me itch to get closer to her. For the last... well, however long we'd been out there on our own... we'd simply been surviving. A mate had been the last thing on my mind, but at the sight of her, a deep, primal need rose up within me, so strong that the haze began to cloud the edges of my vision again.

No! Not now!

Sterling and I both fought against it as hard as we could while our beautiful mate turned to look in our direction. Did she know we were there? Could she smell us? The wind would have been in her favour though it wasn't in ours. I held my breath, waiting to see whether she would recognize my scent for what it was, whether she would come over to find me, but the others with her ushered her inside instead.

Go to her, Sterling growled as we watched the man who had arrived in the truck shift into his wolf form. *She didn't see us so she doesn't know we're here. Go and claim her.*

Oh, sure. I'll just waltz right up there in front of three members of the Ravenstone pack, including the Alpha's daughter, and take her guest as my mate. That won't cause any problems.

Well, you can't let her go!

I didn't want to, but I needed time to think, and the haze encroaching further into my mind didn't help.

It didn't usually come back so quickly. Normally, when I regained consciousness, I had a few days until it hit again. Something about seeing our mate and feeling the mate bond must have awoken it again, and though I tried to fight it, I knew I wouldn't be able to hold it off for long. I never could.

It might try to claim her on our behalf, Sterling warned me, his voice already sounding further away. *It'll feel the bond too.*

Fuck. I hadn't thought of that.

The 'haze' was what I called the feral, animal side of me that had awoken upon our exile from the pack. Although Sterling was a wolf, he was still a werewolf, the same as me. I was a little more animalistic than most humans, and he was a little more civilized than most wolves. The haze didn't possess any of those human characteristics. Pure animal, it took what it wanted without regret, cruel and vicious without its pack for support, pushing me and Sterling out of the way to get what it wanted.

I knew it had to be a part of me, what others might call my baser instincts, but ever since our exile, it had somehow become its own personality, erasing everything good and noble in my character to become the worst version of myself. When it had control, I couldn't do anything to stop it. Often, I blacked out entirely, so I didn't even know *what* it did.

The haze couldn't take my mate. I couldn't bear to think what he'd do to her, what *I'd* do to her under his control.

And so, when she came back out of the cabin in her wolf form, just as beautiful as when she was human, and the haze pushed up, trying to take control, I did the only thing I could think of.

I growled, loudly, drawing the attention of the five werewolves who up until then had been unaware of my presence.

The wind carried my scent over to them as I stood up, and as I hoped, they sent my mate away to safety. The border guards shifted, ready to track me down, and deep weariness hit me again. At least I could stop fighting. With my mate out of harm's way, I could surrender to the haze that swallowed me up as it took over to flee from the guard's angry chase.

CHAPTER FOUR

~Savannah~

Since I couldn't mind-link with Amanda on the way to the Ravenstone pack house, Felix bore the brunt of my questions instead. *What do you think that rogue wolf wanted? Why did it growl at us?*

I don't know, Sav. I've never been a rogue and I'm not a mind reader.

Tala threw her best withering look over her shoulder at Felix's wolf. Amanda led the way since she knew where we were going and Felix took up the rear in case any trouble followed us. That left me in the middle.

Have you dealt with rogues before? I tried next.

Not very often. There aren't many of them around.

He had an annoying habit of only answering the question I asked when I wanted an actual conversation. *Why not?*

Exile from a pack is a pretty big deal, a last resort.

I knew that, but I wanted more specifics. *What happened with the ones you dealt with?*

Normally, we chase them off to make it clear they aren't welcome on our land. That's probably what the guards here will do. In one case, a very small pack's Alpha died without a successor. The whole pack became rogue, so they came to us and we took them in. Luckily, they came before they got too wild so they were still able to negotiate with us rationally.

Wild? I repeated curiously. *What does that mean?*

The longer a wolf is rogue, the less civilized it becomes. I don't know why. Severing the pack bond does a lot of damage: emotionally, mentally, even physically. That's why it's a last resort. Our pack hasn't exiled anyone for more than a hundred years.

So, the rogue out there must have done something pretty terrible to be exiled in the first place? For some reason, that didn't feel right to me. Maybe I just didn't understand how someone who smelled so good could be all that bad.

He must have, Felix agreed. *It might be a sore subject for the pack, and we don't even know for sure if he was exiled from **this** pack, so don't go asking about it, okay? Let's focus on what we came here for.*

Getting me laid, you mean?

Tala threw another look over her shoulder, that one a grin, as Felix's wolf tried not to laugh. *I don't think Vaughan put it to me in quite those terms.*

You mean my brother who still thinks I'm a virgin?

Felix's chuckle echoed inside my head. *I don't envy the man you eventually set your sights on.*

Hey! I'm a catch and you know it.

We teased each other and laughed for the rest of the trip until the main pack settlement came into view. Although Vaughan visited recently, we hadn't had a chance to chat about his visit, and nothing he could have said would have prepared me for the breathtaking beauty of it. Another lake stretched out in front of us, this one a cool, icy blue colour, and the mountains provided a perfect backdrop for it, framing it beneath their snow-covered peaks that soared up to the sky beyond. Closer to us, individual cabins sat along the lakeshore while a large, modern Alpine house dominated the whole scene.

That had to be the pack house, and if I were to actually choose one of the pack's leadership team to be my mate, it would be my new home.

Not too shabby at all, I thought, and Tala readily agreed. News of our arrival had clearly been passed along since two members of staff came out to meet us and direct us to the back door. There, we were each ushered into our own private changing room where we could shift back to our human forms and get dressed again in comfort. Although I had the clothes I'd been wearing earlier, a pretty navy-blue dress and heels had been left for me to wear instead. Somehow, they knew my size perfectly. There were even some toiletries including a hairbrush and some brand-new makeup to make myself presentable. Thoughtful on the part of whoever had arranged it, and I appreciated the gesture.

The Ravenstone pack obviously knew how to look after its guests, which could only be a good sign.

When I looked my best again, I left the room to find a young woman waiting for me. Her long, dark hair hung sleekly over her shoulders, and big, serious brown eyes looked out from a tanned oval face. "Good afternoon, ma'am. Welcome to the Ravenstone pack. My name's Heather and I'll be looking after you during your stay."

The 'ma'am' wasn't really necessary. She didn't look *that* much younger than me. I gave her a warm smile to try to put her at ease. "Hey, Heather. I don't suppose you know where I could find a candy bar? All that running made me hungry."

It didn't help that the sweet smell from the forest lingered in the air around me. It seemed to have gotten stuck in my nose, and my stomach had been rumbling ever since.

My request seemed to scandalize Heather, her eyes widening in surprise. "Dinner will be served very shortly, ma'am. They're waiting for you."

Damn it. I'd have to suffer a little bit longer, it seemed. "Lead the way, then."

I gave her a salute that I thought was rather funny, but she didn't crack a smile at all. I found Amanda was serious, but compared to Heather, she was a barrel of laughs.

From the changing rooms, we walked down a long hallway, past several closed doors. Big wooden beams lined the inside walls, like the outside, but mirrors, lights, and some tasteful art along the hall helped to brighten the place up. All in all, it felt like an upscale hotel, in a good way. Living there would be very comfortable.

Eventually, the hallway opened to a huge, open space that formed the main reception room of the house. The ceiling soared two stories above us and large windows faced the beautiful lake we'd seen earlier, with a set of French doors that opened onto a large, open balcony. Opposite the doors and windows, a wide staircase ascended to the second floor, bordered by beautiful carved wood balustrades. A happy buzz of chatter came from the open doors at the top of the stairs, but at the foot of them, clearly waiting for me, were Felix, Amanda, and an older man who I knew immediately must be Alpha Warren. He and Amanda shared the same high forehead, slim nose and rounded chin, but more than that, I could feel the authority coming from him.

"I hope I haven't kept you waiting, Alpha. Your pack house is beautiful." I bowed to him graciously, ignoring the way Felix's eyebrows raised in surprise. Despite what he thought, I could actually follow proper etiquette... when it suited me.

"You would always be worth waiting for, Lota Savannah," the Alpha replied just as smoothly, reaching for my hand and bringing it to his lips when I placed it in his grasp. "It's delightful to meet you, and our pleasure to welcome you to the Ravenstone pack. There are many people who are very eager to make your acquaintance."

Now we were talking. *Bring on the men!* I announced to Tala, who snickered in my head. We'd always shared the same sense of humour, thank the Goddess. Even when no one else understood me, my wolf always would.

Out loud, I was much more restrained. "I'm eager to meet them. Shall we?"

The Alpha offered me his arm to head up the stairs while Felix and Amanda followed behind us. I was more than ready to sink my teeth into whatever we were having for dinner, and hopefully, a little bit more besides.

Chapter Five

~Jasper~

When the haze faded again, the sun had begun to go down. My mouth felt dry and stale, but thankfully, I'd ended up close to a cobalt lake further from the Ravenstone territory. In my haze, I must have been able to escape the border guards and make my way there instead. Wearily, I padded down to the water's edge to drink.

The cool, fresh water immediately made me feel a little better, and I drank it down greedily before checking in with my wolf. *You okay, Sterling?*

Still tired. Can we sleep soon?

Yeah. We'll find somewhere safe for the night and we'll...

I trailed off as a noise came from behind me, and instantly, I crouched down and spun around, baring my teeth in anticipation of danger.

To my surprise, a man stood there, not far from where I'd just been. Even more surprising, he was completely naked.

Perhaps most surprising of all, I recognized him.

He recognized me too, even in my wolf form, and his lips pressed into a bittersweet half-smile that seemed at odds with his defensive posture. He looked ready to shift at a moment's notice as he spoke to me.

"Hey, Jasper."

Jeremy? I reached out to him in my head before remembering that my pack link had been severed. I couldn't speak to him in my wolf form, so if I wanted to talk, I'd have to become human again.

Is that smart? Sterling asked. *What if he came to hurt us?*

He's unarmed, I pointed out. His hands were out in the open where I could see them, and since he wore no clothes, he couldn't be concealing anything. *If he wanted to hurt me, he wouldn't have gotten my attention. Let's see what he wants.*

It had been so long since I'd shifted that it hurt much more than it should have. My limbs screamed out in discomfort as they grew longer, stretching out muscles that hadn't been exercised in far too long, and I struggled to keep my balance as I stood upright, naked, at the water's clear edge.

"Hey."

Despite having just drank in my wolf form, my voice sounded hoarse, my vocal cords not used to the exercise any more than my body was.

Jeremy obviously heard it too. "Drink," he instructed, gesturing down at the water by my feet, and I immediately took advantage of his consideration. Bending down, I scooped the water up in my hands and brought them, dripping, to my parched lips. It wasn't as effective as drinking in wolf form, but fuck, it felt fantastic.

When I'd had enough that it no longer hurt to swallow, I stood back up, wobbling unsteadily, the rocks on the lake bed digging into the tender soles of my feet. "What are you doing here? Won't you get in trouble for talking to me?"

No one had reached out to me since the exile and I hadn't expected them to. Associating with a rogue was considered treason, and could be punishable with the same exile the rogue had suffered. Only something of the greatest importance made it worth the risk.

Yet, he'd tracked me down anyway.

Jeremy still had that same half-smile on his lips, one that wasn't really amused but suggested he didn't really know what else to do with his face. "I'll only get in trouble if they find out, and I don't plan on telling them."

"I won't either," I promised before realizing how ridiculous that sounded. No one would listen to me anyway. He was the one taking the risk in speaking to me at all.

"Come and sit down," he invited, gesturing to some large, smooth rocks a little further along the water's edge, tucked away beneath some trees. It would be more private there, as well as more comfortable.

A couple of times, I stumbled over my feet, nearly tripping as I got used to walking upright again, and when we reached the rocks, I collapsed gratefully onto one of them as Jeremy sat down too, keeping a safe distance between us. Whether that was for my sake or his, I couldn't be sure.

"You've got to stop provoking the pack," he stated bluntly as soon as we'd gotten settled. "Up to now, their orders have been to keep you out, but after today, we've been told to use deadly force if necessary. They're going to kill you, Jasper. You've got to let it go and move on. Find somewhere else to live. Try a human town, maybe. I don't know, but if you stay here, you're not going to survive."

As part of the border patrol force, he would know what he was talking about, and I believed each word he said.

"After tonight?" I repeated hesitantly. "What happened tonight?"

He raised an eyebrow at me in disbelief as he leaned forward, resting his elbows on his knees. "The way you went for Andrew's throat? You nearly killed him."

"I did?" Honestly, I didn't remember that at all. I thought I simply ran away, but when Jeremy's expression hardened, probably suspecting me of lying or playing dumb, I tried to explain myself. "I have these... blackouts. They affect my memory."

"Is that what happened with those kids?"

My empty stomach heaved so fiercely that I thought I would be sick, even though I had nothing to bring up. Fuck, I was hungry. "What kids? What are you talking about?"

I hadn't hurt any kids, had I? The fact that I couldn't even be sure horrified me.

His look of disapproval gradually melted into concern. "The reason you got exiled, Jasper. The missing kids? You must remember that."

Somewhere deep inside me, a memory stirred. Before I became a rogue, I worked with the pack's internal security, the werewolf equivalent of a police force, and I'd been investigating the disappearance of two very young children. That must have been just before my exile.

I'd forgotten all about it until he mentioned it.

"I remember they were missing, but I don't remember what happened. Were the kids found?"

The look he gave me morphed all the way into pity, like I'd truly lost my mind. "Yeah, they were found. Locked up in *your* basement."

No. Sterling growled in my head, his tone as full of disbelief as I felt. *That can't be right. Someone must have set us up.*

Do you remember any of this? I asked, hoping that maybe, somehow, his memories weren't as affected as mine.

Unfortunately, that wasn't the case. *I don't remember, but we would have never done that.*

I wanted to believe that. I thought the haze didn't start until after we were exiled, but if I couldn't remember the end of my investigation or the exile itself, maybe it had started earlier. Maybe I *had* done it and didn't recall.

"Were they... alive?" I hated that I had to ask, but I needed to know.

"Just barely. It took them months to recover."

Months. That meant it had been months since my exile. I honestly couldn't have said for certain.

Jeremy sighed as he sat back upright. "Look, Jasper, you were always a nice guy. You probably don't even remember because I was no one back then, but you helped me out a lot back in the academy. You helped a lot of us, and we didn't want to believe you'd hurt anyone on purpose. We thought you needed help rather than exile, but the Alpha insisted. All I can do is give you my best advice: go get some help now. Talk to someone, figure out these blackouts, and for the love of the Goddess, stop hanging around the border, especially now. None of us wants to see you dead, alright?"

Despite everything, I appreciated the sentiment.

Something else he'd said stuck out to me, though. "Why especially now?"

"What?"

"You said to stay away from the pack 'especially now'. What's going on now?"

He grimaced as he realized he probably shouldn't have told me anything at all, but after a quick glance around to make sure we were still alone, he leaned closer. "The Alpha's got a special visitor right now. He wants to make a good impression and he's furious that you spoiled her arrival."

Her? Instantly, an image of the beautiful woman I'd seen earlier came back to me, and just as suddenly, I couldn't believe I'd forgotten about her.

How did I forget I found my mate? What the fuck was wrong with my head?

"Who is she?"

I couldn't have sounded cool about it even if I wanted to. My desperation bled through my words, loud and clear, and Jeremy shook his head apologetically. "I can't tell you. I shouldn't have said anything at all, and I have to get back before anyone comes looking for me. Will you think about what I've said, please?"

"I'll think about it," I said, but deep down, I knew I couldn't leave. Not with my mate so close, and not after the clue he'd given me about what led to my exile in the first place.

Somehow, I had to figure out the truth. If I'd done something awful enough to deserve my exile, then I didn't deserve my mate either. But if somehow, I hadn't been to blame, I needed to find a way to prove it so I could claim her as soon as possible.

Nothing in the world had ever felt so important.

Chapter Six

~Savannah~

I spent dinner seated at the head table of the large pack house meeting room, sandwiched between Alpha Warren on one side of me and Beta Chad on the other. Both were perfectly nice men who made perfectly pleasant conversation with me, but both were also mated. The Beta's mate sat on his other side, while Alpha Warren apologized to me for the Luna's absence, saying she had a chronic illness that kept her out of the public eye much of the time.

I came there ready to flirt, and so far, I hadn't had a single opportunity.

It didn't help that my stomach continued to rumble. The food was delicious, but my portions were way too small. I couldn't help noticing that the men were served significantly more than the women, as if we didn't get hungry too. *Did you pack any snacks?* I mind-linked Felix halfway through the meal. *I'm going to need something else to eat after this.*

I'm afraid not, he answered, leaning forward to catch my eye from further down the table. *I can try to get something extra from the kitchen later if you need it. I noticed they're not giving you ladies very much.*

He sat next to Amanda, on Alpha Warren's other side. We all sat on one side of the table, like we were the freaking disciples at the Last Supper or something. It was so that the whole pack could see us, I understood that, but it still felt unnatural. Our own pack didn't stand on that kind of ceremony.

At least it gave me the opportunity to scope out some of the other men in the pack, though I still didn't know who was who. Alpha Warren had suggested I'd be introduced to everyone, but to that point, I hadn't met anyone other than him and the Beta, and dessert had just been brought out. As with the other courses, my tiny slice of cake could barely be called a mouthful.

Spread out in front of us were another six tables, seating ten people each. Since the pack had several thousand members, the guest list that night must have been carefully curated. Men far outnumbered the women, but which of them I was meant to be considering, I still didn't know.

"How did you two meet?" I asked Beta Chad, leaning forward to include his mate in the conversation too.

"We grew up together," he replied, reaching out to place his hand on his mate's. "She's the Alpha's sister."

We had something in common, then, and I gave the woman an encouraging smile.

"It came as a big surprise when we found out we were fated," she added. "We'd known each other almost all our lives."

I wouldn't have guessed that she was Amanda's aunt since there didn't seem to be much of a resemblance, but what she said about being fated caught my attention. "Amanda mentioned to me that often, ranked wolves in the pack don't end up with their fated mates. I guess you were an exception?"

The Beta's eyes darted over my shoulder, but whether they sought Alpha Warren or Amanda, I couldn't be sure. "We all have the choice about whether to accept our fate or not. In our case, it worked out. Others aren't quite so lucky."

The answer sounded almost rehearsed, but I couldn't argue with it. Some people got lucky with a fated mate and some didn't. What I really wanted to know was whether there was going to be a chance for me to get lucky that evening in a different way.

At last, the Alpha got to his feet and all the chatter in the room immediately died off. From where I sat, I had to crane my neck to look up at him. "As you all know, it wasn't that long ago that we were welcoming the Alpha of the Crimsontooth pack here to celebrate him choosing my daughter as his mate."

My eyes immediately dropped to Amanda, whose face remained neutrally blank. Whatever she might be feeling at the reminder of her failed mating, it didn't show.

"Unfortunately, he chose to turn his back on the agreement we made, dishonouring not only Amanda but the entire Ravenstone pack. His true, selfish nature has been revealed."

A rumble of agreement swept the room, several people exchanging dark looks, as I frantically linked Felix in my head again. *Are we supposed to sit here and let him insult Vaughan?*

We're miles deep in their territory, he reminded me, though I could hear the edge in his response. He didn't like the Alpha's words any more than I did. *Let's see where he's going with this.*

Looking satisfied with the response he received, the Alpha held up his hands to quiet the crowd again. "However, we can take the high road. We've agreed to give the Crimsontooth Alpha a second chance to prove his loyalty, and for that reason, he sent the two people sitting here with me tonight: his Beta, Felix, and his sister, Lota Savannah."

The Alpha gestured to Felix and I in turn, and the eyes of everyone in the room followed his movements.

"I trust that you'll all welcome them with the courtesy the Ravenstone pack always shows to its visitors, and hopefully, we can put the ugliness of the past few days behind us for good. Drinks are in the library." With that, he looked down at me and offered me his hand, as if he hadn't just insulted my brother, Alpha, and my entire pack. "Shall we?"

With little choice if I didn't want to make a scene, I let him help me up and escort me next door to a library as big as the room we'd eaten in. Staff were already waiting with glasses of wine, and the Alpha took one for himself and one for me, handing it to me in a way that made it clear I couldn't refuse.

"Now, you'll meet my team. This is my Gamma, Thomas."

A man appeared almost out of thin air, making me gasp in surprise as I tried not to drop the wine glass in my hand. "It's... lovely to meet you," I managed to say as Thomas took my hand and kissed it. They were all very formal.

At least fifty years old with greying hair and deep lines on his face, the Gamma could have easily been my father, but the appraising look he gave me, his eyes examining me from head to toe, couldn't be called fatherly. "I hope you'll feel at home here, Lota. If there's anything I can do to make your stay more... comfortable, please let me know."

"Thomas' mate passed away five years ago," the Alpha informed me bluntly, making it clear if I hadn't already guessed that he was one of my potential matches. "His children are all grown so he lives alone."

Was that supposed to be a selling point?

I tried to be sympathetic. "That must be lonely sometimes."

"It can be," he agreed, his eyes dropping to my body yet again. "Especially at night."

Alright, that's quite enough of that, Tala growled in my head. *What else have we got?*

Two Deltas were next, Michael and Matthew. I hoped I wouldn't be asked to tell them apart because they had the same build, the same buzzcut, and the same dull-as-white-paint personalities. Furtively, I glanced around for Felix, but he had been drawn into a conversation with some of the other men.

"Ian is one of our Epsilons, head of the border guard," the Alpha introduced me, and I shook the hand of the tall, broad, serious-looking man.

"I understand you encountered a rogue wolf outside our territory," he stated, barely moving his lips. His teeth must have been clenched tight. "I can assure you there's nothing to worry about."

I hadn't been worried, but since he brought up the rogue, I couldn't contain my curiosity, even though Felix told me not to ask. "Did he used to belong to your pack?"

Ian immediately glanced over at Alpha Warren, who stepped in to answer on his behalf. "It's hard to say. Once they lose the pack scent, it becomes almost impossible to recognize them. Let's see who you haven't met yet."

He pulled me away from Ian before I got a chance to ask any other questions, and a moment later, I found myself standing in front of a very handsome man, much closer to my own age, with the palest blue eyes I had ever seen.

"Lota, this is Kyle, one of our research scientists, and the pack's scientific advisor."

That sounded impressive, especially for someone so young. Maybe his focus was chemistry, because I definitely felt some. "Hi. I'm Savannah."

I held out my hand, palm down, expecting him to kiss the back of it as the other men had done, but with a bit of a bemused smile, he took it and shook it instead. His hand felt warm against mine, firm but not too rough. "Your parents must have had very good genes."

The words were so unexpected, I blinked in surprise. "Excuse me?"

Looking a little embarrassed, he laughed. "Sorry. I'm a geneticist by trade and that sounded pretty good in my head. It was meant to be a compliment."

"Oh." That must have been his attempt at flirting, apparently, which was actually kind of cute. I decided to play along. "I had the same thought about you. Your eyes are rather striking. You must have inherited them?"

"I did, actually. From my mother." He looked pleased that I'd noticed, or perhaps pleased that I'd made the genetic connection.

"Would you both excuse me for a second?" the Alpha interrupted, his attention drifting away from us. "I'm needed elsewhere."

Finally, a lucky break. Of the men I'd met so far, Kyle was the one I'd be happiest to be abandoned with.

"Yes, of course," I murmured at the same time that Kyle also agreed, bowing his head to his Alpha.

"Have you been out on the balcony yet?" he asked me, gesturing to a set of doors that led outside once the Alpha walked away.

"No, not yet."

"Would you like to go? The view is the best one in the whole territory, in my opinion."

I gave him my sweetest smile. "I'd love to."

Things were definitely looking up as the handsome scientist offered me his arm and led me through the crowd. Maybe it would turn out to be a lucky night for me after all.

Chapter Seven

Vaughan,

We're here.

Sorry not to text sooner but I haven't really had a moment to myself yet. I'm hiding in the restroom right now.

For the most part, they're treating us like honoured guests, but the Alpha talked some shit about you at dinner. Although, you did dump his daughter, so I guess you kind of had it coming.

Sav seems to be enjoying herself, chatting up all the men. She just went out onto the balcony with one of them. Seems like they really will be giving her a choice, but she's playing it cool. So far, so good.

Thanks for the update. I've been worried, and Callie's not much better. She feels responsible for Savannah having to go up there, so if I can tell her that Sav's having a good time, that'll help.

Keep us updated, and if anything changes, let me know right away. I might not be close by, but I've got connections. If you need to get out, we'll get you out.

Chapter Eight

~Savannah~

Kyle promised me the view would be good, but even so, I gasped as we stepped out of the library. The balcony jutted out from the side of the pack house rather than the front, so instead of facing the lake straight on, we got a gorgeous view of the mountains to the northwest, the forest to our right and the lake to the left. Living in Montana, I was no stranger to the beauty of nature, but even I had to admit the view was something special.

"Holy shit, that's gorgeous."

Too late, I remembered I was supposed to be representing my pack as a paragon of feminine grace, and I clamped my hands over my mouth as Kyle chuckled.

"You took the words right out of my mouth. If you come right to the edge, it's even better. You're not afraid of heights, are you?"

I accepted the invitation, moving over to the railing at the edge of the balcony. "As long as you're not planning to push me over the edge, I'll be fine."

"I wouldn't dream of it. That would truly be a waste of such a special woman." His stunning eyes darted down as he said it, just for a second, sneaking a quick glance at my body in a way that I found rather charming. I'd been checking him out too.

"Am I supposed to be looking at something in particular?" I asked, turning my gaze out to the spectacular view. The sun had almost disappeared beneath the tops of the mountains, casting its last golden rays over the blue lake and throwing long shadows behind all the trees. The entire vista was gorgeous, but I didn't know if he wanted to show me something I couldn't have seen from closer to the house.

Kyle quickly confirmed that he did have something in mind. "Look down there, where it looks like a small bay in the lake."

Following his point, I could see the spot a little further along the shoreline. The water sparkled the same icy blue as the rest of the lake, but strangely, what looked like several tall poles extended up from the water, almost as tall as the large fir trees further back from the shore. It almost looked like the masts of an ancient ship that had sunk beneath the water's surface. "What are those things in the water?"

"That's what I wanted to show you. They're spruce trees. There used to be a little patch of them there, probably a hundred years ago or more, until one day, part of the mountain gave way in a rockslide. It wiped out a lot of the trees and formed the little bay, but those trees you can still see there survived."

"Why haven't they rotted?" I wondered. If he was telling me the truth, they'd been there for more than a century. The flooding should have killed them.

"The cold water preserves them. The sun never really reaches that spot in the shadow of the mountain so it's colder than the rest of the lake, which is already pretty cold even in the summer. Beneath the water, the algae grows so thick along the trunks, it almost looks like an underwater forest."

I couldn't quite picture it, but his knowledge impressed me. "I thought you were a geneticist, not a... tree scientist."

Tree scientist? Tala teased me in my head.

What, like you know what it's called?

Kyle smiled at my comment but didn't make fun of me like my wolf did. "I find it fascinating. Those trees should have been wiped out along with the others but they adapted to their new surroundings. In the face of catastrophe, they survived."

Looking out again at the barren shards of wood, I didn't see it quite that way. "They're still there, and they're beautiful in a way, but they're also frozen. Can you really call it surviving when they're dead inside?"

He conceded that point with a gracious smile. "I suppose it depends on how you define survival. Success always depends on the parameters of the goal in the first place."

He had a point too, I supposed, but I was ready to stop talking about dead trees and find out a bit more about him instead. "What does success look like for you, personally?"

As he turned to look at me, I suddenly realized how close we stood to each other. It hadn't seemed all that close until we were face-to-face.

"In general, or tonight?"

He raised an eyebrow as he asked the question, and a warm flush spread through my body. We seemed to be on the same train of thought, and I smiled back at him, tucking my hair behind my ear in a move I knew most men couldn't resist. "Let's start with in general, and depending on how that goes, maybe we can talk about tonight."

His smile widened. "I think my ambitions are pretty standard: doing well at a job that I enjoy, seeing my pack flourish, and raising a family with my gorgeous, irresistible mate."

That answer couldn't have been much smoother, though it actually told me very little. "What about a fated mate?"

He shifted ever-so-slightly closer. "A fated mate isn't always best. You must agree with that if you came up here to choose your mate for yourself."

I didn't want him to get the wrong idea about that. "I came to see what my options were. I haven't made any firm decisions yet about whether I'll accept *any* mate here, let alone who."

"Of course. You just got here and you have every right to be picky."

At least we were in agreement on that, so I moved on. "And tonight? What was your goal for tonight?"

"This."

Closing the small remaining distance between us, Kyle took my face in his hands and pressed his lips against mine in a surprisingly firm kiss.

The move was bold, even risky, but luckily for him, I liked a man who took charge. I'd been sending him signals to show my interest, and having picked up on them, he took action. I respected that, and I would have happily kept kissing him even longer if someone hadn't cleared their throat from behind us, bringing the moment to an abrupt end.

"Am I interrupting something?"

Chapter Nine

~Jasper~

Despite my fatigue, the conversation with Jeremy managed to re-energize me, especially when I remembered that I'd found my mate that evening. Rather than looking for a place to spend the night as I originally intended, I headed for the mountains instead.

What are you thinking? Sterling asked, knowing from my purposeful gait that I had a plan but obviously not sure what it might be.

We need help. I have to get into Ravenstone territory and I can't do it on my own.

I'd shifted back to my wolf since I moved faster that way and the rough ground hurt my paws a lot less than it did my human feet. Even so, I tried to stay away from the rockier patches, following a few of the natural trails that countless other wolves had blazed through the forest over hundreds or even thousands of years. The fresh pine scent from the trees around us sat heavily in the evening air which had started to cool off from the warmth of the day.

Sterling still wasn't following my train of thought. *Who do you think is going to help? Jeremy?*

That didn't seem likely. He'd already taken a risk in talking to me and I didn't expect or want him to put his neck out any further. Besides, he couldn't do what I had in mind anyway.

No one from the pack can help. The problem is that as soon as I cross the border, they'll feel it, right? Even if someone in the pack lets me in, it'll still set off their alarms.

Right. So...?

So, what if there are multiple breaches on their border at the same time? Several different rogues, coming from different directions. They'll have to divide their forces and we might be able to slip through.

At last, Sterling caught on to what I had in mind. *No way,* he growled. *Rogues can't be trusted.*

The irony of that statement made me laugh. *Have you forgotten that* **we're** *rogues?*

That's different.

I didn't see how. *We always assumed that they must have done something awful to be exiled, but maybe they didn't. Or maybe they don't remember either. Maybe they're like us.*

We'd encountered a few other wolves in the months since our exile, or at least signs of a wolf nearby. The scent of a rogue couldn't be mistaken for anything else. Wanting to avoid any trouble, we steered clear of them. Once, we got into a fight that couldn't be helped, and I remembered very well where that particular wolf lived. During a rainstorm, I stumbled upon a cave while looking for shelter, not realizing it already had an occupant. Its inhabitant chased me off after taking a good chunk out of my leg with his teeth. It had stung for days.

I planned to start my recruitment there.

You're going to get us killed, Sterling grumbled in my head.

Maybe, but have you got a better idea? The answers about what happened with those kids are in the pack, and so is our mate. We have to go in.

As I reached the base of the mountain where the wolf in the cave lived, the Ravenstone pack house came into view, as beautiful as ever. Lights shone from within, illuminating the whole building, and from my vantage point, I could make out the silhouettes of two people on the balcony facing my direction. I was too far away to see who they were, and as I watched, a third person came out and called them back inside. Whatever was going on there that evening, it looked important.

My mate would probably be there, and the thought sent a pang of longing through me so strong that it took all my strength not to race towards the house immediately. The Ravenstone pack treated its guests well, and I'd always taken pride in that fact. My pack meant everything to me and my loyalty to it had never been called into question.

Not until they kicked me out.

The sun's about to go down, Sterling pointed out, pulling me out of my thoughts. *If we're going to go talk to this guy, we should get there before dark.*

As usual, he had a point. The light would disappear quickly once the sun dipped below the mountaintops, and approaching a strange wolf at night would only be asking for trouble.

Despite the aching in my limbs, I began to climb, remembering the route I'd taken on that rainy day, and I reached the cave entrance with only a thin sliver of sunlight left in the sky above me. Although I couldn't see the wolf anywhere, I could smell him, which meant he could probably smell me too. If he felt under attack, he'd go on the offensive, so if I wanted to diffuse the situation, making myself less threatening seemed like the way to go.

With that in mind, I shifted back to my human form for the second time that night.

You've officially gone crazy, Sterling howled in my head. *He's going to tear you apart.*

I'd have to take that chance.

"Hello?" I called out, my voice a little stronger than it had been earlier. I almost sounded human again. "I just want to talk to you. I'm not here to fight."

My reward for that opening salvo was a deep growl that echoed from inside the cave, a warning sound sending me a very clear message: *Go away.*

Since I couldn't do that if I wanted to achieve my goal, I tried again. "I don't want anything that's yours. Your cave, your food, anything you're protecting, I'm not interested in it. I only want to talk. When's the last time you talked to anyone?"

Did werewolves who stopped shifting eventually lose the ability entirely? If the haze affected other rogues too, did it eventually take over? Was there even still a man inside the wolf in the cave?

The growling grew louder, and closer. In the fast-fading light, I could make out two eyes staring out at me from the darkness of the cave entrance.

"It's been a few months since the Ravenstone pack exiled me," I explained, holding my hands up so he could clearly see I was unarmed, like Jeremy had done with me. "They're the pack that lives down at the base of the mountain."

The growling stopped as I spoke, so I kept talking.

"The past few months have been pretty brutal. I knew exile was no joke, but fuck, it's been hard. Has it been hard for you? I could really use someone to talk to. I know rogues are supposed to be lone wolves, only looking out for themselves, but fuck that. Who wants to be alone all the time? We're social creatures for a reason, right?"

No response came, but no growling either. The eyes had disappeared, and with nothing else to go on, I carried on.

"Do you ever talk to any of the other wolves around here? I know there are a few. If you've been out here longer than me, you probably know even more than I do. Do you guys ever get together and hang out? No one's ever invited me."

The words coming out of my mouth were nonsense by that point, but I had to say *something* until I got some kind of response.

Finally, I did.

"You talk a lot."

The words were raspy and sore-sounding, a lot like my voice had sounded earlier that night, but they *were* words, which meant the wolf had shifted. That was a really good sign.

In relief, I babbled even more. "Yeah, sorry. I don't usually talk so much but I'm a little worked up tonight, not to mention that I didn't know if you'd kill me on sight. My wolf thought you might."

"Your wolf sounds pretty smart."

Sterling hummed in agreement while I let myself smile. Those muscles felt sore too. It had been a long time since my face had done that. "I'm Jasper. What's your name?"

Tentatively, a foot appeared from the cave, the leg attached to it looking just as unsteady as I'd felt earlier. When the werewolf stepped completely out of the cave, though, I was taken completely by surprise. The raspy voice hadn't given me any clue, but the body in front of me left no shadow of a doubt even with her long hair hanging down over her breasts.

My rogue attacker was actually a woman.

She sized me up too, looking around to make sure I was truly alone. Satisfied in her inspection, she introduced herself. "My name is Myra, and I'm from the Ravenstone pack too. Looks like we might have some things to talk about."

Chapter Ten

~Savannah~

At the sound of her voice, I pulled back from Kyle and turned towards the door where Amanda stood, a hand on her hip and her eyebrows raised, waiting for a response to her question about whether she had walked into something.

"You... uh... no. What?"

The words out of my mouth didn't make much sense, and I could see her trying not to smile at my incoherence.

"Do you need something, Lota?" Kyle asked, his tone polite but restrained, giving me the feeling he didn't appreciate the interruption.

"Yes, actually. Savannah has several other people to meet. My father is still occupied, so he asked me to take over. Shall we?" She gestured back towards the library, and though I would have rather stayed outside with Kyle, I had no good reason to refuse.

As I took a step away from the railing, I had an odd feeling that someone else's eyes were on me. I looked out over the view we'd been admiring earlier, but nothing in particular caught my eye. There was too much to take in, and not enough time.

"Kyle, would you get Savannah and I another drink?" Amanda asked, her tone making it clear he didn't really have a choice. The glass the Alpha had given me had long since disappeared, and my throat had gone a bit dry. I *would* appreciate another.

"Can we get some more food too?" I whispered to her after Kyle had walked away. "I'm starving."

Despite her sympathetic smile, she shook her head. "The nutritionists have worked out what they believe to be the ideal caloric intake for both male and female wolves, and the kitchen staff are instructed to keep to it strictly. I noticed the Crimsontooth pack was a lot more lenient about that, but you'll get used to it."

I didn't *want* to get used to feeling like my stomach was about to eat itself. "They actually control how much you can eat? That's bullshit."

Amanda glanced around furtively, checking that no one had overheard us. "The pack is very concerned about the wellbeing of all its members."

Vaughan was concerned about the wellbeing of his pack members too, but he didn't go around weighing their food. However, I bit those words back to focus on the other thing I wanted to know while I had a moment alone with her.

"You promised you'd give me a heads up about any of the men I needed to watch out for. What's the deal with Kyle?"

Once again, she took a look around, checking that no one could hear and especially that Kyle wasn't on his way back with our drinks yet. "I don't know him very well personally, but I do know that he's never been mated. He's part of the leadership team but not from one of the ranked families so mating with you would definitely raise his profile in the eyes of the pack. I don't think he's a bad guy, but keep that in mind."

So, Kyle wanted the prestige that would come with being mated to an Alpha's daughter. Although I didn't love that, I had to be realistic too: other than my fated mate, everyone would take my status into consideration. I'd have to be naive to think otherwise. It didn't mean there couldn't still be chemistry between us and possibly even more.

Before I could ask anything else, the man himself walked back up to us, a glass of champagne in each hand. As I took mine from him, he let his fingers brush against mine, slowly and deliberately, sending a little zing of attraction through me. He knew damn well what he was doing, and I suspected that meant he'd know what he was doing in other ways too.

"Thank you," Amanda said, curtly dismissing him. "Now, who haven't you met yet?"

She took me through another five men before we reached another one who caught my eye. Tall and strong with a chiselled face that matched his sculpted body, he seemed like a definite possibility, but for some reason, Amanda grew more tense as we walked over to him.

"Savannah, this is Troy. He's the head of our warrior training program."

That didn't surprise me given the excellent shape he seemed to be in and I would have been happy to learn more about him, but he barely glanced at me. All of his attention went straight to Amanda. "What happened with the Crimsontooth Alpha?"

Amanda's lips tightened in disapproval as she attempted to redirect him. "Troy, this is Savannah."

He did glance my way that time, but only for a second before his eyes returned to her. "Did the bastard really reject you?"

The growled and angry words stirred my own anger. After what Alpha Warren said at dinner, I couldn't hold my tongue any longer. "That's my brother you're talking about. Yes, he called off the arrangement with Amanda, but only because he found his fated mate. She's his perfect match, and Amanda accepted his decision gracefully. Everyone admired her for it. You weren't there, you don't know him, and you have no right to pass judgement."

"Sav?" Felix's voice from behind me, curious and a little protective, couldn't have been more welcome. "Is everything alright here?"

A quick look around confirmed that my outburst had attracted a few curious onlookers. I hadn't realized I'd been quite so loud.

"Everything's fine," Amanda assured him, raising an unimpressed eyebrow at Troy. "You were about to apologize, I believe?"

Another growl rumbled in his chest, but with more of the pack watching, Troy couldn't refuse. Amanda clearly outranked him. "I'm sorry, Lota."

"Not to me. Apologize to Savannah."

It couldn't be clearer in their body language, the way Troy's jaw clenched and Amanda held herself so tightly, that they had history between them. Neither wanted to back down, but again, Troy had little choice.

"I'm sorry, Lota Savannah," he grumbled at me, his handsome face looking tormented. "I'm sure your brother isn't a complete bastard."

Felix snorted at the half-apology right as Alpha Warren rejoined our small group, probably having been alerted to the disturbance. "Is there a problem here?"

Immediately, Troy's bravado left him entirely, and he bowed his head in submission. "No, Alpha."

He didn't see it because his eyes were down, but I noticed the look of disdain on Amanda's face as Troy deferred to his Alpha.

"I'm sorry to have left you for so long, Lota," the Alpha apologized to me, turning his back on Troy to box him out of the conversation. "Have you had a chance to meet everyone?"

I couldn't be sure about that, but suddenly, I had no more energy left. Perhaps the champagne had made me sleepy, or the long drive was catching up to me, or maybe it came down to the lack of food. Either way, I didn't want to meet anyone else. "I'm not sure, but I think I'm ready to call it a night, Alpha Warren. It's been a long day."

It seemed almost impossible that just that morning, I'd been at home in my own bed.

The Alpha didn't put up any argument. "Of course. We'll have you shown to your room. Beta Felix?"

"I'm going to pack it in as well," Felix confirmed. "Thank you for your hospitality tonight."

"Our pleasure. Sleep well, both of you. Breakfast is at nine o'clock, you can join me in my private dining room."

With that, we were dismissed, and as soon as we left the library, Heather appeared to show me to my room, along with a male member of staff for Felix. The room they gave me was gorgeous and luxurious, with its own view over the mountains, and my belongings had already been unpacked for me.

It made me a little uncomfortable that someone had been through my things without asking me, but I had nothing to hide. This pack was definitely more hands-on than our pack in a lot of ways, but I had to accept that any pack would have some differences. It didn't mean they were bad or wrong; it would just take some getting used to.

So far, the visit hadn't been boring, at least, and as I lay down in the soft, comfortable bed, I found myself looking forward to what the next day might bring.

Chapter Eleven

~Jasper~

My hopes of making any further progress with Myra that evening were quickly dashed as the sun disappeared completely behind the mountain to the west.

"I have to shift back," she said, nervousness slipping into her tone as she glanced around. "If another wolf snuck up on us suddenly, we'd be in danger. It'll be better to wait and talk in the daylight."

Although that disappointed me, I could understand the logic, and as soon as I let myself think about it, my own exhaustion kicked in. After all the excitement of the day and coming out of the haze twice, I was operating on pure adrenaline. As soon as it began to taper off, I could barely keep my eyes open. "Can I stay here tonight?"

Something close to pity flashed in her dark eyes. "Only because it's already dark. There's room in the cave, but don't think it's a permanent arrangement. You're still a stranger to me."

"Understood."

After shifting back to my wolf, I dragged my tired limbs into the cave. Despite her rather gruff demeanour, I noticed that Myra put herself between me and the cave entrance, essentially standing guard for the both of us so that I could sleep.

Maybe she could tell how much I needed it.

By the time I woke up, the morning light had already crept into the cave. I couldn't remember the last time I slept that long, or that deeply.

You doing okay, Sterling?

Better, he confirmed. *Today's going to be a good day.*

I sure hoped so. When I raised my head, Myra was nowhere to be seen, so after stretching out my limbs, I headed back outside.

The ledge outside the cave had no signs of life either. Just as I started sniffing for a trail to follow, I heard a voice call out from beneath me.

"Stay there. I'm coming back up."

Since she'd obviously taken her human form, I did too. It hurt a bit less that time, though my limbs still felt pretty stiff. Adjusting to being human again would take a little time.

When Myra appeared, she carried two pieces of wood, curved to resemble bowls. One, she'd filled with water, and the other held some berries picked from the forest. In the daylight, I could see her better, the dark brown hair she wore over her shoulders to give her a tiny bit of modesty, though her lower half remained as naked as mine did. Dark brown eyes sat in a round, young face that bore the dirt of many days without a wash. She couldn't have been more than twenty-five.

"Breakfast," she explained, handing both items to me. "I've already eaten."

"Thank you." Though it wasn't much, the fact that she had gone out to get it for me nearly brought me to tears. I hadn't realized how much a toll being starved of any kind of companionship had taken.

Yeah, she's not that bad, Sterling admitted in my head as I took a drink from the makeshift bowl and lifted one of the berries to my mouth. *Unless those are poisonous.*

My hand froze in mid-air. *Why would you say that?*

We have to consider it. I'm just saying it's possible.

"Problem?" Myra asked bluntly, watching me eat. She seemed to be a woman of very few words, but maybe that had to do with how long she'd been alone.

I didn't have any idea how long ago that might have been, so after assuring her the berries looked great and popping one in my mouth for good measure, I started my questions there. "When did you get exiled?"

"About six months ago."

I frowned as I tossed a couple of more berries in my mouth. "That's strange. I worked with internal security and I never heard about anyone being exiled then."

Myra's huff sounded insulted. "They must have covered it up. No one would have missed me."

Her words raised more questions than they answered. "Who covered it up? What did they cover up? What happened?"

Her jaw clenched unhappily, though whether from my nosiness or the memories that came with the questions, I couldn't be sure. "I don't know who. I never saw his face."

She looked like she didn't expect me to believe her, but considering my own circumstances, it sounded entirely plausible that she might not understand the reasons for her exile. "Why don't you start from the beginning? Please?"

With a sigh, she did, speaking more words together than I'd heard from her in total so far. "I was an omega in the pack. My parents both died years ago and I was an only child. Like I said, no one would have missed me. I had a job at the research centre attached to the hospital, cleaning at night. One night, someone was working late when I went in to clean the lab. He smelled incredibly good, and I knew right away that he must be my mate."

After the previous day, I finally knew how that felt, but I also knew that based on where I'd found her, the story probably didn't have a happy ending. I kept my mouth shut to let her continue.

"Like most wolves, I'd imagined that moment so many times, but when it finally happened, I didn't know what to do. I stood in the doorway, frozen, waiting for him to say something. He had a surgical mask on for whatever he was working on, but he must have smelled me through it. His scent hit me so strongly, he couldn't have missed mine."

"But he didn't acknowledge you?" I guessed.

"Not as his mate. He turned and saw me standing there with my cleaning cart, and he asked what I wanted. His tone was so cold. I stuttered out something about needing to clean the room and he told me to come back later after he left. That was it. He didn't say anything else, as if our bond didn't exist at all."

"Fuck. I'm sorry." Our pack didn't used to be so cavalier about the mate bond. That shift in thinking came from the current Alpha. He'd chosen his mate, and he thought everyone should have the opportunity to make an advantageous match for themselves. It led to a lot of heartbreak, some of which I'd seen firsthand.

"That wasn't even the worst part of the night," Myra said, letting out another huff that recognized the absurdity of that statement. "I went back to cleaning, listening to my music through my headphones and trying not to cry, and I guess I didn't hear whoever snuck up on me. The next thing I knew, something grabbed me and jabbed something sharp into me. When I woke up, I found myself outside of pack territory, my pack link gone, and I've been here ever since."

So, she did remember what happened, for the most part, but it made no sense to me. "You think your mate got you exiled? Why wouldn't he have rejected you if he didn't want to accept the bond and left it at that?"

Anger clouded her expression. "You don't think I've asked myself the same question every day for the last six months? And how did he do it? No trial, no appeals process. It had to be someone pretty close to the Alpha to pull that off. Someone who didn't want it known I'd ever been mated to him."

I had to agree, but who? More importantly, why?

Before I could even start to figure it out, a new sound from below us caught our attention, and Myra and I both immediately fell silent, our ears straining to listen. Someone ran through the forest, probably more than one someone, heading our way. A sharp bark rang out, confirming what I'd already suspected: they were wolves.

Without a word between us, Myra and I both immediately shifted back to our wolf forms in case we needed to defend ourselves. Crouching low, we peered over the rocky ledge to try to get a look at the newcomers, and the scent hit me, faintly drifting up towards me, carried on the wind.

I'd never smelled it before, but I still knew exactly what it meant: my mate was down there.

Chapter Twelve

~Savannah~

A soft knock on my door woke me up in the morning, followed by Felix's voice in my head. *Hey Sav, it's me. You up?*

The heavy curtains in my room blocked the outside world so well, it felt like the middle of the night, but I dragged myself out of bed anyway and went to answer the door. Dressed in a hoodie with the hood up, he looked like someone up to no good. The hallway beyond him was still dark and I couldn't hear anyone else around. "What time is it?"

"Early," he confirmed. "I wanted to get here before the staff saw me and stopped me."

"What? Why?" Maybe I was still half asleep but his words made no sense to me.

He held up a brown paper bag and my mouth immediately began to water as the smell of freshly-baked bread hit me.

"I did a little kitchen raid."

"Oh, fuck, that smells good. Come to Mama."

I snatched the bag out of his hand and ran back to my bed to devour the forbidden food in peace, leaving him chuckling as he closed the door behind him. "I had a feeling you'd forgive me for waking you up once you saw why. How're you doing?"

As he came to take a seat on the end of the bed, I knew he didn't just mean my stomach. He wanted to know how I felt about the whole visit so far.

The bread had no butter, but at that point, I didn't care. I shoved so much of it in my mouth that it made answering his question a bit difficult.

"They'resah bitward, bush notta shealbwak."

Felix's laugh came out as a snort. "You want to try that again in English?"

Narrowing my eyes at him, I swallowed the bread in my mouth and repeated myself. "I said: they're a bit weird, but it's not a dealbreaker."

His eyebrows raised in disbelief. "Really? That's what you said?"

"Shut up."

He only managed to dodge the pillow I sent flying at him at the last second, and when he sent it back, it hit me right in the face as I took another bite of the bread.

"Sounds like one of them caught your eye, then?" he asked casually, as if he hadn't sent breadcrumbs up my nose.

Despite the glare I gave him, thinking of Kyle quickly brightened my mood. "Enough that I want to get to know him better, at least. What did you think of last night? You've visited other packs a lot more than I have."

I polished off the last of the bread, having practically inhaled it, and my stomach already felt better. Hopefully, combined with whatever breakfast they gave me that morning, it would be enough to keep me going.

Felix took a moment to consider my question before answering. "I'd say they fall more to the conservative, traditional end of the scale among the packs I've visited, but they also seem to embrace technology. One of the Deltas told me all about their medical research lab, he says it's right on the cutting edge and the pack has even sold some of their research to human pharmaceutical companies to bring in revenue."

That sounded impressive, and I wondered if Kyle's work contributed to that. I hadn't had a chance to ask him much about it the night before. I really hadn't had a chance to find out much about him at all, other than that he had stunning eyes and was a very decent kisser.

"Would you want to live here?" I asked. Might as well get right to the heart of the matter.

Felix grimaced at my bluntness. "That's an impossible question for me to answer since I don't want to live anywhere other than the Crimson-tooth pack. As Beta, my loyalty is there, one hundred percent. My mate will have to be willing to come and live there with me, and before you say it, I know that's sexist, but it's also true. Women get the short end of the stick sometimes."

"In this pack more than most," I pointed out, shaking the crumbs out of the paper bag into my mouth. "Are you going to wait for your fated mate, or would you ever think about choosing one for yourself?"

"After what Vaughan went through? I think I'll wait, thanks." His deadpan delivery made me laugh, but I could tell he really meant it.

"Do you think I'd be crazy for not waiting?"

"I'm not going to judge you, Sav, but I will say that you're still young. Don't let anyone rush you into anything you don't feel ready for, okay?"

I promised not to, and he snuck back to his own room while I got myself ready for the day.

Heather came to collect me to take me to breakfast with Alpha Warren and Amanda in the Alpha's dining room. The Luna still wasn't well, it seemed, but she sent her regrets. My appreciation for Felix's early morning contraband only increased as a plate of fruit was set down in front of me and Amanda while the Alpha and Felix were served bacon and eggs.

"You made quite an impression on several members of my team, Lota Savannah," the Alpha told me after we concluded the obligatory small talk about how we slept, our gratitude for his hospitality, and what the weather would be like that day. "I have several requests for additional meetings so you can spend time with them one-on-one."

That sounded like a good idea but only one request particularly interested me, and as I flipped through the handwritten notes that the Alpha gave me, I was relieved to see Kyle's name there among them.

Savannah, I'd love to continue our conversation from last night. Would you join me for lunch in my office?

By 'conversation', I suspected he meant our interrupted kiss rather than any words that we'd exchanged. Since I would be more than happy to pick that back up where we'd left off, I quickly penned a note back, accepting his offer and passed it to Heather who promised to deliver it. She hovered behind me for the whole meal.

"I'm afraid my work will keep me busy for most of the day," the Alpha informed us. "Perhaps Amanda can give you a tour of the territory this morning."

"I'd be delighted," she agreed, though he didn't really give her much choice. Since she just returned, she might have had other things she'd rather be doing, but he didn't ask. "We could go for a run now and return in time for you to get ready for lunch. There's a rather spectacular view I can show you."

Either she'd been reading the invitations over my shoulder or perhaps she'd been told about them ahead of time and guessed which one I might accept. I *had* been pretty obvious the night before when I asked for her opinion on Kyle and no one else.

With no other plans for the morning, Felix and I accepted her offer, and soon, the three of us were running north towards the mountains that I saw from the balcony the previous evening. The morning dew hadn't dried yet, soaking into our paws as Tala ran through the trees behind Amanda's black wolf, with Felix bringing up the rear again.

Amanda's wolf barked out an order to us, urging us to follow her as she headed towards the base of the foothills. I wondered how high we would go and how much of the mountains fell within the pack's territory, but I didn't get a chance to ask anyone before a new wolf appeared, leaping into our path out of nowhere. With a deep growl, he headed straight for me.

Chapter Thirteen

~Jasper~

As soon as I caught my mate's scent in the air, soft and floral, like lilacs in the spring, the haze began to rise up inside me.

No! Sterling, fuck! Help me!

I couldn't say what I expected him to do since he had no more power over it than I did, but he tried his best anyway. We both tried to fight it, harder than we ever had before, but it was no use. The dark side of myself took over, leaving me helpless to control my actions, just like when Sterling had control of our body.

Perhaps because of how hard I fought, I remained conscious, able to see and hear everything around me but not able to control it. Whether that would turn out to be a good thing or not, I couldn't begin to guess.

Sterling, are you still there?

My wolf didn't answer. Apparently, I was on my own with the consciousness now in charge of my body.

With me unable to resist, my wolf leapt down over the ledge we'd been perched on, seemingly unconcerned about our safety as we raced down the steep mountain slope. Myra's wolf yipped behind me, no doubt wondering what in the fuck I was doing, but I couldn't have answered her even if I wanted to.

I couldn't do anything at all.

Three wolves approached the base of the mountain, just outside the Ravenstone territory. Why they were outside pack land, I had no idea, but it meant that nothing could stop me from charging right at them. The haze had its attention focused entirely on my mate's beautiful brown wolf, and I could see the moment she saw us coming. We were hard to miss, growling like a completely feral beast as we raced towards her.

At that last moment, before I could tackle her, which seemed to be the haze's intent, one of the other wolves intercepted me, ramming me hard from the side. The force of the impact shuddered through me, crushing pain following close behind, but it didn't stop the haze. As the other two wolves ran, the one who'd hit me faced off against me, his teeth bared and his ears flattened, giving me a warning but ready to attack me again if necessary.

He was so focused on me that he didn't see Myra coming until she was almost right behind him.

At the last minute, he dodged out of her way, and with him distracted, I took off in pursuit of my mate, ignoring Myra's warnings once again. My mate's scent in the air practically drew me a map pointing the way she had gone. At some point, she and the other wolf had parted ways, no doubt trying to confuse any pursuers, but with the olfactory breadcrumbs she'd left behind, it didn't slow me down even a little.

She had a decent head start, but I had the speed advantage due to my size, a couple of months of living in the forest, and my pure motivation. My lungs burned as I sprinted through the trees, my limbs that had only barely recovered from the previous day's exertions screaming out in agony, but nothing was going to stop me.

Nothing was going to stop *him.*

A flash of brown fur darted between the trees up ahead of us, honing my path even further. She ran fast, and the idea that I frightened her, that she felt the need to run away from me, pained me to my core. Fuck, I wished I could speak to her and try to explain what was going on. Although, that would require understanding it myself, which I still didn't.

Not knowing the territory as we did, she didn't seem to realize that she was running herself directly into a dead end. One of the many lakes in the area lay ahead, and when she reached its shore, she'd have nowhere else to go. Excitement and adrenaline coursed through my body at the idea, emotions that didn't belong to me but which I understood.

I'd always loved the thrill of the chase.

I just never thought I'd be hunting my mate.

We'd almost reached her when she burst out of the trees and into the cold water's edge. Instantly, she realized her mistake, but by the time she turned around to try to go back, I blocked her path of retreat.

And I could still do nothing but watch.

Chapter Fourteen

~Savannah~

Fuck, I was tired. The lack of a decent meal in the last 24 hours really didn't help when it came to maintaining a sprint, and even running as fast as I could, the unknown wolf kept gaining on me. His pounding footsteps behind me had my heart racing, beating faster than it had ever beat before.

I've barely had time to process what happened when Felix came out of nowhere, barrelling into the charging wolf. *Run, Sav,* he ordered through our mind-link as he and the other wolf rolled over each other on the ground. *Get out of here, back the way we came.*

Which way was that? I'd been following Amanda, not paying attention to any landmarks, and with the tall trees surrounding us, I couldn't even use the sun to work out which way was north.

With no time to figure it out and no direction in mind, I simply ran.

Amanda kept close on my heels, but after I'd gone far enough that I couldn't hear or see Felix anymore, I belatedly realized that I recognized the other wolf's scent. It had been the sweet, marshmallowy smell from the day we arrived, and two realizations hit me at the same time.

First, that wolf must have been the rogue we encountered, the one I smelled but never saw.

Second, and much more significantly, that wolf was my...

Mate. Tala growled the word in my head, as agitated as I'd ever felt her. That explained why he smelled so good to me when rogues were supposed to reek. *Why are you running away from him?*

Uh, because he tried to attack us? I didn't understand much about what happened, but that much seemed clear. Why would he do that? Why wouldn't he just come and introduce himself? I'd never heard of being attacked by your mate in such an uncivilized way.

Did it have to do with the fact that he was a rogue? *Why* was he a rogue? Where did he come from?

Who was he?

I had so many questions, but hidden away among them was one I could barely acknowledge, even to myself: why did I kind of like being chased by him?

Between the sound of his thundering paws and the scent that drifted up to me, it didn't take long for me to realize Amanda had disappeared and my mate was on my tail instead. I could have stopped to let him catch me, as Tala urged me to do, but I still didn't know exactly what his intentions were.

Besides, I didn't want to make it too easy for him.

Summoning all my strength, I pushed myself to keep going, right until the forest gave out around me and cold water splashed in my face as I ran straight into the edge of a lake.

Really cold water.

Fuck, that was freezing, and with a shiver, I turned back to try to find another path, but I didn't get the chance. He'd come up much quicker than I realized, and when I turned, he stood directly in front of me.

Cool, green eyes stared at me, intense and hungry-looking, and he bared his teeth, demanding my submission.

A shiver of excitement slithered through my body, ignoring the pounding of my heart and the thread of fear that hadn't completely disappeared.

If he really wanted my obedience, he'd have to earn it.

Pretending to bow my head, I waited until the tension in his body relaxed as he let his guard down, thinking he'd won. Then, I bolted, running back past him towards the trees.

I only got a few paces before he caught up with me again, and that time, he didn't ask. His big, warm body knocked me over, quickly pinning me beneath him, his front paws holding my body down and triumph flickering in his eyes as the sparks of the mate bond flowed between us, lighting up my whole body like a flash of lightning.

I'd be damned if it wasn't kind of hot.

Since he didn't seem to want to hurt me, I took the initiative and shifted first. We wouldn't be able to speak to each other until we took our human forms, and even though I would be naked, so would he. We'd be on even ground.

His claws quickly retracted as my fur disappeared, replaced by tender human skin, and a moment later, he followed suit, the large grey wolf above me shifting into a rather unkempt man, still with those piercing green eyes. He needed a shave, but I could definitely see potential in the handsome face that stared down at me. On his hands and knees, he straddled me, his knees against my hips and his hands on my shoulders, but no other parts of our bodies touching.

His face was so close to mine, I couldn't see anything of the rest of his body and he couldn't see mine either. We simply stared into each other's eyes, neither of us seeming to know where to begin.

"You could have just said hello," I started us off, still out of breath from the chase. "I'm Savannah."

He didn't answer me. Instead, his lips lowered onto mine with such force and need that I squealed in surprise. It seemed the men around here didn't like to waste any time.

His kiss was greedier than Kyle's had been, more desperate, and instantly, the sparks of our mate bond intensified, accompanied by a primal, pulsing need inside me. *Fuck.* I'd heard the mate bond felt good, but I never knew it would be *that* good. No wonder Vaughan risked pissing off an entire pack to keep his fated mate.

Energy flowed through my body, ignoring the fact that I knew absolutely nothing about the man above me, and that I was cold and naked on the forest floor. None of it seemed to matter when his lips were on mine.

Just as I realized he still hadn't said a word to me, we both heard the noise at the same time: more wolves, at least two of them, heading our way. The man above me lifted his head, letting out a deep groan of frustration.

I had no idea if we were back in the Ravenstone territory or not, but either way, those footsteps were probably looking for me and he knew it as well as I did. Looking back down at me, his green eyes seemed softer than before, a little less intense but kinder somehow. "I'm sorry, I have to go. I'll be back, I promise. Wait for me, Savannah."

With that, he shifted back into his wolf and took off back into the trees before I could get another word out. I called out after him anyway, desperate to know more. "Wait for you? Where? When? Who are you?"

No answer came, and as the wolves came closer, I shifted back to my wolf so no one else would see me naked.

That had to have been the single most confusing and fascinating experience of my life, but I had no idea what to make of it. Who was my mate, why was he a rogue, and what in the world was I supposed to do next?

Chapter Fifteen

~Jasper~

If it weren't for Jeremy's warning the day before, letting me know that my life would be in danger if I were found on Ravenstone territory, I wouldn't have left Savannah for anything.

She was perfect. Completely and utterly perfect.

Beautiful, confident, and willing to give me a chance to explain myself despite the unfortunate circumstances of our meeting, the connection with her helped me get the upper hand and gain control over my body again.

When we caught her, pinning her down in her wolf form, the arousal that raced through my body was so strong, it actually weakened the haze. The baser side of myself was so focused on mating with her that it let its guard down, and I managed to stop him from forcing her right then and there like he wanted to.

We were still in a tug-of-war for control when she shifted, but the sight of her bolstered my strength, letting me take charge again long enough to shift myself. The haze tried to take over again, leaning down with the intent to mark her, to claim her as ours without even saying hello, but at the last moment, I got the upper hand again and diverted towards her mouth instead, kissing her with all the pent-up need of all the different sides of me: man, wolf, and haze alike.

The mate sparks flowed through me, beating the haze back further until finally, at last, I had full control again just in time to hear and smell the advancing Ravenstone warriors, no doubt responding to my incursion into their territory.

With their imminent arrival, I had to leave or face the wrath of the pack that exiled me, but in the brief time I had, I tried to reassure her that I had no intention of rejecting her. I would return, as soon as I could, and we could get to know each other properly then.

You didn't even tell her your name, Sterling grumbled as we raced back towards Myra's cave, safely outside the pack territory. I'd have to lay low for a little while in case they came looking for me, but at least I had a place to run to.

I didn't exactly have the time to get into my life story, I pointed out, though I agreed it had been an oversight not to at least give her my name. I would be thinking of *her* name constantly now that I knew it.

Savannah. Sexy as hell and a little bit wild, it suited her perfectly.

I still didn't know where she came from or what brought her to the Ravenstone, but at least I had her name to tide me over until I could learn more, and that thought had me nearly floating on air as I climbed back up the mountain path.

"What the fuck was that?"

Myra's voice made me jump as I stepped back into the cave, my eyes not adjusted to the darkness yet. To answer her, I had to shift back, willing my body to forget about the look and smell and feel of Savannah, lest I spend the rest of the day walking around with an erection I couldn't hide.

"I'm sorry. Thanks for taking care of that wolf for me." As my weaker human eyes compensated for the lack of light, I could see she held her left arm, cradling it like it might be causing her pain. "Shit, are you alright?"

"Don't pretend to care after you left me alone out there. You're just like the rest of them, only out for yourself."

I didn't know who 'the rest of them' referred to, but I owed her an explanation for my behaviour. "I really am sorry. That... that wasn't me out there. Not fully."

Her voice was laced with suspicion. "What is that supposed to mean?"

"I'll explain it to you as much as I can, but the other thing you need to know is that wolf that I chased after? She's my mate."

From the way Myra's eyes widened, I could tell she hadn't anticipated that, not any more than I had. "Did she reject you too?"

"No. Not yet, anyway. We just met. It's complicated, but let me help you with your shoulder before I get into it. I think it might be dislocated."

Although she still didn't look thrilled with me, she didn't protest when I moved closer to take a look. "Are you a doctor now? I thought you worked with internal security."

"I'm impressed. You don't miss much." I'd only mentioned that briefly but she obviously remembered it. When I tried to gently move her arm, her wince confirmed my diagnosis. "I'm not a doctor but I've done a lot of first-aid training, and I can reset your shoulder if you let me. It'll heal in no time once it's back in place. Will you trust me?"

With a grimace, she nodded, and taking her arm in one hand, I pulled it out to her side before twisting and sliding the joint back into place. She let out a small grunt of pain, but otherwise bore the procedure with stoicism. She might have been an omega but Myra was no pushover.

"How does that feel?"

Stretching out her hand tentatively, Myra raised her arm on her own. "Better. Thanks."

"That other wolf did that to you?" I hadn't recognized him, but with his natural size, he must have been a ranked wolf. I'd seen most of the Ravenstone leadership in their wolf forms before, so perhaps he was the man I'd seen arriving with Savannah the day before.

"I don't think he meant to hurt me. He was trying to shake me off." Myra shook her head at the memory of the whole encounter. "Running straight at them like that was insane. If I didn't step in, you would have got yourself killed. What do you mean that it wasn't fully you?"

As best as I could, I explained the haze to her and how it took control of me. She listened intently, not saying a word until I finished, and I put the question to her: "Has anything like that happened to you?"

She shook her head solemnly. "No, and I've never heard anyone else describe anything like that either. It's not a typical part of being rogue."

I couldn't tell if that made me feel better or not. If it didn't usually happen, what was wrong with me, then? "Who are these others you've talked to? You mentioned them before."

"You don't miss much either," she replied sarcastically, mimicking my earlier compliment before answering my question. "There are other rogue wolves around. I tried to talk to them when I first got exiled. I thought maybe we could help each other but they weren't interested. They all told me to get used to being alone. Eventually, I took their advice."

"You never thought about moving to a human town? It's got to be more comfortable than this." I gestured at the cave around us, which, though better than the accommodation I'd had for the past few months, couldn't really begin to compare to a proper house.

"And do what? I don't have any ID, no identity. I was exiled with nothing. I could go beg on the streets there or I could live as a wolf here. This seemed to be the better option."

I could understand that. As lonely as it might be, at least she could provide for herself. "Listen, I want to be up-front with you: I came to find you because I need help. I need to find out the reason I got exiled, and now, I need to get to my mate too. Everything I need is in the Ravenstone territory, and I know that if I try to go in on my own, I'll be chased off like I was today."

"And what do you think I can do?" Her tone, though blunt, held curiosity in it. She hadn't ruled it out and was genuinely interested in my answer.

"To start, I need you to help me find the other wolves. The two of us won't be enough. We need to overwhelm them with the sheer number of intruders in order to get deep enough into the territory. I know it's a lot to ask but..."

"I'm in, on two conditions."

Her immediate acceptance stunned me into silence. I'd expected a lot more resistance, but I would take what I could get. "What are they?"

"One: I want a chance to speak to the Alpha in person. I want him to tell me to my face why I got exiled."

That seemed fair. "And the second one?"

Her eyes narrowed in determination in the dim light of the cave. "I want to find my mate and give him the same hell he's put me through."

Again, I couldn't find any fault with her demands. He sounded like a complete asshole. "That makes four things we need to do: find out why I was exiled, find out why you were exiled, find my mate, and find your mate. It can't be that hard, can it?"

I meant it as a joke, and Myra almost smiled before returning to business. "In that case, we better go and get ourselves some backup."

CHAPTER SIXTEEN

Felix

We might have been misinformed about the strength of the Ravenstone pack, Vaughan. I don't know if they're as powerful as we were told. They seem to have a real problem with rogue wolves outside their territory. We heard one when we arrived yesterday and this morning, we were attacked by two others. Don't worry, Sav is fine. I'm just concerned that we arranged the alliance for them to have our backs and they can't even control their own borders.

I'm going to try to find out a bit more about the situation and I'll report back to you when I can.

I talked to Callie about your text and she knows a bit about rogue wolves from her hunting days. She says they don't usually go too far away from the pack that exiled them. If there are a bunch hanging around the Ravenstone pack, I'd bet they were exiled from there. That suggests an internal problem at the pack, which is worse than an external one. Stay alert.

Chapter Seventeen

~**Savannah**~

Two wolves I'd never seen before came running out of the trees a few moments after my mate took off. The water from the lake helped to disrupt his scent, so they looked to me for direction, asking me silently which way he had gone.

Jerking my head to the right, I sent them off in the complete opposite direction to the way he'd actually gone. Until I had some proof to the contrary, I would choose to believe that my mate had good intentions.

Are you okay, Sav? Felix's voice asked in my head. He must not have been too far away even though I couldn't see him.

I'm fine. What about you? He'd tried to stop my mate from getting to me, but obviously, he hadn't been successful. Hopefully he hadn't been hurt.

I got a bit scratched up. Nothing I can't handle but I'll have to go visit the medical clinic just in case. Are you okay to head back with Amanda and I'll catch up with you later?

I would have preferred to go back with him and tell him exactly what happened, but I couldn't put myself ahead of his safety. *Of course. I've got plans for lunch but hopefully we can catch up before then.*

Soon afterwards, Amanda's wolf appeared, no doubt having been alerted to my location by the wolves I'd seen earlier. After doing a cursory examination to make sure I was uninjured, she indicated for me to follow her back towards the pack house.

It seemed the view she'd wanted to show us would have to wait.

As soon as we returned to the pack house and I'd shifted back, two men whisked me away to speak to Ian, the Epsilon in charge of the border guard who I'd met briefly at the reception the night before. He assured me then that I had nothing to worry about from rogue wolves along the border, but now that we'd been 'attacked' by one, he changed his tune a little bit.

"Sometimes, wolves who have been exiled can't accept the change in their circumstance. It's sad, but if they're going to attack our guests, we may need to take action. Can you describe the wolf you saw?"

Instinctively, I knew that whatever 'action' he had in mind would be bad news for my mate. Therefore, I lied. "The wolf had brown fur. An average size. Nothing remarkable about him or her."

Ian's eyebrows raised a fraction. "Lota Amanda said the wolf was grey."

Damn it. I didn't realize he'd already talked to her, probably by mind link on the way back, but I refused to change my story, digging in deeper instead. "Things happened pretty fast and she didn't get as good a look as I did. The wolf was definitely brown."

I couldn't tell if he believed me or not, but after a few more questions, he let me go, and I headed back to my room to get changed for my lunch with Kyle. Just as I finished retouching my makeup, someone knocked on my door, and when I opened to find Felix there, I pulled him into my room, my hand digging into his arm in my excitement. If I didn't get to tell someone my news soon, I might burst.

"Felix, I found my mate!"

His startled reaction could have been to my words or it could have been in response to the force with which I shook his arm in agitation.

"You decided already? This morning, you didn't sound sure at all."

Belatedly, I realized where his confusion came from: he thought I meant I'd chosen one of the Ravenstone men, so I quickly set him straight.

"No, I met my *fated* mate. The rogue wolf we saw is my mate!"

"What?" That shocked him even more than the idea that I'd chosen someone. "Are you sure?"

My response came out with all the sarcasm he deserved. "No, now that you mention it, I'm probably wrong. My wolf and I both imagined the scent, sparks and mate bond."

His lips pursed in an exasperated grimace. "You know that's not what I meant. I believe you felt what you felt, but a rogue, Sav? You're going to give your brother a heart attack."

What did Vaughan have to do with anything? "Trust me: my brother is not at the top of my list of concerns right now."

Felix tried not to laugh. "You're right. Sorry. It's my instinct to protect my Alpha, but you're the one who needs me right now. This is... a lot."

"You can say that again."

What were the odds that my mate would be *there*, at the very pack Vaughan had nearly allied with? It seemed both impossible and somehow inevitable. I supposed that was why they called it fate.

"I don't know why he's a rogue or if he came from this pack or what his name is. He told me to wait for him, that's all I got."

Felix's eyebrows shot up again. "You actually talked to him?"

"Barely." It only took me a few seconds to relay the few words my mate had spoken to me. "He seemed to know the territory pretty well. Do you think he was originally from this pack?"

"Vaughan seems to think so." Reaching into his pocket, Felix pulled out his phone and showed me the text he received from my brother after he left the medical clinic. "I think there might be more going on here than we know about."

It certainly felt that way to me. "How do we..."

I didn't get to finish my question before someone else knocked on my door. "Lota Savannah?" Heather's muffled voice came through from the other side. "It's time for your lunch engagement. I'll walk you over to the lab."

"Should I cancel?" I whispered to Felix. As nice as Kyle had been, I didn't really want to be dating other guys until I figured out the situation with my mate.

"It might look suspicious to them," Felix pointed out. "Until we know more about the whole situation, it's probably best to go ahead."

I supposed he was right but I still felt a bit guilty about it as I opened the door to Heather and tried to smile like everything was perfectly fine. "I'm ready. Lead the way."

The Ravenstone pack had no real streets to speak of since cars couldn't make it that far into the forest. Heather led me out of the pack house and away from the lake, weaving through the trees until we reached a large clearing containing a building that rivalled the pack house in size, though it had more of an industrial feel.

"This is the pack medical centre," she explained as we approached. "Both the hospital and the research laboratory are inside. It's all state-of-the-art."

We by-passed the reception desk, the woman there nodding to us in a way that suggested we were expected, and Heather escorted me right to the door of Kyle's lab. Inside, high-tech equipment covered almost every surface, most of it machines I'd never seen before and couldn't identify.

"Lota Savannah." I almost didn't recognize him as he got to his feet and turned to face me, wearing both a surgical mask and goggles over his eyes. He quickly removed both, running a hand through his hair at the same time. "Forgive me, I didn't realize it had gotten so late. I get so caught up in my work that I lose track of time."

I didn't buy that for a second. He must have asked Heather to bring me there so I would see him 'in action' and be impressed. However, because it flattered me that he wanted to make a good impression, I didn't call him out on it. Instead, I walked over to look at the table where he'd been working. Petri dishes were arranged within a temperature-controlled container, all labelled with different codes made up of letters and numbers.

"What's all this?"

He joined me at the table, his body close enough to mine that I could feel his heat. "This is my primary project at the moment. These are all stem cells that contain genetic anomalies and I'm working on a way to use healthy DNA to correct them."

I could just about follow that. Science hadn't been my best subject at school but I'd been a good student all-around and I remembered a little from my biology lessons. "To fix genetic diseases?"

Kyle nodded, looking down at his work with pride. "Yes, and perhaps even more. Some people have a genetic predisposition for beneficial characteristics. To heal faster, for example. Imagine if we could introduce that change to all the wolves of the pack."

I could feel my forehead furrowing as I thought that over. "You want to genetically modify your pack?" That seemed to be veering closer to science fiction than real science, and I could think of a dozen movies where similar experiments went horribly wrong. "Aren't you afraid of creating mutants?"

Kyle let out a bark of amused laughter. "It won't be anything so dramatic, I assure you. Tiny adjustments that will help to protect us all. It's the ultimate preventative medicine."

"I suppose it could be." It still sounded a bit questionable to me, but he obviously knew a lot more about it than I did, and he looked so proud that I didn't want to get into an argument about it. Mostly, I wanted to get our lunch over with so that I could get back to Felix and figure out what to do next about my mate. "Are you busy, or do you have time for lunch?"

"I'll always have time for you."

His smooth reply made me smile, his confidence as strong as it had been the night before when he kissed me. Although it suffered in comparison to the spark-filled one I shared with my fated mate that morning, it *had* been a good kiss. Maybe I shouldn't push Kyle away yet, at least not until I learned more about my fated mate and why he'd been exiled.

I wanted to believe he was a good person, but I had to keep an open mind to all sides until I had more concrete information to go on.

"You can go," Kyle said to Heather, who still hovered at the door. She followed me like a shadow, which would make investigating things in the pack a little more difficult. Was that *why* she stuck so close to me? Were there things they didn't want me to know?

My mind whirled with all my questions and all the possibilities as Kyle led me outside the building to a pretty garden that lay behind the medical centre.

"This is very nice," I observed, looking around with approval.

"It serves a dual purpose: it's good for the wolves who are recovering in the hospital, but also for the staff who work here. I took the liberty of packing us a picnic."

He directed me to a bench where, sure enough, a picnic basket waited, guarded by another man who made himself scarce as soon as Kyle told him he could go. After the excitement of the morning, my stomach felt empty again, but when Kyle began unpacking the food, I noticed that everything had already been portioned out, with him getting a lot more than me.

I couldn't hold my tongue. "Why is your pack trying to starve its women?"

Kyle's pale blue eyes looked up at me in startled surprise, his hand that had been about to hand me a drink freezing in mid-air. "What?"

"You heard me. Why are you feeding the women less than the men?"

"Oh, you mean our prime caloric intake." Looking almost relieved, he finished emptying the basket and sat down beside me. "Our scientists have carefully worked out the optimum number of calories for both male and female wolves to consume each day in order to maintain muscle mass and keep them healthy."

Amanda had said pretty much the same thing, but I didn't buy it. "Every woman is different, though! Every man too, for that matter. You can't pick one number and expect it to be right for everyone."

"Actually, we can." Kyle's tone remained calm as he disagreed with me. "We made a small genetic modification that set everyone's metabolism at the correct level. Based on their job and the level of activity it requires, we tweaked their genetic code so that they would function best off the same amount of food everyone else eats. It simplifies things for our kitchen staff and it keeps everyone in peak physical shape. It's actually quite brilliant, if I do say so myself. We could sell it to the humans and make a fortune."

"How did you make this modification?" I still didn't really understand how what he described would be possible, but he seemed pretty certain about it.

"I'm afraid I can't tell you that. Some things about my work are confidential."

In frustration, I looked down at my small helping. "Well, I haven't had any modification, and this would barely feed a child."

To his credit, Kyle actually agreed with me. "You're right. I'm sorry, I wasn't thinking. Here."

He handed half his sandwich to me, a chicken BLT which disappeared into my mouth in a huge bite as I groaned gratefully.

A moment later, though, another thought occurred to me. "Waitch. Whash aboush u?"

Whereas Felix found it funny that morning when I spoke with my mouth full, Kyle looked less impressed. For the first time, his eyes appeared almost cold. "Excuse me?"

Forcing the food down, I repeated myself. "What about you? If I've taken your sandwich, your intake will be off for the day."

His look of disapproval melted into pleasure, either that I'd made the connection or that I was concerned about him. Maybe both. "I'll speak to the kitchen later and sort it out. Don't worry about me."

I kept my next bite smaller so I could still speak clearly. "Are there any other modifications you've already put into practice? When we were in your lab, I thought those kinds of changes were still hypothetical."

"The specific changes I'm working on in the lab are hypothetical, but we've already introduced a few things into the general population. It's an exciting time, and the Alpha is very appreciative of the work I do. I get paid well, and there's even talk that I might be promoted to a Delta position within the next year. You can rest assured I'm fully able to support a mate."

His blatant sales pitch for himself as a mate made me a little uncomfortable. On the other hand, he couldn't have been making it much clearer that if I were to choose him, he would be in complete agreement. It helped to have things stated so clearly.

However, since I couldn't make any decision until I learned more about my fated mate, I simply smiled and changed the subject.

When Kyle's phone alarm went off to remind him to head back to work for the afternoon, he asked to see me again that evening.

"I'm not sure if the Alpha has other plans for me, but if I'm free, that would be nice. Why don't I give you my number and we can keep in touch?"

He agreed, giving me a much more chaste kiss goodbye than his kiss the previous evening, and I headed back to the pack house, determined to find out as much as I could before that evening. I didn't want to string Kyle along if my fated mate turned out to be the right match for me, but in order to know that, I first had to figure out who the hell he was.

For that, I needed to talk to Amanda.

Chapter Eighteen

~Jasper~

Myra knew exactly where she wanted to go for our first stop. As soon as her shoulder felt up to it, we shifted and headed back down the mountain, carefully skirting the edge of the Ravenstone territory until we approached a narrow corridor that led between two of the foothills, the path carved out by a small stream of water over time. The stream still flowed to one side, with enough space next to it for us to walk comfortably without getting wet.

We've been here before, Sterling reminded me. *Just after the exile.*

I remembered. I also remembered the wolf I encountered on the other side. I tried to talk to him or her, they threatened me, and the haze took over. I couldn't remember what happened after that but I woke up back on the other side of the corridor, so the wolf must have successfully chased us off.

If we were going to see that wolf, hopefully Myra knew some tricks that I didn't.

Eventually, the pathway widened into another thick pine forest, the trees overhead nearly blocking out the sun entirely as we left the hill behind us. As silently as possibly, keeping our ears trained for any sign of trouble, Myra and I followed our noses and it didn't take long to pick up the scent of another rogue wolf.

The scent came from the forest ahead, but a moment later, I could also smell it behind us, which meant only one thing.

There's more than one. Sterling had the exact same thought I did, and I wished I could communicate with Myra to let her know. She continued to move forward even as I glanced over my shoulder.

Suddenly, she came to an abrupt stop, so fast that I nearly ran into her from behind, and lifting her head up to the sky, she let out a loud, plaintive howl.

That seemed to be some kind of signal because in the next few seconds, not one, not even two, but *three* different wolves appeared from the trees around us, making it clear they'd been tracking us the whole time.

Myra shifted first, letting them know, if her howl hadn't been enough, that we weren't there to cause any trouble.

"Come on," she muttered to me as I hesitated, waiting to see if they would attack. "They won't shift until you do."

Although I didn't like it, I would have done the same in their position, so reluctantly, I took my human form.

Before I could even get fully to my feet, the three wolves all shifted to men, one of whom I recognized despite looking a lot scruffier than I remembered the logistics officer who used to work in the same building I did. His missing glasses also altered his appearance, but enough of him remained the same to make the connection.

"Dan?"

He stared closely at me for a moment, perhaps straining to recognize me beneath the beard and dirt as I had with him, or maybe because he couldn't see that well without his glasses. "Jasper?"

"You know this guy?" one of the others asked gruffly. An older, burly man, solidly built, he looked like he could have been one of the Alpha's security detail. I didn't recognize him, but that didn't mean much; those guys were trained to blend into the background.

"I did, in our other life."

The third one hadn't said anything yet. A tall, lean man, he had a long scar across his stomach, and he glanced nervously between all of us while I sized up the situation as well as I could.

"I thought you said everyone kept to themselves," I reminded Myra. I thought we'd have to approach the others one-by-one rather than three at a time.

"We have an agreement to keep other wolves out," the gruff one said, crossing his arms over his broad chest. "And that includes you. Three of us in this area is plenty. We don't need any more."

"We don't want anything from your area," Myra told him, matching his tone exactly. "You know I've left you alone until now."

"What do you want, then?" Dan asked.

She didn't waste any words. "We're planning an incursion into Ravenstone territory and we're looking for people who want in."

The men exchanged glances again, but with curiosity colouring their animosity that time.

"What do you want from them?" the third man asked, the one who had been silent until then. His voice sounded almost as raw as Myra's had the day before, and the other two men looked over at him in surprise, making me think he didn't usually speak up without good reason.

"A few things, but the main one is that we want to know why we were exiled. Do you all know why you were kicked out? Dan?" I started with the man I knew, figuring he might be the most likely to open up to me. "They made an announcement that you'd taken extended leave to visit relatives in another pack."

His thick brown eyebrows drew together in utter bewilderment. "That doesn't make any sense. Why wouldn't they tell the truth?"

"What's the truth?"

Everyone subconsciously leaned a little closer, not wanting to miss any part of his answer. "Some supplies that had been ordered for the medical clinic struck me as odd, so I went to my supervisor about it. Next thing I knew, some of the Alpha's guards arrested me. They told me supplies had gone missing, and because arranging the shipment was my responsibility, they suspected me of being involved in their disappearance. I had *nothing* to do with it, I swear, but they told me they found proof that I'd been siphoning off supplies for years. If I accepted exile, they promised not to take any action against my mate or children."

"Your mate is still in there?" Myra asked in horror, a horror that I shared. What kind of monsters separated a man from his mate? What the fuck was going on in my former pack?

"They said they would tell her what happened, but if they made up a different story for everyone else, I have to wonder exactly what they told her. I've stayed away to keep her safe, but it's killing me to be apart from her and our boys."

Scouring my memory, I tried to place his departure in the timeline I'd started to compile in my head. My old investigative techniques were coming back after lying unused for months, and if we were going to get to the bottom of this, I needed to be on top of my game. With every new piece of information, it grew clearer that whatever was going on didn't only affect me.

"That was about three months ago, right?"

Dan looked almost distraught, his face sagging in defeat. "Is it? I've lost track."

I knew how that felt.

"What about you?" I asked the bigger man. "What's your name?"

His tight lips didn't seem to want to answer, but he grudgingly supplied his name. "Lee."

"What did they kick you out for, Lee?"

"I walked in on a private meeting of the Alpha's. I didn't realize it was confidential. I didn't even hear anything, but the next thing I knew, I was out of the pack."

That reinforced Myra's conclusion that the Alpha, or at least someone very close to him, must have been involved in the exiles.

"And you?" I asked the final man.

Clearing his throat, he shared his story. "I'm Brent. I worked in the medical clinic, but I don't remember what happened. I woke up one day out in the forest, my pack link had vanished, and I had this."

He gestured down at the scar on his torso as my own stomach turned.

Something very, very strange was going on in the Ravenstone pack and they had my mate entirely at their mercy. Somehow, I had to find a way to keep her safe.

87

Chapter Nineteen

~Savannah~

After convincing Heather that I did *not* need a nap in the middle of the day like a toddler, she showed me to the Luna's office where Amanda sat behind a modern-looking desk, all the office furniture in white with the walls painted a cornflower blue. From the large window behind the desk, the office had yet another stunning view over the lake and mountains. The pack house certainly had its fair share of gorgeous vistas, but I'd come there to talk about the people in the pack, not the scenery.

"How are you?" Amanda asked as soon as we were alone together.

I suspected Heather would be hovering outside the door the entire time we spoke, so I glanced back to make sure the door had been fully closed and our conversation wouldn't be overheard. Her constant presence frayed my nerves even though I knew she was only doing her job.

Amanda gave me a curious look when I turned back to her but didn't question what I was checking for. "I'm sorry I didn't get a chance to talk to you when we got back this morning. My father wanted to see me. I heard the doctor discharged Felix with a few scratches but they didn't say anything about you."

"I'm fine. Nobody hurt me. What about you?"

"Absolutely fine too," she agreed, and she certainly looked as impeccably put together as always, her long, brown hair gathered over one shoulder of her pretty pink blouse. "The wolves seemed much more interested in you than me, though, at least the first one that approached us."

I knew exactly why that would have been, but I kept quiet about finding my mate for the time being. First, I wanted to get some information out of her, but I also knew I had to tread lightly. My mother taught me that people were a lot more likely to open up when you connected with them first. Amanda and I had a decent rapport already, despite what happened with my brother, and so far, she'd acted entirely in good faith when it came to choosing a mate for me. I wanted to believe she'd be honest with me, but I also thought it would be better to ease into the conversation rather than diving straight into asking about the rogues.

Besides, there were other things I wanted to know too, and I decided to start with one of those first. "I had lunch with Kyle. He explained about the genetic modifications made to the pack, and how that relates to how much you guys are fed."

A quick smile flashed across Amanda's face. "That's good. I didn't try to explain it to you myself because, to be honest, I don't fully understand it. I only know that since they've put the program in place, everyone's in excellent shape, so it must be working."

That logic felt a bit flawed to me since most werewolves were in good shape to begin with, but I didn't want to argue the details. The big picture interested me much more.

"Were you all told they were making these modifications to your genes?" I had wondered about that when Kyle mentioned it, but I didn't want to ask him directly in case it sounded like an accusation.

Amanda also looked puzzled that I would ask. "Of course. There was a pack-wide meeting and education program about it."

That made me feel a little better about the whole thing, I had to admit. "Did they make any other changes too?"

"No, not yet. I know they're working on more in the lab, but that was the first one they felt was safe. The doctors tested it on themselves first to make sure it worked. Everything's above board, Savannah."

She sounded a little defensive even though I had done my best to keep my tone and questions neutral. "I didn't say anything shady was going on, but out of curiosity: how would you know?"

Her frown looked out of place on her pretty face. "What?"

"If they made other modifications at the same time, how would you know?"

To her credit, she took a moment to think that over. "I guess we wouldn't, but the Alpha trusts the scientists and I trust my Alpha and father. That's how a pack works, right? We all have to trust each other with our lives."

That gave me the perfect opening to the other thing I wanted to ask her about. "Trust is important, but what if someone didn't like the idea of gene modification? Could they say they didn't want it? Is there an opt-out clause?"

"It works best if everyone takes part," she conceded. "That way, the kitchens can stock the right amount of food and the doctors know that everyone's bodies are working the same way. If anyone had objections, they were given the opportunity to ask questions about it until everyone felt comfortable. Eventually, everyone did."

"Everyone? No one was exiled because they wouldn't take part?"

That thought had come to me as I considered the text my brother had sent to Felix, about how there might be an internal problem at the pack. I couldn't say for sure if the two things were related, the gene modification and the presence of rogues on the pack's borders, but given that they were both unusual circumstances, it didn't seem impossible that there might be some kind of correlation.

However, Amanda looked horrified at the suggestion. "Of course not. No one would ever be kicked out of the pack over a simple disagreement. Exile is reserved for the most serious crimes. I don't think anyone's been exiled from Ravenstone since I was a child."

Did she honestly believe that? Assuming my mate had told me the truth, what Amanda said couldn't also be true. One of them had to be wrong, but were they intentionally lying or just misinformed?

Since accusing her of lying probably wouldn't get me very far, I tried a different tactic. "I'm glad to hear that. This is a nice office. It belongs to your mom?"

Amanda glanced around at the same time I did, looking slightly thrown off by the change of subject, but she quickly recomposed herself. "Yes. She's been a wonderful Luna for the pack, but with her health suffering lately, she hasn't used it much. I was looking after some of her responsibilities before the agreement with your pack, and now that I'm back, I guess I'll continue to do so."

"I'm sorry she hasn't been well. Do you mind if I ask what kind of illness she has?"

Amanda's lips tightened unhappily. "They don't actually know but the doctors are working hard to try to figure it out."

That must be difficult for the whole family, but I had a particular reason for asking so I kept going. "Are there pictures of her when you were younger? Family pictures, maybe at an event? I know our pack has decades worth of photos from pack celebrations in our archives. I'd be curious to see them."

Amanda gave me a shrewd look, her expression turning almost amused. "I know what you're up to, Savannah."

I didn't see how she could. I hoped that by looking at pictures of old pack celebrations, I could locate my mate when he'd been part of the pack. *If* he'd been part of the pack. Since there was no way Amanda could have figured that out without knowing about my mate in the first place, I played dumb. "I don't know what you mean."

"Really? This wouldn't have anything to do with looking at pictures of Kyle and his family? You want to see what *his* genes are like?"

Her lips had begun to curl upwards, looking rather pleased with herself for figuring it out, and if she wanted to think that was my intention, I didn't see a problem with that. It would hide my true purpose well enough, so I gave her a sheepish shrug. "You caught me. I'd like to see the whole pack, but maybe one person in particular."

Technically, that wasn't a lie.

"Well, I'm sure that can be arranged." She reached over and pressed a button on her desk, and almost instantly, Heather opened the door. She really *had* been waiting there the whole time. "Can you take Savannah to the library and show her our photo archives?"

"Of course, Lota." Heather bowed her head to Amanda, and I got to my feet, thanking the Alpha's daughter for her time.

"I'm glad you found someone you're interested in," Amanda said before I left, and she really did sound sincere. "I'd like to think there's a happy ending out there for all of us."

"I would too. Thank you."

With that, she went back to her work while I followed Heather to the library, eager to start scouring the photos for any sign of the man I met that morning. Things were still frustratingly unclear, but somehow or another, I intended to get to the bottom of the mystery I'd stumbled into.

Chapter Twenty

~Jasper~

The other rogue wolves all appeared equally taken aback to find out that we'd all been exiled from the pack under shadowy, unusual circumstances. Perhaps they all assumed, much like I had, that they were the exception and everyone else must have done something terrible to deserve their fate. Finding out they hadn't been guilty of much at all only strengthened my conviction that I hadn't done anything all that bad either, even though I still couldn't remember the exact circumstances of my banishment.

While my mind remained clear and focused, I needed to make a plan.

"Based on what you've all said, there seem to be two common denominators: the medical centre and the Alpha. Myra and Brent both worked for the medical clinic or the lab, and Dan was involved in procuring items for them. Meanwhile, Lee worked for the Alpha, and Myra pointed out to me earlier that no one would be exiled without the Alpha's knowledge. He must be aware of what's happening."

"What are you, some kind of detective?" Lee grumbled, apparently not appreciating the way I took charge. As the oldest and strongest in the ragtag group, perhaps he thought that should be his role.

"Actually, he *is* a detective," Dan confirmed. "He used to work in internal security. That's where I know him from."

"What did they kick you out for?" Brent asked me.

I could only grimace. "Like you, I'm not entirely sure. The last thing I remember, I was investigating some kids who had gone missing. A pack member I spoke to recently said he'd been told that I was the one behind their disappearance and they exiled me for that reason."

Immediately, the faces in front of me turned a lot stonier. Werewolves were very protective of any children in the pack, not just their own. If I *had* done anything to those kids, they would have been well within their right to tear me apart. As quickly as possible, I tried to diffuse their concerns and defend myself.

"Like I said, I don't know what happened with my exile, but I do know that I'd never seen those kids before I started investigating their disappearance. I truly believe that I didn't have anything to do with them going missing. Just like Dan got accused of stealing supplies when he didn't, I think someone set me up to take the fall. They're trying to cover their tracks, but where do those tracks lead? Who's behind all of this and why?"

Those were questions I didn't expect answers to, not yet, but it wouldn't hurt to get us all on the same page and thinking about the same things. The more information we had, the better.

"So, you want to get in to find out what happened," Dan summed up, and I nodded in agreement.

"Not only for me, but for all of us. When it was just me, I could accept it might have been bad luck or a personal vendetta. With five of us, it's starting to feel like a conspiracy. We might not be the last ones it happens to either. We deserve answers. We deserve justice, and we need to make sure that nobody else gets hurt. Myra already said she'll help. Are the three of you with us?"

The men all exchanged looks while Myra stood at my side, her arms crossed in a show of support.

Lee spoke first. "It *is* weird that none of us have a strong reason for being exiled. I served the Alpha for a lot of years and I don't want to believe he'd be behind anything underhanded, but it also doesn't make sense that he wouldn't know about it. I've overheard stuff over the years, not on purpose but in the course of things, and I know that the Alpha has a special bond to his pack. He feels it when any pack member dies, and he'd feel it when they're exiled too. There's no way this could be happening without his knowledge."

I'd had my suspicions about that, but hearing it confirmed by someone who knew for sure made it even clearer. "So even if he's not ordering the banishments himself, he's definitely aware of it. What about the medical centre? Do you know anyone there who might be involved?"

I included everyone in the question, and Brent spoke up first. "It'd have to be someone with a lot of access inside the centre and access to the Alpha. There are three men from the clinic on the Alpha's leadership team, but I don't know any of them personally."

"That's okay. Narrowing it down to three is really helpful. If you give us names, it gives us somewhere to start looking."

"What's your plan?" Dan interjected. "Before anyone signs up for this, what exactly are you proposing?"

My answer to that had shifted over the course of the conversation, but I did my best to share my thought process with them. "Originally, I hoped you could create a distraction with the border guards so I could slip through unnoticed, but after everything you've told me, we need to think bigger than that. We need to get into the medical centre or the pack house, and I'm guessing the medical centre might be slightly easier due to the pack house security."

I gave Lee a nod of acknowledgement, and he nodded back, obviously agreeing with me.

"It still won't be easy. We'll need people who know their way around, like Brent and Myra."

Myra had been listening to everything carefully, and when I said her name, she asked a question of her own. "If we all go with you, who's making the distraction? If we're all together, they'll track us down in no time."

She was right: some kind of distraction would still be necessary. "Are there any other rogue wolves around? Maybe ones who *weren't* exiled from the Ravenstone pack?"

"I haven't met any others," Myra replied, and Dan and Brent both shook their heads too.

Lee, however, had a different answer. "I don't know any other werewolves, but there's a wolf pack that lives further north, about ten miles from here."

"Regular wolves? What good does that do us?" Brent asked. His voice sounded stronger every time he spoke, and now that he'd started, he had quite a lot to say.

Lee had an answer for him too. "You want a distraction, right? We run in *with* them. The border guard will know that we're there, but visually, they won't be able to distinguish us from the other wolves. The different scents will make things harder."

I could see the potential, but there was one thing I didn't understand. "How are you going to get a pack of wild wolves to do what you say?"

"They're not so different from us," Lee reminded us all. "They'll do anything to protect their own, and I know for a fact they've got some new pups in the pack. We make them think we've snatched one of their pups and they'll chase us as far as they need to."

Maybe I'd been too long on my own, but that actually made sense to me. If they were intent on catching us, the Ravenstone wolves would only be in their way. They'd be motivated to evade them.

"I'm not putting a pup in danger, wolf or werewolf," Myra stated firmly.

"Neither am I," Lee growled back. "I said we make them *think* we did. Put together a little bundle that looks like a pup from a distance. It'd be enough to fool at least some of 'em."

It might work, and more than that, we didn't have any other ideas at the moment. Every second we spent debating was one more that my mate might be in danger, so in the absence of any better plans, I gave my approval. "Alright. Let's figure out how this is going to work and what we're going to do when we get there. We're only going to get one shot at this, so we need to make it count."

Chapter Twenty-One

After almost two hours of flipping through photos on the computer in the pack house library, my eyes had started to blur. Heather sat next to me 'in case I needed help,' she said, but even she had lost interest in the images on my screen. She started reading on her phone instead, glancing up every now and then, and quickly going back to her own reading when she saw I still hadn't given up yet.

Whoever my mate was, he didn't come from one of the ranked families. They were there in all the photos, front and centre, with the rest of the pack often confined to the background. I spotted Kyle in a picture from about five years earlier, but I quickly scrolled past it before Heather could notice, in case she would wonder why I kept looking after I'd already found one.

Maybe my mate didn't come from this pack after all. He never said he did, he only said he'd be back. Maybe Vaughan and Calista had it wrong.

I'd almost decided the whole exercise was pointless when I clicked on a photo that seemed to show some kind of ceremony, right there in the pack house library where I currently sat. The Alpha had a medal of some kind in his hands, and the man he presented it to...

Yes. It has to be, Tala piped up in my head. *He doesn't have the beard, but look at his eyes. His forehead. His lips. It's him.*

I had to agree, especially once I zoomed in and his green eyes became even clearer. The square jaw surprised me, since it hadn't been clear beneath his beard, but his thick eyebrows were the same, and the eyes staring back at me from the screen sealed the deal. If they weren't the same man, my mate must have had a twin brother. For a second, that thought managed to distract me as I imagined myself mated to *two* of them, making a hot, muscled sandwich around me, but I quickly shook that thought aside to focus on the image in front of me.

"Did you find something?" Heather noticed that I stopped clicking and started studying a particular photo, and I quickly zoomed out before she could get a closer look.

"No, I think I zoned out there for a second," I lied. Instinctively, I suspected that the fewer people who knew about my mate, the better. "I'm going to look for a couple of more minutes and then I'll be done. Would you mind getting me a glass of water? It's pretty dry in here."

She looked relieved to have the chance to stretch her legs after sitting for so long. "Of course. I'll be right back."

As soon as the door clicked shut behind her, I pulled out my phone and took several pictures of the photo on screen, both the wide version and the zoomed-in one. I'd only just shoved my phone back in my pocket when the door opened again and Heather walked back in with my glass of water.

The cool liquid helped to refresh me but did nothing to slow the accelerated beating of my heart as I kept scrolling through photos, keeping up appearances in front of Heather while I tried to connect the dots in my head. Assuming I had the right guy, and I would have sworn I did, he *had* been part of the pack, and fairly recently too. From the way the other wolves reacted to him that morning, he was definitely a rogue. Therefore, it stood to reason that he must have been exiled, despite Amanda saying there hadn't been any banishments in the last decade.

Something didn't add up.

Felix? I reached out to my pack's Beta through our mind-link. *Where are you?*

The response came back almost immediately. *Watching some junior warriors training. Nothing I can't skip. Do you need me?*

Yeah. I'm in the library but I'll be leaving soon. Can you meet me outside and make it look like we ran into each other, not on purpose?

Ohhhh-kay. His drawn-out reply made me smile, though I tried to hide that from Heather too. *Sounds like you're up to something. I'll be there in five minutes.*

The seconds seemed to drag as I waited another five minutes before yawning loudly. "Oh, wow. Sorry. I guess I'm more tired than I thought. Maybe I will go back to my room and have that nap now."

"Certainly, Lota." Heather got to her feet again and led me out of the room, stepping almost straight into Felix as he walked down the hall.

"Oh, hey, Sav." He did his best to sound surprised to see me, as planned.

"Hey. I'm about to head back to my room. Maybe you could walk me there? I'm sure Heather needs a break from me."

I smiled at my shadow to try to make it seem like I really did have her best interests at heart, but she immediately shook her head. "Actually, the Alpha just asked to see you. I'll take you to his office."

Damn it. That wasn't part of my plan.

"Both of us?" Felix asked.

Heather shook her head again. "No, only Lota Savannah. You're free to go, Beta Felix."

A quick glance was all it took for Felix to get the message that I didn't want to go alone. "That's alright, I have nowhere else I need to be. I'll come along too."

She didn't have the authority to argue with Felix even if she wanted to, so without protest, she accompanied us both to the Alpha's office. Next door to the Luna's office where I'd been earlier with Amanda, it was as solid and masculine inside as the Luna's office had been light and feminine. A rusty red colour covered the walls, dark shades of brown made up the furniture, and behind the desk, a large window had the same spectacular view as the room next door.

Alpha Warren sat behind his desk, and Heather bowed deeply as she caught sight of him. A flick of his wrist dismissed her, and she closed the door behind her as she left.

I didn't know why he wanted to see me, but the words that came out of his mouth were unexpected anyway. "Is there a reason you were taking photos of our pack archives, Lota Savannah?"

Felix glanced over at me in surprise while I did my best to maintain a neutral expression. I could have sworn Heather didn't see me, but belatedly, I realized there were probably security cameras in the library. That should have shocked me, but there had been so many odd little things about the Ravenstone pack that I barely felt a twinge of surprise.

I started with an apology, hoping that would satisfy him. "I'm sorry if that's not allowed, Alpha. I didn't realize it would be a problem."

Heather certainly would have told me if she'd seen me taking it, I had no doubt, which was exactly why I'd sent her out of the room.

"What did you take a photo of?" the Alpha asked, his tone not altering at all with my apology. He didn't sound angry, exactly, but not happy either. He definitely expected an answer.

I supposed I would have to come clean. The Alpha could take my phone from me if he really wanted to. We were still on his territory, where his word was law. Maybe by cooperating, I could find a way to ask the Alpha about the man in the photo.

Making up my mind, I reached into my pocket and pulled up the photo. As I tapped on the screen, I airdropped it to Felix's phone as subtly as I could before handing the phone across the Alpha's desk.

His expression didn't change at all as he looked down at the photo for himself, giving me no clue what he might be thinking. "What's your interest in this particular photo?"

"I'm curious about the man in it. Who is he, and what's he being given a medal for? I took the photo so I could ask Amanda, but I suppose you'll know as well as she will."

That sounded like a plausible reason for having taken the photo, and the Alpha didn't disagree. He did, however, question my interest again. "Why did this particular picture catch your eye?"

"Why won't you answer my question?"

The words came out before I had fully thought them through, and Felix quickly stepped in, holding out his hand for the phone. "May I see it, Alpha Warren?"

The Alpha passed the phone to Felix, who peered at it curiously. I had no idea if he'd put together the identity of the man in the photo, but I trusted Felix to have my back.

He didn't let me down. "Ah, I'm not surprised this got Sav's attention. Did you know that Savannah instituted a new recognition program for our warriors?"

That was a complete and total fabrication, and I could have kissed Felix for it.

"No, I didn't, but that's a noble endeavour," the Alpha replied, his eyes moving back over to me as he took the phone back from Felix. "Maintaining pack morale is very important. That particular medal was for services to the pack, but not for a warrior. That's one of our civilian medals."

"You give medals for other types of service too?" I asked curiously, leaning into the cover Felix had provided for me.

"Certainly. Our doctors, our scientists, our engineers, everyone deserves recognition for excelling in their chosen field."

Actually, I rather agreed with that, but he still hadn't answered my initial question. "What was this particular medal for?"

The Alpha's lips tightened a tiny bit. "That man belonged to our internal security team, and he was being recognized for his work in that role."

That was still frustratingly vague. "Could I speak to him? I'd like to know how the recognition made him feel and what he did with the medal afterwards."

"I'm afraid that won't be possible. That particular man has been seconded to work with another pack, but if you're that interested in our recognition program, there are several members of the leadership team who have also been rewarded that you could speak to. Kyle, for instance."

Without asking, the Alpha deleted all the photos I'd taken from my phone and handed it back to me.

"It'll be easier if you don't take any more photos without asking for permission first. My pack's safety and security come first for me, Lota Savannah. Always."

"I understand, Alpha. Thank you."

Bowing our heads in acknowledgement, Felix and I left the room. The hallway was mercifully Heather-free, and Felix and I walked briskly back to my room in silence. As soon as we were inside, I turned to him and said the words I knew we were both thinking: "He's lying. The Alpha's covering something up, and we need to figure out what it is."

Chapter Twenty-Two

~Savannah~

Felix's voice immediately sounded in my head despite him standing right in front of me. *It's not safe for us to talk here. If they have surveillance in the library, they might have it everywhere in the house.*

My arms immediately crossed over my chest as I glanced around, looking for any telltale signs of a camera. *You think someone's been watching me in here? That's creepy as fuck!*

I'd been naked several times in that room already. Sure, as werewolves, we were often naked in front of strangers, but usually only by choice.

Felix took a look around too and thankfully didn't seem to notice anything obvious. *They might not be watching, but they could still be listening.*

Shit. If that's true, then we're already screwed. I told you about finding my mate this morning when we were in here!

Don't panic yet. I'm not certain they've bugged the room but better to be safe than sorry. I'm guessing the guy in the photo is your mate? And you sent a copy of it to me?

With a sigh, I flopped down on the bed, covering my eyes with my hands to block everything else out and try to make some sense of all the thoughts whirling around my head. *Yeah. When I spoke to Amanda earlier, she said no one had been exiled from the pack since she was a kid. Either she's lying or she doesn't know about it. The Alpha is definitely lying, though. No one would be exiled without his knowledge. Why is it a secret?*

The bed sank down beneath me as Felix took a seat on the mattress, thinking things over. *It's going to be difficult to get any information if everyone's in on it together. I think our first step should be finding out exactly what Amanda knows and if she can be trusted.*

You think she can be? That had been my gut feeling, and I suspected Felix wouldn't even bring it up if he didn't have the same intuition.

*What she said was very specific: not since she was a kid. She didn't have to say that if she were lying. She could have said it never happens or it hasn't happened for a while. My gut says that she believes it's true. Let's show her the photo and ask her about it specifically. **Away** from the pack house and any hidden cameras or listening devices.*

That all sounded good to me but we didn't have a lot of time before dinner that night. We'd have to make it quick.

Luckily, Amanda agreed to a walk along the lakeshore with us, and no one from the security team stopped us from leaving or followed us, as far as I could tell. If we'd aroused anyone's suspicions other than the photos I'd taken, I couldn't see any signs of it.

We made small talk about the territory and the pack until we were out of sight of the pack house and out of earshot of anyone who might be interested in our conversation. As soon as Felix gave me a nod confirming he thought it would be safe to go ahead, I dove in.

"I found something interesting in the photo archives this afternoon."

Amanda glanced over at me, curious but not *too* interested. "Other than pictures of Kyle, you mean?"

I let that go, not bothering to correct her. "It's a photo of your father giving a medal to someone from the internal security team."

Her eyebrows drew together, making her look slightly confused. "What makes that interesting?"

"The photo isn't very old. Maybe from two or three years ago? When I asked your father about it and whether I could speak to the man, he said the man in the photo has been seconded to another pack."

She glanced between me and Felix, still looking unsure. "I feel like I'm missing something."

Felix reached into his pocket to pull out his phone, handing the photo to her. "Do you recognize that man?"

Amanda came to a stop to better examine the photo and eventually, she nodded. "Yeah. I don't know him well, but that's Jasper. One of my friends had a big crush on him back in school."

I could see why. When I saw him that morning, he looked ruggedly handsome, and in the photo, clean-shaven and wearing a suit, he looked just as good. I loved a man who looked good both dressed up and dressed down. Or wearing nothing at all, for that matter.

Jasper. It was a good, strong name. I liked it too.

"I didn't know he'd been seconded somewhere else, but I'm not surprised," Amanda continued, handing the phone back to Felix as we resumed our walk. "He's very good at his job. That medal he got was for stopping a smuggling ring that had recruited some of our younger, more impressionable young warriors. He protected not only our pack but the wider region too."

Tala hummed with pride inside my head while my chest swelled with it too. Smart as well as handsome, apparently. So far, so good with my mate, if we forgot the whole rogue thing.

"I'm still not sure what's so interesting about the photo though," she reminded me.

Should I tell her? I asked Felix in my head. Amanda certainly didn't act like someone with something to hide and I couldn't see how we would get the answers we needed if we didn't explain what we knew about Jasper's rogue status.

Go ahead. I've already texted Vaughan to let him know that if he doesn't hear from me hourly for the rest of the night, he should assume we're in trouble.

Well, that makes me feel much better.

I threw Felix a withering glare before turning to Amanda.

"Here's the thing: the Alpha said he's been seconded and *you* said no one's been exiled from the pack recently, right?"

"Right," she confirmed.

"So, how is the man in the photo the rogue wolf that we ran into this morning?"

Again, Amanda came to a stop, but that time, much more abruptly, her eyes wide with surprise. "That can't be true."

I stopped too, coming to stand right in front of her to look her square in the face. "I promise you it is. He shifted in front of me. The rogue wolf was Jasper, which means he wasn't seconded anywhere. He was exiled. You and your father both lied to me today, and as someone who's considering whether or not to join this pack, I can't say that gives me a lot of confidence that it would be the right decision."

She held my gaze, her eyes conflicted and her lips growing tighter with every word I spoke. "I didn't lie," she protested when I'd finished saying my piece. "I had no idea Jasper had been exiled, but if you're really sure..."

"I'm sure."

"Then let's go and ask my father why *he* would lie about it."

Turning sharply on her heel, she headed back towards the pack house while I shrugged over at Felix. *Should we let her go and ask him?*

I don't think we can really stop her at this point. Buckle up, Sav, looks like we're going for a ride.

At the pack house, Amanda marched straight to her father's office, opening the door without knocking. Luckily, he was on his own, reviewing some files, and he looked pleased to see her until he caught sight of me and Felix behind her. "What's going on?"

Making sure the door was closed behind us, Amanda walked over to the solid dark-wood desk, standing over it so her father would have to look up at her from his seat. "Why did you exile Jasper McMillan?"

The Alpha's expression barely altered, but I noticed the way his grip tightened on the armrest of his office chair. "Who told you that?"

To my relief, Amanda kept me out of it. "Someone from the border guard said they saw him outside the territory, as a rogue wolf."

"Really." He said it as a statement, not a question, his eyes flicking over to me for a second. He would have to guess it wasn't a coincidence that

I happened to be looking at a photo of the same man, but I did my best to look unconcerned.

Amanda refused to back down. "Yes, really. Was he lying?"

The Alpha's lips tightened much like his daughter's had earlier, both of them sharing the same mannerism when they didn't like what they were hearing. After what he said before, I thought he'd deny it, but when he answered, his words came as a surprise. "No, he wasn't lying. Jasper was exiled three months ago."

"What? Why?" Amanda sounded so stunned that if I'd had any doubt that she hadn't known about it, that uncertainty would have been erased. If she was acting, she deserved an award.

"We kept it quiet because of the circumstances of his disgrace. We didn't want it to be common knowledge among the pack that someone we'd held up as a hero was actually a monster."

My stomach lurched at the final word and I couldn't stop myself from speaking up. "Monster? What do you mean?"

When his eyes moved back to me, the expression in them was almost apologetic. "I didn't want you to be concerned about this, Lota Savannah. I understand it can be distressing to hear about these kinds of things, and I didn't want you to get the wrong idea about our pack."

"What did the man do, Alpha Warren?" Felix asked from beside me. As Beta of our own pack, he would know as well as anyone what reasonable punishments were.

The Alpha leaned back in his chair with a sigh. "He abducted two pups, young ones."

The gasp that echoed around the room made me jump, and I realized a second later it had actually come from me.

Amanda also turned a little paler. "What did he do to them?"

"Thankfully, we found them before he could do anything. He was actually in charge of the investigation to find them, so we don't know if he set the whole thing up to make himself look like a hero, or if he had more sinister intentions the whole time. The children were drugged and a little malnourished, but luckily, we got to them in time and they've made a full recovery."

No. Tala's voice was firm in my head, rejecting the explanation the Alpha offered as much as my own heart wanted to. *He wouldn't do something like that.*

I wanted to believe that, but what did I really know about him? Absolutely nothing, and it *did* make sense why the Alpha wouldn't have been keen to share that particular piece of news with me until we forced his hand.

Could I really be mated to someone... evil?

Before any of us could ask any follow-up questions, the Alpha's door burst open and Beta Chad came rushing in. A brief look of surprise flashed across his face when he saw us all there, but he didn't stop, hurrying straight over to stand next to Amanda in front of the Alpha's desk.

"Alpha, we've had a report from the border guard. There's been another rogue incursion."

Jasper? He said he'd be back. Those words that I'd taken as a promise suddenly seemed a bit more sinister.

"And?" the Alpha asked, making it clear he thought they should be able to handle it on their own without his input.

"And they're not alone. There are dozens of wild wolves with them, and they're heading right for the pack house."

Chapter Twenty-Three

~Jasper~

In the end, getting the wolves to chase us turned out to be easier than I would have guessed. We all agreed that we'd give our own wolves control over our bodies since they had stronger wolf instincts than the human sides of us did. When split-second decisions were required, they were more likely to make the right ones.

First, we had to make our decoy pup, and there, Myra far outshone the rest of us. Finding a thick, short piece of wood on the forest floor, she used her wolf claws to tap into the sap of one of the nearby pine trees. When the wood had been coated in the sap, she rubbed it over Lee's wolf, covering it in fur. Close up, it didn't look anything like a wolf pup, but from a distance, carried in the mouth of a wolf moving fast, it could pass.

Since the wolves would focus on the one carrying the 'pup', and the whole thing had been my idea in the first place, I volunteered to be the one carrying it. I would stay in the middle of our small group, hidden from view as we made our foray into the wolves' territory, and only when we reached the pups would I make a break for it, making it look like I'd snatched one of their young.

You've got this, I assured Sterling, watching as he and the others moved at a steady trot, following Lee to where he knew the pups would be kept. *We're going to get some answers and we're going to get to our mate and make sure she's safe.*

I won't let us down, he promised.

Soon, the scent of the wild wolves reached us and we slowed our pace, moving as quietly as possible through the trees so as not to alert them of our presence too early. At last, Lee made the prearranged signal, bowing his head twice, deeply, before jerking his head to the right. Everyone looked in that direction and sure enough, we could see a large den where two wolves had their backs to us. Beyond them, we would find the pups.

Nodding once more, Lee broke into a run with the rest of us close behind, no longer trying to hide. We wanted all the animals to see us, and me in particular. The terror in the young pup's eyes as Sterling brushed against him sent a twinge of regret through me, but he didn't actually cause him any harm. Instead, he broke free from the others, heading back the way we came with the fur-covered wood in his mouth.

As Lee predicted, all hell broke loose. Howls, growls and barks echoed behind me, accompanied by the steady drumbeat of paws on the forest floor as my companions followed me back towards the Raven-stone pack with a much bigger contingent of wolves than I'd expected on our tail. There had to be at least thirty of them, and they were about as happy as I'd expect them to be, thinking that I'd taken one of their pups. Those left behind would quickly realize none of the pups were missing, but without the ability to mind-link that werewolves had, they would have no way of passing that information on. As far as the wolves behind me were concerned, they were engaged in a battle for the life of one of their pack members, and they had no intention of letting me win.

Back through the narrow canyon passage we ran, along the stream, and back to the foot of the mountain with Myra's cave. From there, the roof of the pack house could be seen, and I headed straight for it, knowing as soon as we crossed the border, an alert would go up. Hopefully, the presence of all the extra wolves with us would confuse and distract them.

As soon as we see the security team, run right at them and drop the 'pup,' I advised Sterling. They'll get caught up with the other wolves, and we can make our break for it.

The others had already peeled off from the group, splitting up and making their own way to the medical centre as we planned. We all knew the protocol for an attack within the pack: everyone would be ordered to shelter indoors wherever they were, other than the warriors who would come out to fight. The work day would have already ended, so the medical centre should be relatively quiet. We planned it all out as best we could with the time we had; now, we had to hope it worked.

My lungs burned as Sterling continued his sprint, getting within a mile of the pack house before the Ravenstone warriors finally appeared. Any other day, I would have run away from them, but at that moment, they were exactly who I wanted to see.

As I drew closer, I could see the confusion on their faces, wondering why I kept running straight at them, but they didn't stop either, and at the last minute, as late as I could leave it, I dropped the furry wood on the ground and took a sharp left, veering out of the way.

The momentum of the Ravenstone wolves was too great to stop, and as they trampled over the piece of wood, the wolves behind me howled in fury, their teeth bared and their minds set on revenge as they ran straight into the Ravenstone defense.

I didn't stick around to watch what happened next.

Running like his life depended on it, which in many ways it did, Sterling darted through the trees, through all the shortcuts we knew from a lifetime in these lands, avoiding detection as we made our way not to the pack house where even more warriors would be waiting, but to the medical centre instead.

Myra, Brent and Dan were already there when I got there, as out of breath as I was, and we all shifted in unison, retaking our human forms as adrenaline ran through my veins. I wanted to celebrate that we'd actually gotten that far, but I knew there was much more still to be done.

"Where's Lee?" I asked, looking around while Brent used his security codes to open one of the back doors into the centre, close to the laboratories and away from any patient or doctor areas.

"I lost sight of him," Myra admitted. "We split up in case we were being followed."

"We have to go in," Dan pointed out, casting a nervous glance over his shoulder. "If they find us out here like this…"

"We're going in," Myra assured him. "It's what he would tell us to do."

She had that right, but I couldn't help looking back one more time before I followed Brent through the door, hoping that wherever the big man had ended up, he wasn't in any trouble.

"This way," Myra whispered as soon as we were inside, leading us down the darkened, quiet hallway to one of the supply rooms. There, we found extra clothes we could wear and cleaning supplies which would help to cover our rogue scents, at least temporarily. Everything was where they predicted it would be, and all their old access codes still worked. Pack security must not have thought there was any chance the rogue wolves would ever come back so they hadn't bothered to change the codes.

"Hopefully, my computer login still works too," Dan whispered as I stuck my head cautiously back into the hallway, making sure the coast was clear before we ran down it, looking for an open office we could use.

As we reached a corner, I suddenly put my hand up, silently telling the others to stop. Ahead of us, voices could be heard.

"Someone accessed the south door," a male voice said, sounding out of breath. "We need to verify who it was."

"Why can't the guards do it?" another voice whined. "If I wanted to be in security, I'd have joined their team instead."

"They're all out fighting off the wolf pack. It's probably one of the cleaners but we need to check."

I'd heard enough. They were heading straight for us, but as far as they knew, they were only looking for one of us. Just as I was about to suggest we split up and hide, Brent spoke up first, having obviously reached the same conclusion.

"It was my code that was used. They'll figure it out eventually. I'll let them catch me. Go and hide so they don't see you."

Instinct told me to argue that we could all hide, but the pointed look Myra shot me made it clear she knew better. So did I, if I were honest with myself. If they knew *someone* was there, they wouldn't stop looking until they found us, but they *might* stop looking if they found one of us.

"Thanks," I said simply instead, patting him on the shoulder before nodding at the other two. We managed to duck into an empty office before the men rounded the corner, their shoes skidding on the linoleum floor as they came to an abrupt halt at the sight of Brent.

"Who are you?"

"I'm one of the interns. I work here." He sounded convincing to me but a long pause followed during which none of us in the room dared to even breathe.

"You smell funny," the other man, the whiny one, finally said.

"Yeah, I spilled some of the cleaning fluid on me when we got the alert about the attack. This is crazy, right?"

"It is," the first man agreed, sounding a little more relaxed. "Come with us, we're all supposed to be sheltering in the dining hall."

It sounded like they left, their footsteps getting quieter as they walked away down the hall, and about twenty seconds after I couldn't hear them anymore, I could finally breathe again.

"Let's get into the computer," I whispered to Dan, pointing at the machine on the desk in the office we'd ended up in. "I'll go out and stand guard."

Dan had told us he had access to the pack's personnel records under his old login, so we were going to start there, looking up each of our records to see what had been recorded about us, and looking at who had made any changes to our records. It wouldn't be a lot to go on, but we had to start somewhere, and knowing who the players were seemed like a good first step.

Leaving him and Myra to it, I returned to the hallway, keeping my ears tuned for the sound of anyone else approaching. Next door to the office we'd ended up in, a little further along the hall, sat a large laboratory of some kind, with tubes and vials that looked like something out of a science-fiction movie.

Curiously, I took a step closer, peering through the window to try to make out what might be happening inside. There seemed to be some mice in glass cages, scurrying around, and even a couple of dogs towards the rear of the room, which was odd. Our scientists used to experiment on dogs since their genetic makeup was similar to wolves, but the practice had ended a long time ago. Maybe they were pets of the people who worked there.

Suddenly, out of nowhere, a person appeared in the room, making me nearly jump out of my skin. I hadn't thought anyone would be in the darkened room, especially after what we overheard about people sheltering in the dining hall. Luckily, the person had their back to the door so they didn't see me, but I quickly ducked to the side anyway, staying out of sight.

My heart still racing, my ears picked up a new sound of someone running down the hall at a high speed. In a split second, I did the calculations in my head, figuring out how much time it would take me to get back to the office where the others were versus the speed at which the owner of the footsteps seemed to be approaching. It didn't seem likely I'd make it, at least not without attracting some attention, and I cursed myself inwardly for getting distracted by the lab.

I couldn't hide, so I'd have to fight instead. Across the hall was another office, its door sitting open and its lights off, and with my whole body tensed, I waited until the footsteps got closer...

And closer...

Three, two, one...

As soon as the person rounded the corner, I slammed into them, my hand going around their neck as I pushed them into the dark office across the hall, closing the door behind me with my other hand. The entire maneuver took no more than three seconds.

Only when the lilac scent hit my nose did I realize exactly whose throat my hand was wrapped around, and I took a step back in surprise, squinting to try to make out her face in the dim light that filtered in beneath the office door.

"Savannah?"

Chapter Twenty-Four

~Savannah~

Alpha Warren wasted no time in getting down to business when Beta Chad told him about the extent of the rogue incursion. I'd never heard of a rogue working with wild wolves before, but then, I didn't know much about rogues at all. Felix said they went a little wild over time, so maybe it made sense.

The Alpha's eyes instantly glazed over, sending out the alert to the whole pack that only the highest-ranked members had the ability to do. Though Felix and I couldn't hear it, I could imagine it would be brief and to the point, telling people a threat had been identified and to follow the procedures they'd been trained to do. Every wolf pack, no matter where they lived, prepared and drilled for emergencies. We all had enemies.

"Is everyone from the L-team accounted for?" the Alpha asked his Beta once his message had been conveyed, keeping his words brisk and clipped.

"All but Kyle. He must be in his lab."

As if I weren't already paying close attention, the mention of Kyle intrigued me even more. Why would he be one of the first people the Alpha asked about after being informed of an attack on the pack?

The Alpha glanced over his shoulder for a second, looking out the window as if he might see the invaders from there, before turning to Amanda. "The lab has special insulation that's necessary for the work he does, but it also stops mind-links from getting through. Kyle won't have heard the alert. Go and tell him to follow the Code Grey protocol. He'll know what that means."

He might, but I had no idea what it meant, other than that it all sounded rather mysterious. What were they worried about the rogue getting access to?

Amanda, however, had her own concerns. "*My* protocol is to secure the pack house staff and children, since Mom isn't well enough to do it. That takes precedence."

The Alpha had his mouth open to argue, but I saw an easy solution to their impasse so I piped up even though no one had asked me to. "I know where Kyle's lab is. I visited him there this morning. I can go."

Alpha Warren raised an eyebrow at me, obviously questioning whether I could be entrusted with such an important task, so I repeated his instructions to confirm I'd been paying attention.

"When I get to his lab, I'll tell him to follow the Code Grey protocol. Anything else?"

He and the Beta exchanged quick glances before the Alpha gave me a short nod. "That's all. Thank you, Lota Savannah. One of the guards will meet you at the back door to accompany you over in case there's trouble. Beta Felix, will you join me and my team?"

Felix nodded in agreement, keeping his eyes on the Alpha as his voice sounded in my head. *Be careful, Sav. Any trouble, call for me immediately.*

I will. Don't worry.

With all our tasks assigned, the Alpha's office quickly emptied, and I raced to the back door where one of the guards met me as promised, armed with a rifle. Werewolf law prevented us from using guns against other werewolves, but regular wolves, along with other wild animals, were a different story. The sight of the weapon in his hands made my stomach twist, knowing that my mate might well be among the wolves being shot at.

After what the Alpha revealed, did he deserve my concern, though? I had no idea what to think, and no time to think of it anyway.

We raced the short distance to the medical clinic where the guard used a security code to let me in the main doors that had been locked down. Inside, the place felt like a ghost town compared to the hustle and bustle of that morning, but I paid no attention, sprinting down the empty hallway towards Kyle's lab, fully focused on the task at hand.

As I rounded the corner before the lab, the air in my lungs suddenly emptied, the world moving sideways as I was grabbed and pushed by an unknown assailant into a dark room that got even darker as he closed the door behind us, his hand around my throat.

It happened so fast that I barely had a chance to breathe, but as soon as I inhaled, the sweet marshmallow scent of my mate, along with the sharp chemical smell of cleaning supplies, overwhelmed me at the same time he said my name.

"Savannah?"

"Jasper? What are you... how did you... why..."

All the different questions I wanted to ask competed to get out of my mouth first, pushing past each other so that no one question got out in its entirety. The sparks from his hand against my throat still tingled even after he'd removed it and my heart raced both from the adrenaline of his sudden appearance and from being so close to him again, even in the dark. My body was going haywire, making it very, very difficult to concentrate.

He let out a low, rumbling, satisfied growl that seemed to reverberate through my body, warming my blood as it moved through my veins. "Fuck, my name has never sounded so good as when you say it. How do you know it? I forgot to tell you earlier."

The question immediately brought the conversation with the Alpha back to my mind, reminding me not only of what he said but also that there was likely a massive manhunt on for Jasper right at that moment. That had to take priority, no matter how desperate I might be to understand everything else.

"Why did you come here? You're in danger. The pack knows you're inside the territory."

"You think I don't know that?"

My eyes had begun to adjust to the lower lighting and I could make out the way his lips curled as he asked the question, ending in a sexy smirk that sent another shot of excitement through me, a purely physical reaction I couldn't control. When he spoke again, I had to force myself to concentrate on his words.

"I came because something strange is happening in the pack. I'm not alone. There are others with me, others who were also kicked out under false pretenses. We need to figure out why."

"False pretenses?" Was that a line or did he actually mean it? Was there more to the story than what I'd been told? Could the Alpha have been misinformed?

"Yes. Five of us exiled in the last year, all for seeing something they shouldn't have or being somewhere at the wrong time. Apparently, the pack is being fed lies about what happened to us. I know it probably sounds like I'm crazy, and honestly, I'm not 100% sure that I'm not, but when it comes to this, I'm pretty sure I'm right."

Five exiles? That certainly put things in a new light. Amanda said there hadn't been any until we forced the Alpha to tell us about Jasper. What would he say if I asked him about the others? The omission called everything else the Alpha told me into question too.

It might be worth finding out as much as I could. "What are the names of the others?"

"It's not important, but..."

"Yes, it is." I cut him off. "I'm staying inside the pack house. I can do some digging and find out what the official story is."

A pause followed my words, and when he spoke again, his voice sounded thicker, full of an emotion I couldn't quite name. "You would be willing to help me? You don't even know me."

"I don't, but I agree that we need to get to the bottom of this. For all our sakes."

He couldn't argue with that, but he did sigh in frustration. "I don't want you anywhere near the pack house."

His possessive, protective words brought to mind the way he kissed me that morning, and I couldn't help leaning a little closer to him and teasing him, giving in to the chemistry I felt between us. "No? Where would you like me instead?"

That ridiculously sexy growl came out of him again. "That's a dangerous question, Savannah."

"I like to live on the edge."

"I can tell." He sounded almost impressed as he said it, definitely meaning it as a compliment instead of the way other men sometimes said it.

"You haven't answered my question."

He stepped closer to me, so close I could feel the heat his body gave off. "You really want me to?"

"I wouldn't have asked otherwise."

"Fine."

The next thing I knew, his strong arms were around me, lifting me off the ground as I gasped in surprise. Sparks immediately flared to life everywhere his skin touched mine, sending another wave of longing through me.

"If we'd met under better circumstances, I'd want you on a bed somewhere, pinned beneath me as I put these sparks to good use. Or I could be pinned beneath you; I'm equal opportunity that way."

Even in the darkness, it didn't take more than a second for his lips to find mine, and almost instantly, my body melted against him, our hard edges seeming to run together in the heat of our kiss.

It felt a bit sweeter than the kiss that morning but equally full of need, and for a brief moment, I could almost forget everything else around us.

Unfortunately, a noise outside the door brought us both crashing back to reality, and Jasper reluctantly put me back down. "You should go before anyone comes looking for you. I have to help the others, but as soon as my name is cleared, nothing will keep me from you."

He hadn't even asked if I would accept him. He assumed I would, and damn if I didn't find that confidence appealing. "Before I go, what are the names of the others who were exiled?"

He'd obviously forgotten about that question, as I nearly had, but he answered it that time. "I don't know their surnames, but Myra was a cleaner, Lee worked security, Dan was in procurement and Brent worked here in the clinic. It's not much to go on."

"It's something," I assured him. "I'll see what I can find out. If I can sneak away after sunset, can you meet me on the lakeshore?"

"Assuming I haven't been captured and killed? Yes. I'll see you there."

His dark humour appealed to me, along with just about everything else about him. *Fuck.* I hoped my gut had it right and he wasn't a bad guy after all.

After whispering goodbye, I opened the door to continue heading to Kyle's lab, but almost exactly as I closed it behind me, the lab door opened and Kyle walked out, spotting me instantly and giving me a curious look. Although I still found him handsome, especially his stunning eyes, he didn't make my stomach flutter the way that Jasper did.

"Savannah? What are you doing here? And what were you doing in there?"

He cast a curious look over my shoulder at the door I had come out of, and the room beyond where Jasper still waited for the coast to clear.

"I was looking for you and I chose the wrong door," I lied, raising my voice a touch so that Jasper would hear me and understand I had his back. "The Alpha asked me to come and tell you to implement the Code Grey protocol."

Kyle's eyes widened in surprise. "Really? It must be serious."

"It sure sounded that way. Is there anything I could do to help?"

Kyle was the only pack member I'd seen in the clinic, so if I could help to keep him busy, it should give Jasper time to finish doing whatever he was doing in the building. With that in mind, I followed Kyle back into his lab, pasting a smile on my face even as my mind continued to race.

Research had never been my strong suit; I wanted all the answers right away but I would have to take what I could get.

Was my mate crazy? Were *all* the rogue wolves crazy? Why exactly had they been exiled from the pack? Those questions and more swirled around in my head, and I hoped it wouldn't be too long before we finally started getting some concrete answers.

Chapter Twenty-Five

~Jasper~

A new energy and determination flowed through my veins as I pressed my ear against the door, listening to Savannah cover for me. With every second I spent with her, she seemed even more perfect to me than before. The way she teased me, the way she *kissed* me, and especially her confidence despite the highly unusual circumstances we found ourselves in: every action made me fall a little bit further for her and soon, I knew, there'd be no way back. I'd have to have her or it would break me, and I had no intention of letting it be the latter.

The haze tried to surface at the first scent of her, but for the first time ever, I managed to push it back down. That strength came from Savannah and from the strength of our bond, I knew it as surely as I knew anything.

I couldn't see the man she spoke to, but I heard them move further away, followed by the sound of a door closing. Waiting a few more seconds to be sure the coast was clear, I darted back down the hall to the room where Dan and Myra were still working.

"There are people around," I told them bluntly as soon as I walked in. "We're okay for the moment, but the faster we can get out of here, the better."

"I think I've got something," Dan answered quickly. "Look at this."

He pointed at something on the screen and I quickly rounded the desk to look at the files he had open. The document looked to be an approved leave of absence form, in Dan's name, authorizing him to leave the pack to visit relatives. That matched exactly with the story I'd been told about why Dan suddenly disappeared.

Though I didn't want to be negative, it wasn't quite the smoking gun I'd been hoping for. "What good does that do us? They're covering their tracks, like we expected."

"It all looks legit," Dan had to agree. "But look at who signed it."

I followed his point to the signature at the bottom of the document. "K Lewison? I don't know who that is."

If he had a point, I didn't get it, but Dan quickly tabbed over to another document. That one was in Myra's name, stating that she'd found her mate in another pack and the Alpha granted her permission to go and live with him. Obviously, it was as much a fabrication as the first, meant to stem any questions that might arise from Myra's disappearance, but when Dan pointed at the signature on the form, I started to understand.

"The same guy signed it."

"That's not all." Next, Dan pulled up my own record. That one actually did state I'd been exiled, charged with kidnapping and endangering the two young pups I'd been trying to find. Seeing it in black and white made my stomach turn, but the bile turned to anger as Dan pointed to the signature on the paperwork, the same as the other two. "I've got Lee's and Brent's too. He signed all of them."

"Who is he?" I suspected Dan would have already figured that out and he didn't let me down. He pulled up yet another personnel record complete with a picture of a man with unusually pale blue eyes and a rather smarmy-looking smirk.

"Kyle Lewison. He's a member of the Alpha's team and he works here in the medical centre. There's a whole bio on him here and the work he's doing."

We'd been looking for a link between the Alpha and the medical centre, and it looked like we found it. He looked vaguely familiar, but no more than vaguely. I must have seen him at pack functions or perhaps during the course of my work, but as far as I could remember, we'd never had a conversation. How did he come to be involved in the exile of all five of us?

Was he carrying out orders or was there something more sinister about it? What could he be covering up?

"I printed copies of everything," Dan said as Myra went to the printer to grab the stack of papers from it. "It's not a full answer, but it's a start."

"It's great work," I assured him. "At least we know where to start looking."

Before running into Savannah, I would have suggested that we go track down this Lewison guy right then and there, but after speaking with her, I didn't want to take any additional risks that might get me caught and not able to meet up with her later. Besides, she said she'd do some digging on her end. If I could share what we'd learned, maybe the two of us could come up with a plan together.

Already, I trusted her implicitly, and at the moment, it seemed like our best option would be to retreat.

"We should get Brent and get out of here before they figure out exactly who he is. Myra, do you know where the dining hall is and the nearest exit to it?"

"What if they catch all of us?" Dan spoke up before Myra could answer me. "We should get out while we still can."

"We're not leaving anyone behind if we can help it," I growled back. I already didn't like the fact that we'd lost track of Lee, and I had no intention of letting Brent pay the price for keeping the rest of us safe. "Myra?"

She gave me a nod that confirmed her agreement with me. "There are a couple of exits but they might be guarded because of the attack. We'll need to play it by ear."

We'd pretty much been winging it all day, so why change? "Alright. You both stay behind me and follow my lead."

When I stuck my head back out the door, the hallway was still empty. Outside the lab that Savannah had gone in, it took all my self-control to keep walking past it and not go in, knowing she was so close but still out of reach. Hopefully, it wouldn't be long until we had some real time together. I couldn't wait to get to know her, but first, I had to get my new friends somewhere safe.

Following Myra's directions, we arrived at the dining hall and we all took a quick note of the nearest exit before we went in. Thankfully, no one stood guard near it, just as there had been no one by the one we came in through. It would probably trigger an alarm when we opened it, but that wouldn't matter when we only wanted to get away anyway.

Even with my wolf hearing, I couldn't hear much noise from within the dining hall, but that didn't surprise me. In the event of a pack-wide lockdown, everyone would be waiting for additional orders from the Alpha.

The door didn't give when I pushed it, so I knocked instead, loudly and firmly.

"Who's there?" a gruff voice asked from the other side.

I came up with a cover story on the spot. "We're new interns and we got lost. Is this where we're supposed to be gathering?"

I did my best to sound younger and more naive than usual, and it seemed to work because a moment later, the door opened, revealing a large, grumpy-looking man who blocked our path. "What are your names?"

"Our names?" I repeated, mostly to buy myself time to try to look past him to find Brent.

Looking down at his phone, his finger flicked across the screen, making the lines of text scroll. "Yeah, your names. I've already got one person who's not on the sign-up list today, so who are you?"

Brent was obviously the one person he meant, and over the man's shoulder, I could see him standing a short distance away, separated from the rest of the crowd with another person close to him, probably keeping an eye on him. It looked like they were already suspicious, even if they didn't suspect him of being a rogue yet, so we'd have to move fast.

I caught Brent's eye and gave him a small nod, letting him know to be ready to move, and he nodded back to tell me he'd got the message.

"We must be on there," I told the man with the last, grabbing the phone from his hands. "Let me see."

"Hey! Give that back, you can't..."

He trailed off as I wound up and threw the phone as far as I could into the room. When he turned in disbelief to watch it go, it created an opening just big enough for Brent to sneak through, stumbling into the hall with us as I yelled at the others. "Go! Now!"

They didn't need any further encouragement. As the men we'd left behind took a second to react, the four of us headed for the door with Myra in the lead.

"Shift as soon as we're outside," she yelled over her shoulder. "I've got the papers."

While running, she rolled them up and put them in her mouth, and as soon as she pushed the door open in front of her, she shifted, her clothes falling away but the printed papers safe in her jaw.

We were all right behind her, shifting and taking off at a sprint as shouts rang out from behind us. No doubt they'd be mind-linking to let their superiors know what happened, so we had no time to waste.

Myra knew her way around as well as I did, if not better, and she led us safely out of the territory without encountering any Ravenstone wolves. Even after we crossed the border, we didn't stop, running all the way back to her cave and the relative safety it provided.

Part of me hoped we would find Lee there, but there was no sign of him as the rest of us shifted back and shared our relief over our mutual escape. If he hadn't returned by the time I met with Savannah, I'd have to ask her to try to get that information for me too. A lot rode on my mate helping us, but rather than making me nervous, that prospect only excited me.

From the moment I first saw her face, I knew that if anyone could save me, it would be her.

CHAPTER TWENTY-SIX

~Savannah~

In his lab, Kyle immediately set to work to carry out the protocol the Alpha had ordered.

"Can I help?" I offered again.

"It'll take me longer to explain what needs to be done than to do it," Kyle replied, not unkindly but with his attention firmly focused on the screen in front of him.

Being of no use there, I stood out of the way, in front of the door, so that if Jasper happened to walk by, Kyle wouldn't notice him.

My heart still thudded heavily in my chest, remembering the feel of Jasper's arms around me in the darkened room and the spark of his lips against mine. Hopefully, I made the right call in agreeing to help him. The mate bond might have been influencing my judgement, but something still didn't feel right about the whole situation.

"You seem to have a problem with rogues here," I said, trying to sound like I was simply making conversation as Kyle tapped away at his computer touch screen, locking down various parts of the lab. Silver bars descended from the ceiling in front of some of the storage units, ensuring no werewolves would be able to access them. "Do they attack often?"

"No," he answered shortly, his eyes still on the screen. "This is unusual. Our security will take care of it, but better safe than sorry."

"Why would the rogues be interested in any of the stuff in your lab?" I asked next. The stem cell samples he'd shown me earlier were lowered into the table they'd been resting on and a silver lid slid into place over top of them. All of this security couldn't be cheap, and I couldn't imagine they'd do it if they didn't have a reason to suspect real danger.

"They won't be," he contradicted. "Rogues only care about their own survival. These measures are in case we're attacked by another pack. The Alpha's being cautious in case the rogues are working for someone else."

"Does that happen?"

"It can. If rogues are desperate and hungry enough, they can take work as mercenaries. I'm not saying that's what's happening here, but it's something we need to be cautious about."

It certainly hadn't sounded like Jasper worked for another pack; he merely wanted to know why he and the others were exiled. That reminded me that one of the men he mentioned had worked in the clinic, so Kyle might have known him. Maybe I could start my investigation there.

"Do you know someone named Brent who works here?"

For the first time since he started the protocol, Kyle glanced over at me. "Who?"

"Brent. I'm not sure of his surname, but he works in the clinic."

Kyle's eyes remained on me. "It doesn't sound familiar. Why do you ask?"

I grabbed for the first explanation I could come up with. "A friend of a friend of mine knew his family, and I said I'd say hi if I saw him. Sorry, I know that's random, but I just remembered about it. My train of thought often takes detours."

I smiled to let him know I meant it as a joke, but he didn't return the smile, turning back to his computer instead. "Hundreds of people work here and I usually stay in my lab. I don't know them all."

So much for that idea. I'd have to try with Amanda instead.

I lapsed into silence as Kyle finished the last of his computer commands, watching over his shoulder curiously. After tapping in a six-digit code, he turned to me. "The lab will lock down in ten seconds whether we're in here or not. Let's make sure we're not."

Since I had no desire to get locked inside, I hurried out into the hall with Kyle on my heels. Sure enough, almost as soon as he closed the door, I could hear the locks engaging and a maze of motion-detector lasers crisscrossed the entire room. No one was getting in there without someone in charge knowing about it.

Outside the lab, Kyle's eyes almost immediately glazed over as he received a mind-link from someone else in the pack. "The Alpha needs me at the pack house. I'll accompany you back there."

Since I wanted to go there anyway, I agreed readily, and as soon as we arrived, Kyle veered off to find the Alpha while I went in search of Amanda. I found her in the basement with the non-fighting staff and children, and almost as soon as I walked in, Amanda announced that the danger had passed.

"Everyone can return to their work. Thank you all for staying calm, and our thanks to the Alpha and his security team for keeping us all safe."

Instantly, my heart began pounding again, wondering what it meant for Jasper that the alert had been called off. Did he simply leave the territory, or had someone found him in the clinic when he tried to leave?

"Thank you, Alpha," the others all murmured in chorus, looking re-lieved as they filed out of the room, until only Amanda and I remained.

"Did they catch the rogue?" I asked, trying to keep my voice from shaking.

"They caught one," she confirmed, and my stomach lurched until she added another sentence. "It's not Jasper, though."

She looked so confused about that, she must have missed the look of relief that spread across my face. Quickly, I rearranged my expression to a more neutral one. "There are others? But I thought you said..."

"I know what I said," she cut me off, her jaw clenched. "Obviously, there's more I don't know, but I'm going to find out now. Are you coming?"

Hell, yes. Let's go and get some answers, Tala growled, she and I in total agreement.

Following Amanda, we went through a series of doors in the basement, each opened by her fingerprint, until we ended up in a holding cell similar to the one our pack had, where Felix had locked up my brother's mate not that long ago. Thankfully, she didn't hold a grudge about that, but based on the glowering expression on the face of the man sitting behind the bars in the Ravenstone cell, his hands bound behind his back and his mouth gagged, I would have placed a bet he wouldn't be quite so forgiving.

The others in the room all turned to look at us as we walked in: Alpha Warren, Beta Chad, Epsilon Ian, Felix, and Kyle.

The last one took me by surprise. I knew Kyle went to find the Alpha, but why would he be involved in questioning the rogue when he was only a junior member of the Alpha's team? What did it have to do with his area of expertise?

Whatever the reason for his presence, he didn't look pleased to see me and Amanda, and neither did the Alpha.

"What are you doing here?" Alpha Warren growled at his daughter. "This doesn't concern you."

Amanda was as defiant as she'd been in the Alpha's office earlier. "The fact that you lied to me, *again*, doesn't concern me? I know this man, he's one of your security guards. Why is he a rogue? Why did he get exiled? What is going on?"

Jasper mentioned someone that worked in security: Lee, I thought he said, which must have been the man in front of me. If he was as innocent as Jasper claimed, hopefully no harm would come to him. I wanted to hear what he had to say, but unfortunately, it didn't look like that would happen.

"Beta, I'll leave you in charge here," the Alpha commanded. "Amanda, Beta Felix, and Lota Savannah, come with me."

Amanda began to protest but the Alpha held up his hand to silence her.

"I'll answer your questions, but not here. It's a long story and it's past suppertime. We can talk over dinner."

I glanced over my shoulder one last time as the Alpha ushered us all from the room, just in time to see a syringe in Kyle's hand and the look of panic in Lee's eyes before the door closed behind us.

Chapter Twenty-Seven

Things are getting messier. A rogue wolf led a group of wild wolves in an attack. I didn't even know that was possible, but whoever he is, he's not happy about having been exiled. The guards have captured him and we're about to go question him. I'm sticking close to the Alpha.

Sav's had some concerning news. I don't want to go into any details in case my phone is confiscated or this text is being monitored, but she needs to stick around a little longer to figure it out. Otherwise, I'd be hauling her out of here right now.

You said you have contacts nearby, right? If you don't hear from me in the morning, send them in to look for us.

CHAPTER TWENTY-EIGHT

~Savannah~

Dinner had already been brought to the Alpha's private dining room but I had no appetite as we walked into the room. "What are they going to do to that man?"

"What man?" The Alpha's eyes betrayed his disapproval at my tone but I didn't have time for civility.

"The rogue! Kyle had a syringe. What was he going to do to him?"

We didn't have to interrogate people often at the Crimsontooth pack, but I knew for fucking certain that no one ever got injected with anything when we did.

The Alpha waved my concern away with a flourish of his hand as he dropped into his seat. "It's a mild sedative to calm him down so he can answer some questions. Nothing more."

He took the glass of wine that stood in front of his place and took a long sip from it, perhaps bracing for the conversation still ahead of us. Amanda still had questions and I had even more of them, even if I accepted his answer that the syringe only contained a sedative. "He looked pretty scared when he saw it," I pointed out.

"Some people don't like needles," the Alpha replied coolly. "Even big, rough-looking rogues. Sit, all of you. The food will get cold."

Since he obviously wouldn't start giving us answers until we did, Amanda, Felix and I all took seats around the circular table, Felix and Amanda on either side of the Alpha while I sat across from him. Felix grabbed a piece of the fresh bread that had been set out, the same kind of bread he brought to my room that morning, and took a big bite of it while I shook my head at him. *Seriously? How can you eat right now?*

I'm hungry, he answered in my head. *I was out chasing rogues. You should eat too, Sav. Keep your strength up. We don't know what the evening might still bring.*

That was for damn sure. I promised Jasper I would do my best to meet with him later, once I got some information for him, and being hungry and irritable when the time came wouldn't help matters any. Reluctantly, I picked up my fork and put a small bite of the moose stew in my mouth, forcing myself to swallow past the lump in my throat.

Amanda's hands remained at her sides, and she addressed her father in a calm, even tone that sounded even more dangerous to me than if she'd yelled. In some ways, Amanda and I had a lot in common, and like me, I suspected that when she got quiet, people needed to worry.

"How many others are there?"

"What?" the Alpha asked before shovelling a forkful of his own supper into his mouth. He sat leaning forward, his elbows on the table and his shoulders hunched, and I suspected he knew as well as I did what she meant. He just wanted to buy himself a few seconds to decide how to answer.

She clarified the question as if his confusion were genuine. "How many others have been exiled in secret? The truth, this time."

He took another pause before answering, chewing and swallowing the food in his mouth and taking another mouthful of wine before finally responding.

"Six."

"Six?!" All three of us asked the question in unison, in varying degrees of dismay. Thanks to my conversation with Jasper, I had been more prepared than the other two for a larger number, though I didn't know if the Alpha would admit to it, but six was even more than I thought. There must have been one Jasper didn't know about.

"How have you exiled six people without anyone noticing?" Amanda asked, sounding utterly bewildered. "Didn't their families notice? Their friends? Their colleagues?"

Those were good questions, but not the one I wanted answered the most, so I threw that one in too. "*Why* were they exiled?"

Finally, the Alpha put his fork down and gave us his full attention. His shoulders straightened and he looked each of us in the eyes, ready to defend his actions. "They were exiled because they put the pack in danger. You know the situation for all packs in the region, not just us. Pressures on our borders are significant, but the things the team in the science lab are working on are going to be huge. The potential in the human *and* werewolf worlds is unparalleled. I've thrown a huge amount of the pack's resources and finances behind this project, and the people who were exiled all tried, in one way or another, to sabotage or expose that work. I had to put the pack first. As for why no one knows about it: we made up other excuses to explain their absences. It had to remain a secret to avoid tipping off anyone else about the transformatory work being done."

Although he'd said a lot of words, he actually hadn't told us very much at all. I wanted to get much more specific. "What did Lee do, exactly?"

Alpha Warren's eyes narrowed thoughtfully as he looked over at me. "How do you know his name?"

Fuck. I wouldn't have known it except that Jasper told me, but I quickly made up a lie to explain it. "I heard Beta Chad say it when we were leaving the cell."

"Stop avoiding the question," Amanda interjected. "What did he do?"

"He eavesdropped on one of my private conversations with the chief scientists, and we found contact numbers for other packs in his phone. He must have been intending to sell them the information."

"Did he confess to that?" Felix asked, and when the Alpha shook his head, Felix frowned. "Why wouldn't you put him in prison, then? Why jump all the way to exile?"

"All the people involved in running the prison would be aware of his incarceration. There would have been more questions. We tried to contain it, to stop anything from spreading, but unfortunately, the potential leaks didn't stop there. We had a man in procurement and three people at the medical clinic who were also potential security risks."

"That's only five," Felix pointed out, keeping track in his head just as I was.

"Five plus the man I told you about earlier. I already explained the reason for his exile to you. The others, we may be able to bring back into the pack once the research is complete and the danger has passed, but Jasper is a separate case. He won't be coming back."

Again, my stomach twisted uncomfortably at the idea that there could be any truth to the accusations against Jasper. He certainly seemed to lump himself in with the others. Was that wishful thinking on his part? Delusion? Or were there still things the Alpha was trying to hide?

Felix found another part of what the Alpha said concerning. "If you believe that they were trying to sabotage you, believe it strongly enough to exile them in the first place, why would you intend to bring them back?"

"The nature of the project allows for it. I can't say more than that, Beta Felix. You've already seen how seriously we take our intellectual property."

With that, the Alpha picked up his fork and started eating again while an uneasy silence descended over the room, each of us lost in our own thoughts.

What do you think? I asked Felix in my head, looking down at my meal so the Alpha wouldn't see my eyes glaze over.

It doesn't add up for me. What are they working on that could be so important, and why do they think it will eliminate all their worries afterwards?

I don't know, but I intend to find out. I'm meeting with my mate this evening as long as I can sneak out of the house.

What? How did you arrange that?

I hadn't had a chance to tell him about my encounter with Jasper in the clinic yet, and this wasn't the time either. *I'll explain later, but the important thing is that I get to see him. Will you help me?*

Glancing up, I caught the smile that flashed across Felix's face before he took another bite of bread to hide it. *Your brother would kill me if he found out. He'll probably already kill me for not telling him about your mate.*

Then we'll make sure he doesn't find out. It seemed simple enough to me. *I have to give Jasper a chance to explain himself. As my mate, he deserves that much.*

You always see the best in people, Sav. Hopefully, he's worth the trouble.

I hoped so too, and most of all, I hoped that by the time the night was over, I would know one way or the other.

Chapter Twenty-Nine

~Jasper~

Using a few long blades of grass, I tied the papers we'd printed at the medical clinic together and Myra helped to attach them to my ear in my wolf form. She'd done her best to keep them safe on the way back to the cave, but a wolf's mouth wasn't the driest place. To avoid any further damage, I wanted to keep them away from any more saliva.

The lakeshore where Savannah and I had our brief encounter earlier that morning sat right on the edge of the Ravenstone territory. By paying careful attention, I could skirt the border, making sure not to set off any further alarms when I would rather avoid detection.

She might not be able to come, Sterling pointed out as we found a quiet, mostly hidden spot next to some trees where we could see the shore but not be readily seen, in case anyone else happened to come that way. *You should have told her not to put herself in danger.*

She doesn't need me to tell her that. She's a smart, capable woman, I'm sure she'll be careful.

Though I barely knew a thing about her, not even where she came from or why she came to the Ravenstone pack in the first place, I already knew that much about her. She didn't need me to look after her; she could do a damn good job of that all on her own.

The ability to size people up quickly and accurately had been important in my investigative work, and even though everything else in my life had fallen apart, I still trusted my gut. It told me loud and clear that Savannah was something special.

The adrenaline that had fuelled me during our incursion into the Ravenstone territory earlier had worn off, leaving me tired even in spite of the anticipation of seeing my mate again. The wind blew against the lake, making the water lap gently at the shore, and my eyelids began to feel heavy as the sun dipped lower in the sky. Blinks took longer, my eyes staying closed a little bit longer each time.

"What have you done to them?"

The voice sounded far away, in the dark somewhere, but I knew it. I should. It belonged to me.

*"I'm making them better. I'm making us **all** better."*

That voice, I didn't quite recognize, but something about it sounded familiar anyway.

*"I'd say you're insane but I don't think you are. You just have a god complex. You think the rules don't apply to you, but there **are** limits. I'm calling the Alpha in and he can…"*

"You're not calling anyone."

The snap of a branch shook me awake again, my eyes snapping open and my heart rate immediately kicking up several notches. Had I dreamed that conversation or had a memory come back to me?

And of more concern at that exact moment, who snapped the tree branch?

"Jasper?"

That voice, whispered and urgent, I recognized immediately, and I stepped forward, still in my wolf form, so she'd see I was there but wouldn't be startled if I suddenly appeared in my naked human form.

Savannah wore loose clothes I recognized from our pack, her brown hair curling naturally over the shoulders of the grey sweatshirt, and when she caught sight of me, the smile that bloomed on her face sent a shot of desire through my body. In the last fading light of the day, she couldn't look more gorgeous.

"I brought an extra set of clothes for you," she said, holding up a bag I hadn't noticed in her hand. "So you can shift and be comfortable while we talk."

Thoughtful, and practical too. Speaking to her while naked would have been distracting for us both.

Snatching the bag from her hand with my mouth, I retreated to my sheltered spot and shifted, putting on the set of non-descript clothes and removing the tied papers from around my ear before I went to join her.

While I'd been changing, Savannah had found a fallen tree trunk, big enough for us both to sit on and far enough back from the shore that we wouldn't immediately be seen if anyone else happened to venture outside of the territory for an evening drink from the lake.

"I've got some new information," I told her, holding up the papers in my hand as I took a seat on the moss-covered tree next to her. "But you can go first. It looks like you have news too."

I'd gathered that from the way she leaned forward when I settled and the way her toes tapped on the ground.

"I've found out a few things. First of all, the Alpha has Lee."

My stomach lurched painfully hard. *Fuck.* I knew it could be a possibility when he didn't return, but hearing it confirmed made me feel even worse. If I hadn't suggested the whole thing, he wouldn't be in that position. "Do you know what they're going to do to him?"

I had no idea how much access she had, since I still didn't know exactly who she was, but I needed to ask anyway.

"They're questioning him, that's all I know. They injected him with something too. The Alpha called it a sedative, but I'm not sure."

I wouldn't be sure either. I didn't think they would kill Lee, since if they'd wanted to do that, they would have done it instead of exiling him in the first place, but the mention of an injection certainly made me uneasy. My frustration with the gaps in my information couldn't get any stronger.

Dwelling on what might or might not be happening to Lee wouldn't change anything, though, so I forced myself to move on. "What else?"

"The Alpha said six people had been exiled but you only mentioned five. There must be another one out here somewhere."

Savannah glanced around as she said it, her hair swishing over her shoulder, and her scent filled my nose again with the movement. It took all my self-control to focus on what she said and not take her in my arms like I had that afternoon. "That's good to know, thank you. None of us have seen another one, but we'll keep an eye out. Did he say anything about why we'd all been exiled?"

It impressed me that she got the Alpha to talk about it at all.

Her pretty mouth tightened into an unhappy grimace. "He said the others had all been trying to sabotage something the scientists are working on."

I caught the words she left unsaid immediately. "But not me?"

Savannah's brown eyes met mine with both confidence and uncertainty, a beguiling, contradictory mix of emotions. "No. He said you endangered some children and that's why you were kicked out."

Well, at least they were sticking with the same story, even a bullshit one. "And you still came to meet with me?" I asked, not sure whether to be pleased by that or concerned about her judgement.

Savannah simply shrugged. "I'd like to hear your side of the story."

I really appreciated that, but it also posed a problem. "I don't remember exactly what happened, but I do know one thing: I would have never intentionally put anyone in harm's way."

I hoped she would hear the sincerity in my voice but she focused on the first part of what I'd said instead. "What do you mean you don't remember?"

"Exactly that. My memory is fuzzy both before and after my exile. And there's something else too, something that started happening after the exile. There's this... darkness... that takes hold of me. It's like when my wolf takes over, but different. I don't know what it is, but I lose control and..."

No sooner had I mentioned it than I felt the haze pushing up, stronger and faster than it had for a long time, so quickly that I didn't have time to fight it off. The next thing I knew, I became a passenger in my own body again, watching helplessly as the thing in control of me leaned closer to Savannah.

For the first time, the haze spoke, the voice coming out of me sounding deeper and painfully raw.

"It's about time he introduced me. I've been dying to meet you properly, *mate*."

Chapter Thirty

~**Savannah**~

The change in Jasper was immediate and total. Though he still had the same green eyes beneath his shaggy, unkempt hair, their expression grew harder and sharper. The earnest look on his face turned to a smirk, and the controlled way he held himself melted away as he leaned closer, looking ready to devour me any moment.

It reminded me of the soap operas my mom used to watch, where a character had an evil twin played by the same actor and they had to exaggerate the 'bad' one's characteristics. Coupled with what Jasper said about some other being taking control of him, it all added up to one conclusion: either my mate had some kind of personality disorder or something crazy had been done *to* him.

Given everything else I'd seen since arriving at the Ravenstone, I couldn't rule out the latter.

"Hello," I said warily, speaking to him as if he were in fact a completely different person. "What do I call you?"

"You can call me whatever you like." The way his eyes moved over me made it clear, even if his tone already hadn't, that he meant it in a flirtatious way. The grey, shapeless, unisex clothes I'd borrowed from the pack house couldn't be any less flattering, but he stared at me like they were the most enticing thing he'd ever seen.

Felix helped me procure the clothes and evade Heather so that I could sneak out for this meeting. Though he hated the idea of me going alone, he stayed behind to cover for me, urging me to be careful. What would he think if he could see the man in front of me who seemed to be

"

possessed? What would my brother think? Probably a good thing several hundred miles separated us at the moment.

"Do you have a name?" I tried again.

"Not that I know of. Why don't you give me one? Make it something you'd feel comfortable screaming out when we mate."

His hand went around my waist, pulling me closer to him and he leaned towards my neck, as if he intended to mark me right there and then.

"Okay, hold on. Back up a second."

I tried to push him back but his solid form didn't budge, and as his warm breath hit my neck, a spike of fear and adrenaline rushed through me. As much as I liked a take-charge man, no one would be marking me without my permission.

He might have been stronger than me, but I had a few tricks up my sleeve. Vaughan arranged self-defense classes not only for me but for all the women in the pack, and I used one of the tactics we'd been taught to slip out of his grasp and spring to my feet, taking a few steps back as I kept my eyes on him in the fading dusk.

Maybe Vaughan's insistence on looking out for me wasn't *all* bad after all.

"Where's Jasper?" I kept my hands up and my stance tense, ready to move or even shift if he came at me again.

"Oh, he's still here. As weak and useless as usual."

A growl rumbled in my chest, partly from me and partly from Tala, neither of us appreciating the insult to our mate. "You think you're better than him?"

"I'm the *best* of him. All the best parts: the confidence, the lust, the ambition, the wheat separated from the chaff. He's my useless leftovers. Trust me, Savannah: between the two of us, you want me, not him."

"There's such a thing as *too* much confidence," I pointed out, taking another step back as he got to his feet. "Stay there or I'll call for help."

"Why would you do that when we're starting to get to know each other?" His smirk straddled the line between sexy and creepy. It could honestly go either way. "I'm getting stronger all the time. Soon, he'll be nothing but a memory. If you bond with me now, me and not him, you can help it happen even sooner."

"Does that mean if I bond with him instead of you, he gets a boost?"

His expression instantly darkened, the smirk falling away as he stepped towards me again. "This isn't a game."

"I never said it was. You're the one who..."

I trailed off as he suddenly bent over, his whole body seeming to collapse in on itself for a second before, with a gasp, he stood back up.

"Fuck, Savannah, I'm so sorry. I didn't even know he could talk. I didn't know he would..."

Jasper stumbled back, obviously still fighting against whatever forces were at work inside him, and I stepped forward to help steady him, the sparks flowing between us as I made contact. "Sit back down. It's okay."

I lowered myself down beside him until we both sat on the log as before, with the unsettling memory of what happened lingering between us.

"You must think I'm crazy." Jasper's voice came out hoarse and full of frustration. "This never happened until my exile. I don't know what he is."

I had a couple of ideas about that, neither of them good.

"You said you don't remember what happened before you were exiled," I reminded him. "Is it possible that this other side of you took control and did the things you were accused of? I'm not blaming you if that's the case. I just want to consider all the possibilities."

"I hadn't considered that," Jasper admitted, and I appreciated how he took the time to think about it rather than dismissing my question out of hand. "I suppose it's possible. That might explain why I don't remember it. On the other hand, every other time I've come out of the haze, I know that I've been in it. It takes me a while to recover. When I woke from the exile, I didn't feel that way."

"Haze?" The word sounded like it had a special meaning for him, so I asked him to clarify.

"That's what I call it. Him. The being inside me. It's almost like a hangover when I get control back from him, but like I said, when I first became aware of being exiled, I didn't feel that way."

Every word sounded sincere, so I shared my other idea instead. "Did you hear everything he said to me just now?"

Jasper nodded unhappily. "Like I said, I've never heard him speak before. He hasn't taken over very often in my human form."

"He said he's the best of you, a part of you that was separated somehow."

"I've had that feeling at times, that he's part of me like my wolf is. But how is that possible? Was the exile so traumatic that it caused some kind of psychotic break?"

"I suppose it's possible," I said, repeating his earlier words back to him. "But I'm not convinced it happened naturally. Do you know about the genetic manipulation that the pack scientists are working on?"

Jasper's brow furrowed, his eyebrows drawing down over his green eyes. "You mean the caloric intake stuff? I'm aware of it but I don't know all the details."

"That's part of it, yes, but they're working on more than that too. The Alpha said their discoveries are unparalleled. He wouldn't say exactly what those discoveries are, and I don't pretend to understand all the details either, but based on what you've said, I have an idea."

Jasper gave me an appreciative smile. "It sounds like you're going somewhere with this, but I'm not following. Why don't you lay it out for me?"

I did it the best way I knew how: "Do you know the story of Jekyll and Hyde?"

The parallels jumped out at me as I spoke with 'the haze'. I read a lot growing up, since I wasn't allowed to do much else, and the similarities were striking.

Jasper blinked in surprise, obviously not having expected that question. "I think so. Guy with a dual personality, one good and one evil?"

"Kind of. Jekyll was a doctor who wanted to eliminate the baser parts of human nature and he developed a treatment that would separate those parts out and get rid of them. He tested it on himself, but rather than destroying those parts, they became a separate personality, Hyde, made up of all the dark parts that Jekyll rejected."

Jasper's eyes grew wider with each word I spoke. "That sounds familiar."

"I thought so too. What if the scientists are trying to find a way to control different parts of a person's personality, the same way they used their genes to control their reaction to food, and you were given a prototype of that treatment? What if someone did this to you?"

Chapter Thirty-One

~Jasper~

I couldn't pretend that I understood how Savannah's suggestion would be possible, but I sure as hell knew that it rang true. Something truly messed up was happening in the Ravenstone pack, and after the haze spoke in its own voice, I had to accept that I was pretty messed up too.

It made sense that the two things would be related.

Although I knew that I lost control to the haze at times, I hadn't really understood that it had its own consciousness until the interaction with Savannah. She compared that consciousness inside me to Jekyll and Hyde, and again, it made some sense to me. I wouldn't have called the haze evil, necessarily, but he certainly had fewer inhibitions than I did. He was a part of me that did what he wanted, said what he wanted, and had nearly marked Savannah whether she wanted it or not.

As he stepped towards her, I fought harder than I'd ever fought for anything before to wrest control back. I would never force myself on her, but apparently, he had no such compunction, which made finding out how to stop him more urgent than ever before.

If someone did this to me on purpose to cover up whatever was going on in the pack, they were going to pay, for me and for all the others.

Most of all, I wanted some fucking answers.

The papers I brought with me had fallen to the ground during the haze's takeover, but with him under control, I picked them up again and unrolled them to show them to my mate.

"When we were in the medical centre earlier, we found some information about our exiles in the personnel database. They were all signed by the same person: Kyle Lewison. I read his bio and it sounds like he might be involved in genetic research. If you're right about something being done to me, I think he'd be the best place to start."

Savannah's face paled as she took the papers from me, glancing down at them in dismay. "Kyle? Are you sure?"

"Do you know him?" I still didn't have a clue what her connection to the pack was. I wanted to know, along with a million other things about her; there just hadn't been time to ask her about it yet.

Savannah swallowed hard as she flipped through the papers, seeing the signature on each one the same as I had. "We just met, but yeah, I've spent a bit of time with him. You're right about his scientific leanings: he's the one who told me about the genetic manipulation, so that's definitely in his wheelhouse. He's the one I saw giving Lee the injection too."

Fuck. All the signs pointed towards this bastard being right at the heart of things, and the idea of Savannah being anywhere near him roused every protective instinct I'd ever had. "It's not safe for you to go back there. You should come with me."

My mate's warm brown eyes returned to me, looking both appreciative and amused. "You're not in any position to be protecting me at the moment. The answers we need are still in the pack, and you can't get in. I can. Not to mention they'd send out a search party for me if I didn't return. I can handle myself, Jasper."

I knew that. I'd told Sterling the same thing earlier, but it didn't make the gnawing worry in the pit of my stomach lessen in any way. "If we're right about this, if *you're* right, then this guy is fucking dangerous. You can't let your guard down around him for a second."

"I understand," she assured me. "I'll try not to be alone with him again."

Again? Why had she been alone with him before? The idea of her being anywhere close to him at all nearly made me sick.

"He doesn't know I've been in touch with you," Savannah continued, her gaze returning to the papers in her hands. "And he's really proud of his work. If I can get him to start talking, he might let some things slip that I can..."

Whatever the rest of that sentence was going to be, I didn't get to find out. A deep growl echoed from the trees behind us, accompanied by the stench of a rogue. Even though I carried the same scent myself, it still smelled awful to me.

"Shift!" I whispered to Savannah. "Now!"

"The papers..." she protested, still holding them in her hand.

"It's too dangerous for you to take them. Leave them. Shift. Go!"

Looking almost as reluctant to leave me as I felt about being parted from her, she obeyed, shifting into her beautiful brown wolf before I shoved the papers beneath the fallen tree we'd been sitting on and took my wolf form too.

From the trees, Lee's wolf appeared, snarling and growling. My first reaction was relief that they hadn't killed him. Not only that, they'd set him free again, but my delight over that quickly faded into concern as he advanced, his eyes fixed on us with deadly intent.

I don't think he recognizes us, Sterling said in my head, a moment before the same thought crossed my mind. *If they injected him with something...*

It probably affected his memory, at the very least, I agreed. *We have to assume he's dangerous.*

With one last look at Savannah, I gestured to the trees with my head, telling her to make her escape, and thankfully, she not only understood, she accepted my instruction. Giving me a slight nod, she waited for me to make my move, and when I did, she took off, away from the dangers of the angry rogue but back towards the Ravenstone pack and all the potential dangers it held.

I honestly couldn't say which one would be worse, but at that moment, I had my hands full with the wolf in front of me.

I darted towards him to distract him from Savannah, giving her time to escape, and as soon as I saw her go, I turned around and took off back the way I came, counting on the fact that he'd chase after me. He didn't disappoint me. Paws thundered against the dry forest floor, his growls ringing in my ears and his rotten smell following after me as he pursued me further out of the Ravenstone territory.

Hot on my heels, Lee chased me back to the base of the mountain where the others were still resting from our earlier incursion. I hoped they'd hear us coming, and again, my expectations were met. Before I could even start to climb, the others appeared ahead of me with Myra leading the way, also in her wolf form.

With four of us against him and the benefit of the higher ground, Lee's wolf quickly realized his weaker position, and with one last frustrated growl, he took off, running towards the narrow passage that led to where I'd met him earlier that day. My heart panged with guilt and regret as I watched him go.

Hopefully, whatever they'd done to him would be temporary or could be reversed as soon as we had the answers we were looking for. Those answers felt closer than ever, and as the sun disappeared behind the mountains, the rest of us headed back to the cave where I could fill them in on what I'd learned and we could all decide what the fuck we should do next.

Chapter Thirty-Two

~**Savannah**~

My heart continued to pound as I ran back towards the Ravenstone pack house, though the rushed rhythm didn't stem from the rogue we'd encountered or from the possibility of being caught by the Ravenstone security patrol. It didn't even have anything to do with the close call with Jasper's 'haze' nearly marking me.

No, the drumming of my heart had everything to do with what had been done to Jasper, if our suspicions were correct, and the idea that I'd kissed the man responsible for it.

At that point, I didn't know for sure how big a role Kyle played, but he definitely seemed involved and it made his interest in me seem sinister rather than flattering, as I'd originally taken it. He couldn't have known about my connection with Jasper, since *I* didn't even know until that morning, so what else could he want from me? What good did separating Jasper's personality into two parts do? Why exile him and the others from the pack?

What was the point of *any* of it?

Those thoughts all continued to swirl around my head as I drew nearer to the pack house, no closer to the answers I wanted so desperately. As the impressive log house came into view, I slowed my pace, keeping as quiet as possible and sticking to the shadows until I could see a clear opening to approach with attracting the attention of any of the patrols. When I shifted as Jasper instructed, the clothes I'd been wearing had torn, so I had nothing to cover me while I climbed back up to the window that Felix had left open for me. Behind the drawn curtains, I could see his shadow inside, pacing the room, and knowing that he had my back made me feel a little more confident that I could eventually get to the bottom of all of this.

Jasper had me, I had Felix, and together, we would figure it out.

At last, the guard at the back of the house went around the side to continue his patrol, and after one more quick look around, I sprinted across the open space between the trees and the rear of the house, still in my wolf form. Once I got into the shadows there, I shifted back to my human self, shivering as the cool night air blew across my naked body. My skin puckered into goosebumps and my nipples tightened, not in a pleasurable way.

It hadn't felt so cold at the lake with Jasper around.

Glancing up again at the window to judge the distance, I grabbed hold of the drainpipe I'd used to climb down, and pulled myself up off the ground.

"Do you need a boost?"

A startled yelp burst from my lips as the voice spoke from behind me, and my hands slipped off the pipe, sending me back to the ground with a thud, the impact shuddering through my legs. My heart beat even faster as I shrank back into the shadows again, trying to cover my nakedness as much as possible as I turned around to see who had snuck up on me.

In the moonlight, Kyle's pale blue eyes looked eerier than I'd ever seen them before. Fully clothed, he stood with his eyebrows raised, his hands behind his back, and his eyes scanning me from head to toe. Even though the shadows provided some cover, I knew that werewolf night vision worked pretty damn well. He could definitely see me; the appreciation on his face made that clear even if nothing else did.

Since I couldn't think of any plausible excuse for why I would be outside on my own, naked, I decided not to try to make one and answered only the question he'd asked me instead. "No, thanks. I think I've got it. Have a good night."

Turning my back to him, I went to grab the drainpipe again, but I hadn't even managed to pull myself up before he spoke. "Where were you, Savannah?"

Although quiet and calm, a hint of warning underpinned his tone, letting me know he didn't appreciate me trying to avoid him. It looked like I would need to come up with an excuse after all so, reluctantly, I let my hands drop again and looked back over my shoulder to answer him. "My wolf wanted to go for a quick run. All the excitement of the day had her worked up."

"Alone?"

It *did* seem unlikely, but I stuck to my story. "Everyone else seemed busy with this whole rogue attack thing. I didn't want to be a bother. But she's satisfied now and I'm pretty tired, so I'm going to..."

He didn't let me finish. "You knew there were rogues on the loose, yet you went out on your own anyway? I'm not sure if that's brave or reckless."

He took a step closer to me and I shivered again, that time less from the cold than from the intensity of his gaze. "Why can't it be both?" I replied, still trying to keep the mood light. Glancing up at the open window above me, I wondered if Felix could hear our conversation. I'd be happy for his assistance, but he didn't know anything about the suspicions about Kyle, so even if he did hear us, he probably wouldn't interfere.

Kyle's eyes dropped to my body again, having noticed me shiver. His gaze rested entirely too long on my bare ass. "Where are your clothes?"

I didn't have a good explanation for that either, so I tried to put the focus back on him. "A gentleman would get me something to wear rather than watching me freeze."

His eyebrows raised once more, the hint of a smile on his face. "You don't want a gentleman though, do you?"

How he'd come to that conclusion, I couldn't imagine. "You think you know what I want?"

"Better." He stepped even closer, and I turned around to try to defend myself. My back hit the pack house wall, leaving me nowhere else to retreat. "I know what you need."

With that, he closed the remaining distance between us, leaning down to kiss me again as he had on the balcony the night we first met. Unlike then, however, I wanted nothing to do with him. Instinctively, I tried to push him away, but something sharp stung my arm when I did.

Shoving him back with all my might, I looked down in dismay at the syringe in his hand, which he'd clearly injected into my arm. "What the hell is that?"

Kyle's smile sent a deep chill through my body, cooling it even more than the night air did. "Something to calm you down. Don't worry. When we're done, I'll make sure you don't remember any of it."

Done? *Done what?* I tried to ask the question out loud but my mouth refused to cooperate, and as the edges of my vision began to blacken, I tried to send a message to Felix by mind-link. I should have done it earlier, it just hadn't occurred to me, and I cursed my lapse of judgement even as I tried to get my message through. *Jasper... Kyle... injection...*

Unfortunately, my thoughts didn't form any better than my words had, and the last thing I saw before the darkness claimed me was Kyle's pale blue eyes, watching dispassionately as my legs gave way. I was out cold before I even hit the ground.

Chapter Thirty-Three

~Jasper~

Myra, Dan and Brent exchanged worried, unhappy looks when I finished my explanation about what I'd learned since I saw them last.

Nothing got left out; I told them all about my haze, Savannah's theory about it, what she'd been told by the Alpha and seen happening to Lee, and my encounter with Lee afterwards. They'd started a small fire in the cave while I'd been away, its warmth helping to keep away the chill of the night air as we all sat with our arms wrapped around our knees, trying to conserve as much body heat in our human forms as possible. The light from the fire threw shadows across the walls of the caves, dancing with each flicker of the flames.

"We're fucked," Brent stated bluntly, the first one to break the silence. "They can do whatever they want to us. If the Alpha's behind it..."

"I don't think he is," Dan countered, cutting him off. "He might have known about the exile, but Kyle could have lied to him to get him to agree."

"We can't know that for sure," Myra pointed out. "We have to assume everyone knows about it. We can't trust anyone."

"Which means we're fucked," Brent repeated, his hands clenching in frustration. "I always knew there was something creepy about that guy."

Those words immediately caught my attention. Brent hadn't been with us when we discovered the connection to Kyle in the files, so I hadn't had a chance yet to ask him what he knew, but since I assumed he was talking about Kyle and not the Alpha, I quickly remedied that. "Do you know Kyle? Were you friends?"

"I don't know if anyone is 'friends' with Kyle. The other interns were all terrified of him because he'd freak out if they did anything wrong. He always acted like he was better than anyone else in the lab, and when he got added to the Alpha's leadership team, he became even more insufferable. I steered clear of him whenever possible."

None of that surprised me too much, but my focus remained on how we could use this connection, however tenuous, to our advantage. "Do you know which lab he uses?"

Brent shrugged. "Yeah, of course. Everyone knew so they could avoid it."

"What are you thinking?" Myra asked warily, already getting to know me well enough that she knew I had something in mind.

My train of thought wasn't hard to follow. "The answers we need are in that lab."

Dan hopped aboard immediately. "So, we get proof about what he's doing, the injections, the memory loss and your haze and all the rest of it, and we take it to the Alpha."

Brent would take a lot more convincing, growling over at Dan. "The Alpha's in on it! We take it to him, we'll end up like Lee. It's better to cut our losses and leave this whole pack behind while we still can."

"I'm not going anywhere while my mate is still in there!"

The two men began talking over each other, each unwilling to take the other's point of view into consideration, while Myra tried to mediate and get her own opinions heard. Meanwhile, my nose twitched as a new scent drifted over to me from the cave entrance.

"Quiet! Now!"

The words came out in a hushed whisper but their tone still managed to stop the others, all of whom turned to look at me in confusion.

"There's something outside," I whispered. "Get ready to shift."

"Is it Lee again?" Myra asked, keeping her voice down too. "Maybe we can talk to him this time and help jog his memory."

"It's not Lee. It's not a rogue and it's not a Ravenstone wolf. It smells different."

As the scent grew stronger, the rest of them smelled it too, and we all shifted, ready to defend ourselves and our home, such as it was. The fire inside made it difficult to see anything outside the black hole of the cave's entrance, so we stayed near the back of the cave, waiting to see who or what had found us.

"Hello?"

The voice, when it came, took me by surprise. Masculine and strong, whoever it belonged to must not have come there to attack us or he wouldn't have shifted back to his human form. What did he want, then?

"Jasper?" the voice said next, and all the other wolves in the cave immediately turned to look at me, looking for an explanation, though I didn't have one. "Are you in there? It's important. It's about Sav."

'Sav'? Does he mean Savannah? Sterling growled in my head at the sound of another man saying our mate's name, and his possessiveness over a woman we barely knew would have made me laugh if I didn't feel the same.

I wouldn't get any answers in my wolf form, so I shifted back again, the process getting smoother and easier each time I did it. "Who are you?" I called out, remaining in the cave with the others until I had more information.

"My name is Felix. I'm the Beta from Sav's pack. I think she's in trouble, and I don't know who the fuck I can trust in there. I thought you might be able to..."

Before he'd finished that thought, I strode out of the cave, ignoring Myra's growled protests behind me. Just to the side of the cave entrance, illuminated by the moon, stood the man I'd seen arrive with Savannah the day before. He was telling the truth about knowing her, at least, so I had no reason to doubt the rest of what he said. "What kind of trouble is she in?"

His eyes widened as he took in my appearance, and it made me wince, wondering how bad I must look. I hadn't seen a comb or a mirror in weeks, and yet, Savannah hadn't seemed put off by me at all.

Thankfully, Felix recovered from his surprise quickly and got down to business. "While I was waiting for her to come back from meeting with you, I heard her talking to someone outside the pack house. She sent me a few words by mind-link, but then everything went quiet, and when I looked out the window, she was gone. One of the words she sent me was your name, and I figured you'd be as motivated as I am to track her down."

He had that right. I was ready to run straight back into the Ravenstone territory immediately, but I forced myself to ask some questions first. "What else did she say?"

"I only heard 'Jasper', 'Kyle' and 'injection'."

That didn't help much. Had she been trying to tell him about our theory about me being drugged somehow? Or did it mean something else?

"Who was she talking to?" I tried next.

He answered with one word, the worst word I could imagine in that situation: "Kyle."

The growl that came out of me was so strong, Felix took a step back, and the other three came out of the cave, still in their wolf forms, curious enough to see what was going on.

"She was talking to Kyle, alone, and then disappeared?" I repeated slowly and clearly, wanting to make sure I had understood completely correctly.

When Felix nodded, that was all the information I needed. Turning to the others, I laid it out for them: "I'm going back in, right now. I'm going to that lab, I'm finding my mate, and I don't care if the whole pack tries to stop me. Who's coming with me?"

Chapter Thirty-Four

~Savannah~

Slowly, the fog around my thoughts began to recede. It felt like waking up from a long sleep, so long that it somehow made you tired again, or maybe more like waking up with a hangover where the world seemed a little too loud and bright.

With my eyes still closed, I could hear beeping sounds, sounding far off in the distance, and a shiver ran through me as I became more aware of my body. The surface I lay on felt hard and cold, and I had nothing covering me, not a blanket and not even clothes.

Where the fuck was I?

Beep.

My eyelids resisted my attempt to open them, feeling leaden and heavy.

Beep.

My lips had dried out and a chalky, stale taste filled my mouth.

Beep.

With a groan, I managed to open my eyes a little and immediately squeezed them shut again, the light sending a piercing, sharp pain through my head.

"Your genes really are good. That dose would have knocked out a lesser wolf for another hour, at least."

The voice sounded familiar, but it wasn't until I forced my eyes open again and Kyle's lab took shape around me that the rest of it came flooding back too. I remembered the conversation with Jasper, the papers he'd shown me, and the conversation with Kyle outside the pack house. Most of all, I remembered the syringe in his hand and the look on his face as I collapsed.

"What did you inject me with?"

The words came out slurred and mumbled, but at least I could speak again. Maybe it hadn't worked if I could still remember everything? He'd implied I wouldn't be able to.

Kyle stood at his lab table, his body in profile to me so I could only see him from the side. He didn't look at me at all, continuing to focus on whatever sat on the table in front of him. Between us, a row of metal bars restricted my view, and as I took a better look around, I realized they were part of a cage like the ones he kept his animals in, except this one held *me*.

He put us in a fucking cage! Tala sounded as outraged as I felt, though her thoughts weren't as clear as usual either. Whatever he gave us clearly affected us both.

Take it easy, I advised her. *I got this.*

Wires ran through the bars, wires connected to the beeping machine on one side and to electrodes attached to my chest on my side. Reaching down, I ripped them off, my body responding sluggishly to my commands, and the machine immediately let out a shrill alarm that made me wince. With a sigh, Kyle left his work station and went to the machine, pressing a button that turned the alarm off. Still without looking at me, he returned to what he'd been doing before.

"That's a waste of time and energy, Savannah. I'll have to put them back on later. Just relax. I'll have the compound ready soon."

"Compound?" The word sent another chill through me, one that had nothing to do with the cool metal floor of the cage. "What compound?"

As I painfully pushed myself up to a sitting position, I could see that Kyle had a dropper in his hand, dripping liquid into a container I couldn't see. The cage wasn't tall enough for me to stand up, so my view of his table remained limited to the only angle I had. Still naked, I had no way of covering my body but it didn't seem to matter. He must have already seen everything when he brought me to the lab, and I didn't think he'd taken advantage of me in a sexual way while I'd been unconscious. His intentions seemed much more clinical and somehow even more sinister.

His eyes never left his work. "You don't need to worry about that. It would have been better if you kept sleeping while I finished this. You can try to rest again if you want. It'll all be over soon."

Well, that sounded creepy as fuck. A sarcastic retort sat on the tip of my tongue, but at the last second, I pulled it back, trying to think strategically rather than emotionally. Locked in the cage, I didn't have much hope of escape. He would have made sure of that while I was unconscious.

Alpha Warren had mentioned before that Kyle's lab had some kind of soundproofing that stopped mind-links from going in or out, so even if Felix were in range, I wouldn't be able to reach him.

At first glance, my situation seemed pretty hopeless.

However, when I didn't return, Felix would get worried. Maybe he'd even overheard part of our conversation beneath my bedroom window. Eventually, he'd come looking for me, and given enough time, I felt sure he'd find me. I just had to give him that time, which meant trying to delay whatever Kyle had planned for me as long as I could.

I needed to stall, and as I watched the man who I'd originally considered rather handsome but who now made my stomach turn, I remembered how proud he'd been to show me his work earlier that day. Maybe I could get him talking about it as a means of distraction. He might even let some things slip that could be useful as long as I could keep my memories of the conversation afterwards.

It might not have been much of a plan, but since I didn't have a better one, I started talking.

"Is that compound going to erase my memories just like you did to the rogues?"

Though he still didn't look at me, I could see the corners of Kyle's mouth pull upwards. "I had a feeling you spoke to one of them tonight.

The Alpha told me about the questions you've been asking. You really are rather clever in your own way. You'll make an excellent mate."

The words carried a hint of pride that disgusted me, not to mention the implication that I'd be *his* mate, but I did my best to maintain a neutral expression in case he glanced my way, and stuck to the questions I wanted answered. "What exactly did you do to them?"

He tutted at me as he added a few more drops of another liquid to his work. "Your curiosity is a trait we can do without, though. I won't be able to edit it out this time, but maybe with a bit more practice, I can find the right gene."

The calm, impersonal way he spoke of 'editing' my personality had to be one of the scariest things I'd ever heard, and I swallowed down the lump in my throat, trying to keep my panic at bay. "Is that what you did to Jasper? Edited out the things that you didn't want him to have?"

He didn't immediately answer me, so I tried again.

"You say I'm not going to remember any of this, so why not take the opportunity to tell me about it? It must be killing you that your groundbreaking work has to be a secret. Wouldn't it be nice to tell someone?"

That was exactly the right thing to say. At last, Kyle looked over at me, his pale blue eyes full of passion, not for me, but for his work. "You really want to know?"

"I'd love to hear all about it. Every last detail."

Chapter Thirty-Five

~**Savannah**~

I hoped Kyle would stop working while he explained his grand designs to me, but he wasn't quite that stupid. His eyes returned to the table in front of him, his hands keeping busy with whatever concoction he had in front of him, but at least he began to talk.

"I told you earlier about the genetic engineering we've done and how we used it to optimize caloric intake, but that's only the tip of the iceberg. The more I studied, the more I realized that every single part of us is controlled by our DNA. Change the DNA, change the wolf. It's simple."

And unethical, I thought, but I refrained from stating that out loud. Instead, I leaned closer, pulling my knees to my chest to cover myself as much as possible while doing my best to look fascinated.

Kyle didn't need much of an audience anyway once he got going. "Darwin explained natural selection over a hundred years ago, how certain genetic traits increase the odds of survival, and as a result, species evolve. What I'm doing is no different, except instead of it taking hundreds or thousands of years to evolve, I'm making those changes happen immediately. Every one of us can be improved right now, and those changes, built into the very fabric of our DNA, will also be passed to our children. I'm creating a whole new species of super-wolves, Savannah. Weaknesses will be eliminated, strengths enhanced. The world will never be the same."

Well, as long as he stayed humble about it, what could go wrong? *Fuck.* He might not have been crazy, but he'd certainly lost his moral compass. Insanity might have been easier to deal with.

"How do you know these changes can work?" I asked, trying to sound only interested rather than disgusted. "Working on cells in your lab is one thing. Altering a whole functioning werewolf is something else."

"You're absolutely right," he agreed, sounding almost proud of me for understanding that. "That's why testing the treatments on live werewolves is so important."

My chest grew tighter as I realized what he meant. "You tested it on the rogues?"

"Some of it, yes." He answered me so calmly, without a hint of guilt or regret, that I had to believe he truly didn't see a problem with it. "I tested the memory alteration first. Rather than permanent genetic editing, that particular treatment temporarily disrupts the delivery of proteins to the part of the brain involved in short-term memory. The half-life of the treatment inside the body is fairly short. When it degrades, their memories return to normal functioning, but the memories that didn't get stored are lost forever. It worked perfectly."

It certainly seemed to have, since none of the rogues were able to remember exactly what had happened to them. "And since that was a success, you moved on to testing other things too?" I guessed.

Again, a hint of pride tinged his reply. "Precisely. It's been a bit of trial and error. The first dose went to Jasper. I assume he's the one you've been speaking to?"

I supposed by mentioning his name earlier, I'd given that away, so I didn't bother to deny it. Kyle didn't know about Jasper being my mate; to him, he was just another wolf. "What did you do to him?"

Kyle sighed, his hands stilling for a moment in his frustration. "The treatment was meant to suppress the independent part of the human entirely, but it wasn't quite ready when I gave it to him. My incubators hadn't quite finished producing the cells I needed yet, so it separated parts of his personality instead, suppressing those pieces but not the whole. It was a setback."

"For him, you mean?" I couldn't help asking, and Kyle glanced over at me with a rather condescending smile.

"He played a key role in helping me understand what was needed to perfect the treatment. He should be honoured to have been involved in something so significant."

It didn't seem likely that Jasper would see it that way, but I let that comment slide, focusing on something else he'd said. "If Jasper was the first, does that mean you've done it successfully on others?"

His temporary distraction disappeared as he returned to his work. "The second time was better but still not perfect. The suppression worked but there were side effects. Unfortunately, they proved fatal. Still, I learned a lot. We learn more from our mistakes than from our successes sometimes."

My arms tightened around my knees as I realized what he meant. The sixth rogue, the one Jasper didn't know about, must have been that wolf, and the unfortunate person actually lost their life after being injected. As before, Kyle didn't even seem upset about it for the affected person's sake, only frustrated that his 'treatment' hadn't fully worked.

"Lee tolerated it much better this afternoon. I tagged him before releasing him, and I'll follow up in a few days to see how he's been affected."

So, he *had* dosed Lee with more than a sedative. I knew it! Hopefully, it wouldn't end the same way for him as it had for the other wolf.

"This is why your genes are going to be so valuable," he continued, putting the dropper he'd been using down and picking up a syringe instead. "Alpha blood can be used to create stronger stem cells. That will result in a better, more reliable outcome. I think that's the biggest problem remaining."

"You want my genes?" I sputtered in disbelief. "What about *your* Alpha? Or Amanda, for that matter? They both have Alpha blood!"

The condescending smile reappeared as he slowly drew the liquid up from the container in front of him into the syringe. "Yes, but the younger the subject, the better. It's not *you* I need. It's your child."

"My *child?*" Maybe he had gone insane after all, because he wasn't making any sense. "News flash, Kyle: I'm not pregnant."

"Not yet," he agreed. "The plan had been to use Amanda's child after she mated with your brother. That would have been ideal since both parents had Alpha blood, but when he called off the mating, that option disappeared. You're the next best thing."

At last, the pieces fell into place about why the Alpha had been so insistent on getting me in exchange for my brother. It had nothing to do with an alliance or any of the other bullshit he suggested it did. They wanted my body. My genes. My child.

"Did Amanda know about this?" The idea horrified me that not only had Kyle fooled me, but Amanda might have as well.

However, to my relief, Kyle shook his head. "No. I couldn't trust her not to overreact."

Overreact? Why would she possibly overreact about someone wanting to use her child to grow genes?

That sarcastic response stayed inside my head as my thoughts continued to whirl. What about me? Were they ever actually going to give me a choice about choosing a mate and staying in the pack? Or would Kyle have found a way to force me to, no matter what?

The whole thing had been a set-up, and if he succeeded in wiping all of this from my memory, I might still fall prey to it. My fingernails dug into my arms that I'd wrapped around my knees, trying to stay calm.

That wasn't all, either. The puzzle continued to take shape in my head, new connections being formed, and something else he said stood out: *the younger the subject, the better.*

"Jasper was exiled for abducting some children," I said slowly, connecting the dots as I spoke out loud. "But it was you, wasn't it? *You* abducted them."

It never sat right with me that Jasper had done something like that, even if it had been his 'haze'.

Kyle didn't deny it, and I remembered what he said about the treatment he gave to Jasper not being quite ready yet because his 'incubators' hadn't finished producing the cells yet. At the time, I thought he meant regular, mechanical incubators, but as I learned more about the depth of his depravity, I realized exactly what he'd used the children for.

"You used them as live incubators for your treatment, but Jasper discovered it. He found them and you, and so you drugged him, framed him, and had him exiled."

For the first time, anger flashed in Kyle's eyes as they turned back to me, the syringe still held in his hand, the clear liquid inside it looking all the more sinister for its innocuousness. "He didn't understand my vision. He would have exposed everything."

"Exposed it to who? Does the Alpha know about all of this?"

Kyle took a step towards me, his white lab coat, swishing against his legs. "He knows that I'm the only one who can give him what he wants most. He trusts me."

That wasn't a yes. There must be at least part of it the Alpha wasn't aware of, but at the moment, my attention remained fixed on the syringe in Kyle's hand, the tip of the needle glistening beneath the lab's lights as he crouched down, closer to my level.

"I'm not a bad person, Savannah. Everything I've done has been to help my Alpha and help my pack. It'll all be worth it in the end."

I doubted the wolf who died would agree with that. "And now what?" I asked, trying to sound a hell of a lot braver than I felt. "You're going to take away my memory and try to convince me that you love me so I'll take you as my mate?"

"Oh, I don't have to convince you." His proud smile returned, looking out of place beneath his pale, heartless eyes. "This compound will increase your body's production of dopamine, oxytocin and serotonin, and you'll associate that feeling with me. You'll fall in love with me without me doing anything at all. I guess you could call it a love potion, but there's nothing magical about it. It's 100% science."

Right about now would be a good time for Felix to show up, Tala murmured nervously in my head, and I could only nod, scrambling back in the cage as far as I could, trying to stay out of reach.

Kyle sighed as he watched me. "You underestimate me, Savannah."

Reaching up, he pressed a button on the top of the cage, something I couldn't see from my position, and immediately, the cage began to shrink, the bars closing in tighter around me. In a matter of seconds, I'd be within his reach, and if he managed to stick that needle into me, my life as I knew it would be over.

Chapter Thirty-Six

~Jasper~

The uneasy looks that Myra, Dan and Brent exchanged when I announced I was going back into Ravenstone territory had Sterling howling impatiently in my head. *Stop wasting time! Go! She needs us.*

I know that, but we're no good to her dead or captured. It would be better if we had some backup. We have to be smart about this. That's what she deserves.

Felix was with me, at least. "I didn't know where Kyle would have taken her, but you think they're at his lab?"

I nodded firmly. "I'm certain of it. Have you got anyone else with you?"

Unfortunately, Felix shook his head. "Only the two of us came from our pack. If I'd had any idea of the situation here... well, it's too late for that. Earlier tonight, I let my Alpha know we could use some help in the morning, but when I realized Sav was gone, I didn't update him. I came straight here and left my phone behind."

I could understand that. In a panic, I'd have done the same, and there was no fucking way we were waiting until morning anyway. "Looks like it's the two of us then. Let's go."

"Three," Myra's voice called out from behind me. "I'm coming too."

"And me," Dan quickly agreed.

Their support meant a lot to me, and everyone turned to look at Brent, the last holdout.

"Fine," he muttered reluctantly. "But if you all get me killed, I'm haunting you for the rest of your lives. In my wolf form so I can mark all your stuff."

Having him along would be handy since he had the access codes to the medical centre and knew exactly where to find Kyle's lab, so I appreciated his agreement, no matter how reluctantly he gave it.

"They'll be on high alert after this afternoon," I pointed out. "We'll need another distraction but we don't have time to piss off another wolf pack."

"Maybe we don't need a whole pack," Myra said, speaking slowly as she thought it over. "Maybe we just need one wolf."

I understood her immediately. "Lee."

She nodded in confirmation. "I know where he'll be: exactly where we found him earlier today. Instinct will guide him that much, no matter how his memory's affected. Based on the way he reacted to you earlier, I'm guessing I can get him to chase me into their territory."

"I'll help," Dan quickly offered, giving Myra a supportive nod. "You shouldn't go alone."

That left me, Felix and Brent to go to the lab. I would have liked to have a whole fucking army at my back, but it would have to do. "Let's do it."

It would only take a few minutes for Myra and Dan to get back to where we found Lee that afternoon, following their noses, but I had no intention of waiting those few minutes. Even the seconds we'd stood around so far felt far too long. The Ravenstone wolves would be alerted when the three of us crossed the border, but they'd get another alert when the others did, which would hopefully confuse and distract them.

So, without any further discussion, I shifted and took off back towards the Ravenstone territory with Felix and Brent close behind me. As much as I wanted to head straight for the lab when we crossed the border, we had to stay out of sight, so I forced myself to detour. Each step I took off the path tugged at my heart, the worry building stronger with each passing second. What did that sick bastard take her for? Was she still okay? Since we hadn't marked each other yet, would I even feel it if she wasn't?

Fear tightened my chest, making it harder to breathe. No, I couldn't let myself go down that path. Savannah was a fighter, she had a fire in her that I'd already seen, and if there was any chance of her getting the upper hand, she'd find a way to do it. I just wanted to be there to back her up, just in case.

By taking my unconventional route to the medical clinic, we managed to arrive there undetected. Midnight had come and gone by then, so although the lights were still on in the hospital part of the building, the research area looked empty and locked up tight.

Sticking close to the shadows by the wall, I shifted back to my human form. "You can get us in again, right?" I whispered to Brent as he shifted too.

"I'll try," he muttered, going to enter his security code while Felix remained in his wolf form, keeping a wary eye out for any sign of trouble.

That afternoon, the control panel had immediately turned green after Brent entered his code. That time, though, it remained stubbornly red. With a frown, Brent entered it again.

"It's not working." I could hear the panic rising in his voice. "They must have disabled it after what happened earlier."

It certainly would have been the smart thing to do, I had to admit. If I were investigating, I would have recommended exactly the same thing.

There were other ways to get in, ways to cut power to the building or circumvent the alarm system, but they would have all taken too long and we didn't have the necessary tools anyway. My mate was inside with a psychopath and I wasn't waiting any longer. Picking up a large rock that sat on the ground nearby, I hurled it at one of the nearby windows with all my might, putting all my anxiety and frustration behind the throw.

The window shattered and an alarm immediately sounded. There would probably be security on site as well as the pack's internal security team who would hear that alarm too. We'd have to move fast.

Breaking the remains of the pane with my elbow, I ensured we had a safe hole to get through, and in our wolf forms, all three of us leapt inside. The room we ended up in was a regular office, dark and useless. Shifting back, my heart pounding more with every passing second, we raced out into the hall.

"This way," Brent directed, leading us down the corridor towards a room I recognized: the one Savannah had gone into earlier that day. Light spilled out from beneath the door and I ran toward it as fast as I'd ever moved before, hoping with every fibre of my being that whatever I found on the other side, I wouldn't be too late.

Chapter Thirty-Seven

~**Savannah**~

Just as the cage stopped moving, the bars close enough to me I had nowhere to go to stay out of Kyle's reach, one of his machines began to beep loudly.

Frowning, he stepped away from me to go check on it while my eyes remained glued to the syringe in his hand, my heart pounding violently as I tried to figure out how I could avoid it.

"That's odd," he muttered before pressing something that made the beeping stop.

"What is?" I honestly didn't care, but each second I could keep him talking would be one more that might bring Felix closer to me.

He still felt confident enough to confide in me. "The rogue I dosed earlier is moving back into our territory. That shouldn't happen. He should be acting purely on instinct now, and instinct would tell him to stay away. Something must have gone wrong."

The frustration practically flowed off him, evident in the tightness in his shoulders and the clenching of his jaw, but my focus was still on trying to stay undosed myself.

"Maybe you should go deal with that," I suggested as innocently as possible, but it didn't work. Kyle simply smirked as he turned back to me.

"The border guards will pick him up and I can deal with it then. I wouldn't want to keep you waiting any longer."

He stepped towards me again, the syringe still steady in his hand, but before he could jab me with it, a siren started to blare outside the door.

"What the fuck?" His eyebrows drew together in even more frustration as he turned towards the sound. Quickly, I tried to calculate if I could reach through the bars and grab the syringe from him, but it seemed too risky. With my arms exposed, he'd have more surface area to aim for. Better to keep myself as difficult to reach as possible and adopt a defensive position.

Kyle's eyes flitted back over to his screen and back to the door, obviously trying to decide how concerned he needed to be, and a moment later, that question was answered for him as someone tried to open the lab door. When they found it locked, they pounded on it instead.

"Savannah? Are you in there?"

The voice didn't belong to Felix but I recognized it all the same, and my heart soared with relief and disbelief. How on earth did Jasper find me? How had he gotten to the lab without being stopped? How did he know I needed help? I had no idea, but at that moment, I could only be grateful that he had.

"I'm here! Hurry!"

"Shut up," Kyle hissed, obviously feeling differently about the turn of events than I did, his eyes blazing in anger. A second later, the door rattled on its hinges, likely caused by a large, angry werewolf ramming his body into it. "That rogue just signed his death sentence, but first, you're going to forget all about this."

With determination, he walked back over to the cage, but I had no intention of giving in with backup so close at hand. Before he reached me, I shifted, and as he reached through the bars, I snapped at his hand with my jaw, making him pull back quickly before he lost the hand for good.

"No!" His panic grew as the door continued to creak beneath the assault from the other side, no doubt understanding as well as I did how much trouble he'd be in if I kept my memories of the conversation we'd had. "Stay still!"

Not likely. Tala took control of our body and she growled at him, every muscle in her body coiled, ready to respond to any move he might make. When he tried to go around the side of the cage, she anticipated it, and when he tried to fake her out, reaching with his left hand while his right went around, she wasn't fooled for a second, almost managing to snatch the syringe from him with her teeth.

Just a little longer, I encouraged her. The door couldn't hold up much longer under the assault being levelled at it.

In fact, no sooner had the thought crossed my mind than the door finally gave, slamming to the floor inside the lab as it was ripped clean off the wall. Behind it, Jasper, Felix, and another man I'd never seen before quickly rushed into the room, all naked from their own shifts.

Felix's presence helped to explain how Jasper knew I was in trouble, and I had never been so glad to see my brother's best friend before.

However, as Tala turned to look at them, Kyle remained focused on his task.

The syringe pierced the skin of her shoulder as my stomach sank, hard and fast.

"No!" The roar that came out of Jasper was so loud, the vials in the storage unit next to me rattled in their containers. In a second, he was at my side, tossing Kyle to the side as if he were a gnat in his way, and pulling the syringe from my skin. "What the fuck is this?"

He directed those words to Kyle, who Felix quickly picked up off the floor from where Jasper had tossed him.

"What did you give her?"

He held the syringe up as he demanded answers, and thankfully, I could see most of the liquid still remained inside it. Kyle hadn't been able to get very much into me, but I had no idea what a partial dose would do. Would I lose *some* of my memories? Or for a shorter time? Whatever the case might be, I needed to pass on what I knew before I lost the chance.

Shakily, I shifted back to my human form while Jasper searched for a way to open the cage. "I'll get you out of there, hang on."

"No." The word came out croakily, and I tried to clear my throat as Jasper bent down to see me better.

"What do you mean?"

"It's more important that I tell you... experiments... the kids... Alpha..."

Fuck! The sedative part was starting to work on me at the very least, as quickly as it had before, and I couldn't seem to get the words out properly.

"Tell Felix by mind-link if it's easier," he encouraged me, and gratefully, I nodded. That would be easier.

Felix, Kyle's behind all of it. He framed Jasper. He abducted the kids to experiment on them, and that's why the pack wanted me too. They want my genes, my child's genes. The Alpha doesn't know everything. He knows some of it but not all. We have to tell him... the rogues... fatal...

My thoughts became disrupted, just like before, and across the room, I gave Felix a pleading look, hoping he'd gotten enough of it to understand.

Don't worry, Sav. He's not getting away, Felix promised, still holding Kyle tightly. *You're going to be fine. We're going to...*

His thoughts started to fade away too, and my eyelids began to close as Jasper's face reappeared before me. "Stay awake, Savannah. Please. Whatever he did to you, we'll undo it. Stay with me."

I wanted to. I really did, but my body had other ideas. The last thing I heard before the darkness took me again was the sound of more voices shouting in the hall, and Jasper quickly got to his feet, steeling himself for whatever might be coming next.

Chapter Thirty-Eight

~Jasper~

I'd never felt so helpless as I did standing there watching my mate slip into unconsciousness, the bars of the cage separating us. I couldn't get to her and I couldn't help her.

If only I'd gotten through the door a few seconds earlier. Even though Kyle hadn't managed to give her the full dose of whatever the hell was in that syringe, it had been enough. I still felt like a complete failure.

There was no time for self-pity, though, not when shouts came from outside the hall, shouts belonging to the pack's security, tipped off to our presence by the alarm we'd tripped. Whatever Savannah managed to tell Felix, I hoped it would be enough to convince the approaching men that Kyle was the one who should be locked up, not us.

Even if I wanted to run, I couldn't, not when my mate lay helpless beside me. The time had come to take a stand.

"Get behind me," I ordered Brent, seeing the fear in his eyes as the people outside the door drew closer. He'd done his part and I would protect him as much as I could. He was a victim as much as me or Savannah.

Kyle had a lot to answer for.

Brent didn't argue, ducking behind me as I stood next to the cage, taking a deep breath to steady myself while Felix continued to hold onto Kyle who looked a lot calmer now that Savannah had lost consciousness. Whatever she'd been trying to tell me must have been important.

We're going to tear that bastard limb-from-limb if he hurt her, Sterling snarled in my head.

We're on the same page, don't worry, I assured him. Though I generally believed in due process, if the Alpha gave me five minutes alone with him, I would take great pleasure in making the fucker suffer.

The voices grew closer until, in a burst of sound and movement, a group of people stormed into the room. The ones at the front, I recognized: they were my former colleagues from the internal security team, and I held up my hands to show I was unarmed as they aimed their weapons at me and Felix.

Following close behind them were a man and woman I'd never seen before, though the man, tall with curly brown hair and brown eyes blazing with indignation, looked vaguely familiar to me anyway. The woman at his side, blonde and blue-eyed, was a complete stranger.

"Vaughan?" Felix exhaled the name in relief and confusion, looking at the tall man who pushed his way to the front of the group, past the security officers. "What are you doing here?"

"We left home as soon as you felt the need to start checking in with us hourly. Callie convinced me to listen to my gut. Where's Sav?"

His eyes scanned the room until they landed on the cage behind me where my unconscious mate was laid out on the floor, naked, and he let out a growled roar that had all the men in the room bowing their heads in subconscious submission.

Only an Alpha could command that kind of authority, which gave me a good idea who the man might be. Felix had mentioned being in touch with the Alpha of his pack, and it made sense that the furious man in front of me would be that man.

"Why the fuck is my sister in a cage?!"

His *sister?* Savannah was the daughter of an Alpha? I definitely hadn't known that, but now that I did, I could see the family resemblance. *That* was why he seemed familiar.

Shoving me out of the way nearly as roughly as I'd done to Kyle, he bent down to reach in and feel Savannah's pulse, letting out a small sigh of relief as he confirmed her heart continued to beat. It didn't temper his anger very much though.

"What the hell did you do to her?" he asked next, springing back to his feet and turning his angry brown eyes on me.

"Vaughan, stop. It wasn't him. This is the one responsible," Felix called out, giving Kyle a rough shake, and I felt certain that if the Alpha were thinking straight, he would have realized that. Felix had to be holding him for a reason. I kept my hands up in submission anyway, just in case.

"Everybody stand down," the man at the front of the group ordered, trying to keep some control over the situation. "You too, Alpha Vaughan. We'll take everyone to the pack house and get this sorted out with the Alpha."

Though Brent swore softly behind me, the prospect of coming face-to-face with my Alpha and finally getting some answers after all this time didn't scare me. At the moment, all my worry was wrapped up in the woman at my feet. "What about Savannah?" I asked.

"We'll have her taken to the medical clinic," the man suggested.

"No," Vaughan and I protested at the same time, and he flashed me a warning look that told me to back off. I did, only because I knew that he cared as much about her wellbeing as I did.

"She doesn't leave my sight," Vaughan ordered. "Get this cage open and I'll bring her to the pack house myself. The doctors can see her there."

The man nodded in agreement as the others with him brought out their handcuffs. Filled with a silver centre, they weakened the person wearing them so they were unable to shift. I'd used them on people myself before, but I'd never been the one wearing them. Eager to move things along, though, I held out my wrists willingly and encouraged Brent to do the same.

"Let him go," the man ordered Felix, who still had a death grip on Kyle, making it impossible for the men to cuff either of them.

"No," Felix refused, perfectly reasonably in my eyes. "I'll come with you willingly, but he's coming with me."

That answer didn't satisfy the man in charge. "You're still a guest in our territory, Beta Felix. You're subject to our rules, the same as everyone else. I said: let him go."

Kyle still hadn't said a word, obviously not wanting to draw any additional attention to himself. Felix looked over at Vaughan, his eyes clouding over as they communicated with each other through their link, and reluctantly, Felix loosened his grip.

That was all it took. Almost instantly, the room plunged into darkness, and shouts of surprise rang out, along with the sounds of a scuffle. Though I couldn't see a thing, I bent down to try to protect Savannah anyway, putting my body in front of the cage in case anyone tried to attack her.

It only lasted a few seconds before the lights came back on, but when they did, we all noticed the same thing immediately.

Kyle was nowhere to be seen.

Chapter Thirty-Nine

~**Jasper**~

It took the team leader a couple of minutes to restore order after we all realized Kyle had gone missing. I tried to break free, but the cuffs around my wrists were strong enough that I couldn't get loose from the man holding me. Felix also wanted to leave and track the bastard down, but his Alpha told him to stay put.

"We need to make sure Sav's okay," I heard Vaughan say. "And we should speak to Alpha Warren. After that, we can deal with the rest of it."

Logically, I knew that made sense, so I stopped struggling and so did Felix. Savannah came first, no question.

"You three, search the building," my former colleague ordered when he finally had everyone quiet again. "The rest of you, come with me. The Alpha's waiting for us."

With my hands cuffed, I could only watch as the others got Savannah's cage open and Alpha Vaughan gently picked her up. The blonde woman with him, who must have been his Luna based on the marks they both bore, found a blanket from somewhere to drape across Savannah, covering her up and keeping her warm as we stepped back out into the chilly night air.

We should be carrying her, Sterling grumbled in my head as we walked the short distance back to the pack house, the paved asphalt road cool on my bare feet. *We're her mate.*

And her brother doesn't know that yet, I reminded him. It wasn't my place to tell him, not when we still didn't know what would happen next, and not when Savannah couldn't make the choice for herself. *Besides, it would be a little tricky with these cuffs on.*

He had to concede that point, but he didn't do it happily.

Inside the pack house, we were led straight to the Alpha's office, a room I'd never been in before, and there, we found Myra and Dan, already cuffed and sitting on chairs, dressed in the pack's grey shifting clothes. Two wolves stood guard over them, and we all nodded to each other grimly. It appeared the pack had been prepared for us that time around. I wondered what happened to Lee, but I couldn't ask in front of the others so I kept my mouth shut.

Felix, Brent and I were also offered pants to cover up with, which we had to be helped into with our hands tied, and Vaughan laid Savannah down on the couch where the doctor started to check her over.

Before the man could give us any update on her condition, Alpha Warren entered the room, accompanied by his daughter, Amanda.

"Is this all of them?" he asked the man in charge, who nodded in confirmation.

"Yes, Alpha."

That wasn't exactly true, since we were missing Kyle, and I pointed that out at the same time that pretty much everyone else in the room started talking. Voices got louder, talking over each other in an attempt to be heard, until the Alpha shouted at us all to stop.

"Enough! No one speaks unless spoken to."

He glared at all of us, his authority making us bow our heads in submission to him, before turning to the man at Savannah's side.

"Alpha Vaughan, how is your sister?"

"That shouldn't be a question you have to ask," the visiting Alpha growled at him. "Why wasn't she protected?"

The implied insult in the question made Alpha Warren stiffen. For a pack that prided itself on its hospitality, having an injured guest meant he'd failed in that duty of care and we all knew it.

"Her vital signs are good," the doctor spoke up before the Alpha could respond. "It appears she's been sedated, but nothing more sinister than that."

I wouldn't have put any money on that. Physically, she might be fine, but what had Kyle done to her mentally? That question would haunt me until she woke up and I found out for myself.

"I'm sorry, Vaughan," Amanda spoke up, saying his name in a way that suggested they had met before that night. "Things have gotten out of hand and Savannah... well, you know she doesn't sit on the sidelines."

That definitely fit in with what I knew of her, and her brother couldn't argue with that either. He simply gave Amanda a curt nod before turning back to Alpha Warren. "My Beta can be released now. He was only trying to find Savannah."

The Alpha nodded his assent, and the guards quickly undid Felix's cuffs. Seeing him rub his wrists made my cuffs feel even tighter.

Vaughan wasn't finished with the Alpha yet. "What the hell is going on in your pack? Why were these people exiled, and why are they trying to get back in?"

"I think I can answer that," Felix interjected, drawing all attention to him. "Just before Savannah lost consciousness, she told me that Kyle is behind all of it. He's been experimenting on people. He's the one who drugged her. It all comes back to him, that's what she said."

Alpha Warren's lips grew tight, flattening across his face as he glanced around the room. "Where's Kyle now?"

"We lost him, Alpha," the man from internal security admitted, bowing his head apologetically. "I don't know why he ran, but these men were being rather aggressive with him. He probably feared for his life."

I hadn't begun to be anywhere near as 'aggressive' with him as I wanted to be, and I still didn't have a clue how the fuck he had escaped either. I'd been watching him carefully as Felix let him go, and I didn't see him do anything that would have caused the lights to go out. It was almost as though...

"You helped him escape." It suddenly seemed crystal clear to me, and I spoke the words out loud despite the Alpha's order not to speak until he addressed me. "You commanded Beta Felix to let him go and you must have turned the lights off somehow. You two are working together."

"That's ridiculous," the man snarled back at me, an indignant flush of red creeping into his cheeks. "You lost all rights to accuse anyone of anything when you were exiled. No one believes you."

"I believe him," Felix piped up again. "Makes sense to me. Why else were you so insistent that I let him go?"

The man turned to him in exasperation. "Because it's protocol to secure everyone at the scene when we don't know the situation. You should know that."

The last sentence, he directed angrily at me, and although he had a point, my gut still told me I was on the right track.

"In which case, all your men would know you would do it. Maybe one of them was in on it and they waited for you to give the order. Kyle had help to get away, I'm sure of it."

The man didn't immediately respond to that, letting me know I'd struck a nerve. He must have had the same doubts, even if he didn't admit them out loud.

"Back up a second," Amanda requested, her gaze still on Felix. "What do you mean that Kyle experimented on people?"

I suspected I knew, given my earlier conversation with Savannah about my haze, but Felix's words took me completely by surprise.

"I don't know all the details," he admitted. "Sav didn't have a lot of time before she passed out, but she said that he abducted children, the ones Jasper was accused of taking, in order to experiment on them."

"What?" My blood somehow turned cold and hot at the same time, icy shock running through my veins at the same time that it began to boil.

We're going to fucking kill him, Sterling growled, and I didn't disagree. If that man showed his face in front of me again, he was as good as dead.

"Alright, everyone listen." The Alpha took control of the room again, though he sounded more tired than before. "I don't want to hear things second hand. We've got people out looking for Kyle. Lota Savannah needs to rest and so do I. We'll reconvene in the morning to sort this all out, hopefully with Savannah and Kyle speaking for themselves. The rogues can go to the prison where they can't cause any more trouble tonight."

That sounded fair, except for one thing: I couldn't let Savannah out of my sight. "Alpha, I'd like to stand guard over Savannah until she wakes up."

His unimpressed expression would have struck fear into the hearts of most members of the pack. "You're a prisoner. You don't get to make any requests."

I stood my ground. "I'm not going anywhere. I'll keep the cuffs on if I have to. I need to make sure she's okay."

Silently, I prayed he wouldn't ask me why it mattered to me so much, since I still didn't want to tell anyone we were mates until Savannah had a chance to agree to it.

To my relief, Felix stepped in once again. "I'll keep watch over them both. I'll vouch for him."

He threw a meaningful look at his alpha, and Vaughan spoke up too, looking slightly confused. "So will I."

Faced with a united front, the Alpha gave in. "Fine. I'll have my own men outside the room too, but if anything happens to her, it's on you, Alpha Vaughan. Now, everyone, go to sleep. We'll meet back here in the morning."

I gave Myra, Brent and Dan encouraging nods as they were led away to the prison. They looked exhausted, and I couldn't blame them. It had been a long fucking day, but I couldn't imagine myself going to sleep. I would keep watch over Savannah as long as I needed to, to make sure nothing ever hurt her again.

Chapter Forty

~Savannah~

Jasper's scent woke me up.

I didn't consider that a bad thing; far from it, actually. The sweet, mouthwatering smell almost had me moaning in anticipation even before I realized where it came from. A hungry pang gripped my stomach, which had started to become a common occurrence since arriving at the Ravenstone pack, and I wanted to devour the source of that delicious scent until I realized exactly what I smelled.

Actually, I still kind of wanted to devour it then too.

My eyes opened curiously, and to my surprise, I found myself in my guest room at the Ravenstone pack house, wearing my pajamas. How did I get there? The last thing I remembered...

Huh. Actually, I couldn't remember the last thing I remembered.

I did, at least, recognize the man sitting in the chair next to my bed, his shaggy hair still uncombed, his chest bare, and a pair of grey sweatpants covering his lower half. His arms drooped down between his legs, and he was, rather adorably, fast asleep.

Jasper looked like a kid who tried really hard to stay awake for his parents to come home but didn't quite make it, and the thought sent a wave of affection through me.

Nothing else about him looked like a kid, though. For the first time, I got to really take a look at my mate as I pulled myself up to a sitting position, examining him in the early morning sunshine that had started to drift in through the slightly open curtain.

Physically, he wasn't as big as the ranked wolves like my brother and Felix, his body leaner and slimmer but still firm and defined. I had no doubt he could handle me if he wanted to and the thought had Tala humming in my head as I inched a little closer. Dirty from his time in the wild, he probably smelled too, but my nose only picked up his mate scent, overpowering everything else in its wake.

How was he there? None of our present situation made sense to me, and when I leaned forward to touch him, to make sure he really *was* there and not a figment of my imagination, his head suddenly snapped up, his arms raising defensively, as if I might have been trying to hurt him. His expressive green eyes were wary and guarded, and for the first time, I saw that his hands had been cuffed together.

What in the world did I miss?

"Savannah?" My name came out as a croak, and he quickly cleared his throat, lowering his arms again. "Shit, I didn't mean to fall asleep. How long have you been awake?"

"Only a minute. I wasn't sure you were real, I was going to pinch you to make sure."

A short, startled laugh came out of his mouth. "I think you're supposed to pinch yourself, not the other person."

"Maybe," I agreed with a shrug. "But pinching you sounds like more fun."

"It does to me too." We shared a brief, heated smile before his expression melted into concern. "How are you feeling?"

It was sweet of him to ask, but unnecessary. "Fine. Shouldn't I be?"

Jasper's lips tightened. "I don't know. I don't know what kind of injection Kyle gave you."

"Injection?" That didn't clear anything up on my end.

"Shit," he swore again, his jaw clenching in frustration. "You don't remember?"

"Obviously not. Why don't you tell me what happened?"

"I wish I could," he muttered under his breath before sighing. "What's the last thing you remember?"

Trying my best to access my memories, which seemed far foggier than usual, I thought back. "I talked to you by the lake last night, Lee came, and you sent me back here."

"Good." He nodded encouragingly. "What else?"

It got fuzzier after that but I tried my best to push through. "I tried to climb back through the window, but Kyle found me. He started talking to me and..."

The memory faded into darkness with nothing more to find.

"That's all I remember. Did he inject me with something?"

Indignation rose up inside me at the possibility. How dare he? Hopefully, he'd been caught and would be punished, which might explain Jasper's presence but not the handcuffs on his wrists. There had to be more to the story.

"I think he probably did at that point," Jasper agreed. "He definitely injected you with something else later, at his lab."

"His lab?" I'd been in Kyle's lab? I didn't remember that at all.

Jasper's jaw clenched so hard, I thought he might chip his teeth. "We found you there; me and Brent and Felix. He had you in a cage. You spoke to me."

None of that sounded familiar but one word stuck out most of all from what he said. "He put me in a *cage?*"

The words came out forcefully as Tala growled in my head.

Do you remember any of this? I asked her.

No, but when we see him again, I'm going to make him wish he'd never met us.

"Keep your voice down," Jasper urged, fighting a smile. "If no one else knows you're awake yet, they might leave us alone for a while longer."

That sounded good to me, especially since I still had a lot of questions. "Why are you wearing handcuffs? Where's Kyle now? Did you get the evidence you needed?"

"Kyle got away." Jasper scowled, clearly livid about it. He could look quite frightening when anger darkened his expression, yet I felt completely safe with him. "Last I heard, they hadn't found him yet. They brought me back here as a prisoner until the Alpha can determine what's going on. Myra, Dan and Brent are down in the prisons. They only let me stay here with you instead because Felix and Vaughan vouched for me."

"Vaughan?" Maybe I *was* dreaming after all. What would my brother be doing there, and how would Jasper know anything about him?

However, he nodded. "Yeah. He and his mate got to the lab after we did, just after you passed out."

Every word raised more questions. Could Vaughan and Calista really be there? "Does he know you're my mate?"

"No. I didn't think it was my place to tell him."

I appreciated that but I still had so many questions. "And he let you stay in here with me? Alone?"

That didn't sound like my brother at all.

"Felix insisted on it," Jasper explained sheepishly. "He made up something about you saving my life and how I felt an obligation to you. He's keeping our secret."

I owed Felix a big kiss for that, since I didn't even want to imagine what my brother would have done if he knew the handcuffed rogue was my mate. I had a lot to tell him and a lot I still needed to figure out myself.

"You managed to tell Felix a few things before you passed out," Jasper added, his eyes searching mine, hoping to see a spark of recognition as he told me about it. "You said that Kyle confessed to being the one who abducted those kids and that he framed me for it."

I knew it, Tala crowed triumphantly, and I felt a surge of vindication too. It never sat right with me that Jasper would have done anything like that.

Fuck, I wished I could remember exactly what Kyle said.

"So, the Alpha will have to let you return to the pack," I exclaimed happily. "You're cleared."

Jasper smiled at my enthusiasm, but he remained a bit more cautious. "It's not quite that simple. All he's got is your word, via Felix. Without any evidence or a chance to question Kyle, it's not much to go on."

"We'll figure it out," I promised. "You're innocent, Jasper, and we'll make sure everyone knows it. We'll find Kyle and we'll have him undo whatever he did to you..."

Before I could finish that sentence, Jasper's whole countenance changed, his eyes taking on the arrogant, aggressive look that I'd seen the night before when his haze took over.

"You're not getting rid of me that easily," he snarled at me, licking his lips. "But now that we're alone together, maybe we can have a little fun."

Chapter Forty-One

~Jasper~

Distracted by the pleasure of being close to Savannah and my concern about the fact that she couldn't remember what happened the night before, not to mention the silver in my handcuffs having weakened me throughout the night, I didn't feel the haze coming until it was too late.

When Felix pleaded my case with his Alpha on my behalf the night before, doing his best to convince the suspicious Vaughan that I had Savannah's best interests at heart, Felix said I could be trusted. He put his reputation on the line for me, and as I sat there watching her sleep, I'd been on high alert, doing my very best to keep the haze at bay. Only when Savannah distracted me, simply by being herself, did I let my guard down, and that was all it took to lose control.

However, if I thought Savannah would panic at being in close quarters with such an unpredictable adversary, I would have been mistaken.

"I don't want to get rid of you," she told the haze, shuffling a little further away on her bed, but not completely out of reach as she spoke to him in a calm, reasonable tone. "You're part of Jasper. The reckless, ruthless part, maybe, but sometimes, he needs that. We all do."

I could feel the grin that pulled at my lips even though I had no control over it. "I had a feeling you could be a little reckless too. We could definitely have some fun together."

Savannah hadn't finished though. "Be that as it may, you need *him* too. You need his thoughtfulness, his kindness, his loyalty and his honour."

"Honour?" the haze scoffed. "What good has honour ever done a rogue? It's a wolf-eat-wolf world and I intend to be the one doing the eating."

His gaze dropped down to her body beneath its blankets as he licked his lips, making his double meaning abundantly clear.

"You won't *be* a rogue once we clear Jasper's name," she argued back, ignoring the innuendo. "Things can go back to the way they were before."

"Well, that sounds great," he said, surprising us both until it became clear he meant it sarcastically. "I'm not going anywhere. Why would I want to be locked up again, restrained by his weakness? If I have control all the time, I can take whatever I want, *be* whoever I want to be. Don't you want a mate like that, Savannah? I'd burn the world for you. Just say the word."

"I don't need you to burn anything for me," she shot back. "I've got enough fire for the both of us."

She sure as hell did, but the haze seemed unimpressed. "You only think that because you don't know how good it could be if we let go."

With that, he sprang forward off the chair. Savannah's hands instinctively went up to fend him off, but he'd anticipated that. Catching her wrists within his own bound hands, he lifted them up over her head, pinning her down onto the bed and leaning down over her, a satisfied smile on his face and heat rushing through his body.

Though I fought as hard as I ever had, I couldn't stop him. Tired and weakened, I could only watch in dismay as he kissed her, harder and rougher than I would have. It didn't feel like Savannah resisted too much, but I didn't blame her for that. Even trapped in the back of my own mind, I could feel the sparks of our bond that flowed through my body, and it felt fucking amazing. It was still me who kissed her, but not *me*, and it must have been confusing for her when I barely understood it myself.

However, when his lips left hers and began to trail down to her neck, she began to struggle. "Hold up there, Romeo. No one's getting marked today."

Despite her strong, self-assured tone, I could tell by how hard she fought to free her arms that she truly didn't want him to mark her, no more than I did. I struggled from the inside to stop him while she kept trying externally.

"Get off," she ordered, her voice rising in panic as he licked her neck, slowly and deliberately, still fully in control. "Don't! Stop!"

He inhaled deeply, savouring her scent, but as his canine teeth began to extend, the door to the room burst open. My head turned to see one very angry Alpha storming in, wearing only a pair of flannel pants, and with the haze distracted, Savannah managed to jam her knee very convincingly into my groin.

"Fuck," the haze muttered, or maybe I did. Through the pain, I managed to take control back, but a moment later, two large hands gripped me, pulling me off Savannah like I weighed no more than a rag doll.

"You have five seconds to explain to me why I should let you live." Vaughan's brown eyes, so like his sister's, blazed in fury as he held me up to his face with a hand around my neck. "Five... four..."

I couldn't get any words out, mostly because his grip cut off my air.

"Vaughan, stop," Savannah commanded.

He ignored her. "Three... two..."

She got to her knees on the bed, her hands on her hips, letting out a remarkably sexy growl. "Vaughan! It wasn't him. Put him down."

"One." He reached the end of his countdown before fully registering what his sister said, at which point he turned to look at her in bewilderment. "What do you mean it wasn't him? I literally walked in and saw him on top of you with you saying 'stop'. Are you going to tell me I imagined that?"

It certainly looked bad, I had to give him that. "I've been drugged," I managed to choke out from beneath his grip that loosened a little when he addressed Savannah. "Part of me... needs help... but he's... quiet now."

Vaughan looked at me like I'd lost my mind, which wasn't far off the truth, but Savannah backed me up. "He's telling the truth. It's a long story, but he's my mate and if you kill him, I will never give you and Calista another uninterrupted night for the rest of your lives. I might move my bed into your room. Do you want that, Vaughan? Really?"

The creative threat achieved its goal, making Vaughan take a step back in surprise. "Your mate? Are you sure?"

Letting me go, he looked me up and down as if truly seeing me for the first time, and his nose wrinkled, no doubt from the very real stench that must have been coming off me.

"I know how the mate bond works," Savannah replied in a deadpan voice. "Yeah, I'm sure. Are you alright, Jasper?"

I nodded, rubbing at the skin of my throat with my cuffed hands, over the spot where Vaughan's hand had been. Though I considered myself pretty strong, Alphas were on a different level. The idea of my mate having one for a brother would take some getting used to.

"Obviously, we have some things to catch up on," a female voice from the doorway said, and we all looked over to find the Alpha's mate standing there, still in her nightgown. The white lacy fabric and her long blonde hair made her look a bit like an angel. The two of them must have still been in bed when they heard Savannah call out. "We don't need to talk right now, though. It's still early. Maybe we can give them a few minutes alone before everything gets crazy again. I'm Calista, by the way."

She offered me a kind smile, one that almost brought tears to my eyes. No one had smiled at me like I was a real person in a long time.

"You could use a shower," she suggested gently. "Take your time. Sav, use your link if you need anything."

Pulling a still-stunned Vaughan from the room, she closed the door behind them, leaving me alone with my mate once again.

"I'm sorry about him," Savannah apologized with a sigh. "He's always been overprotective, but he did back off pretty fast when I said you were my mate. He might be softening."

I could only hope so. "I'm sorry about the haze, I couldn't..."

She hopped out of the bed, striding over to me in a few short steps and placing a finger on my lips. "Don't apologize. It's not your fault. You do, however, seem to stink, at least to everyone other than me. That shower might be a good idea."

It actually sounded amazing. I hadn't been around running water for months. There was just one problem: "I don't want to be away from you a second longer than I have to."

Savannah offered me a mischievous grin that would have me eating out of the palm of her hand any day of the week. "Who said I'm not coming with you?"

Chapter Forty-Two

~Savannah~

Lust and excitement filled Jasper's eyes so strongly that for a brief second, I thought the haze had returned.

It hadn't, though; he was simply turned on by my suggestion that I join him in the shower.

I'd been thinking about a way to get a little more intimate with him ever since I woke up and found him half-naked beside my bed. Hell, I'd been thinking about it long before then, ever since I realized he was my mate and he first kissed me by the lake. But with everything else hanging over us, the timing had never seemed right, not to mention that I didn't know for sure whether he actually did the things he'd been accused of.

However, after spending more time with him and with Felix's endorsement that he could be trusted, I felt certain that my initial gut feeling had been right and he was completely innocent. With nothing to disturb us for the next little while, I didn't see any reason to put it off any longer. We were mates, and I was ready to take a minute to enjoy that before the day brought whatever crazy new surprises it had in store for us.

The handcuffs were a bit of an issue, unfortunately. Although sexy in the right circumstances, having him restrained and weakened by someone else's order did put a damper on things.

Jasper's train of thought trailed mine exactly. "The things I'd love to do for you in the shower..." he murmured, letting himself imagine it the same way I had. "The things I'd do *to* you. You have no idea. Fuck, I hate this."

By 'this', he meant the cuffs, raising his arms in frustration.

I stepped closer. "The cuffs just mean you have to wait your turn. Maybe I'll get to do some things for you first."

A deep, appreciative groan rumbled from his throat. "You're so sexy, Savannah."

"I know."

My agreement took him by surprise, and he laughed, his voice still low and full of arousal. "I don't know how you ended up mated to me, but fuck, I must have done something right."

On the way to the Ravenstone pack, I'd been worried about the men there only being interested in me because of my position. Jasper, on the other hand, hadn't even known my family history, probably not until he met Vaughan. He wanted me before that, his desire for me rooted in the mate bond, naturally, but growing stronger the more time we spent together, just as my longing for him had.

His eyes burned with the passion I'd always imagined from my mate, and everything about it felt right.

"Let's go before we waste all our time talking," I invited, heading into the ensuite bathroom attached to my guest room. My heart began to thump harder, flooding my body with excitement and anticipation as I turned the shower on, getting the temperature perfect before turning back to face him. Jasper stood in the doorway, leaning against the door frame as he watched me. His hands still hung in front of his body in their cuffs, but they couldn't entirely hide his growing arousal, already evident in his grey sweatpants.

Noticing my gaze focusing there, he gave me a heated smile. "You can't blame me. You've got my imagination working overtime and my body's trying to keep up."

"Well, before we give either a workout, let's get you clean." Doing my best to keep my mind out of the gutter where it desperately wanted to wallow, I pulled the drawstring on his sweatpants and tugged them down, gently lifting them over his rapidly swelling cock. He must have been sleeping in the dirt out in the wild because he was really quite filthy, especially on the soles of his feet, and that helped to keep me focused on the task at hand. I'd get him nice and clean first, and *then* I could do what I really wanted.

Letting him step into the walk-in shower first, I pulled my pajamas off, smiling as he groaned in pleasure as the water hit his skin. "Fuck, that feels good."

"Just you wait," I teased, stepping into the shower after him. "You're about to feel a lot better."

"I believe it." Turning to face me, he took a minute to look over my body, his eyes exploring each curve that his hands itched to touch. His fingers literally twitched but he held back, letting me take the lead. "I'm beginning to think maybe I died last night and this is heaven. It seems too good to be real."

"I promise you I'm very real. Now, close your eyes."

He obeyed me without question as I pushed his head back, letting the water wash over his hair and face. For shampoo, we only had the rather girly scent the pack staff had given me, but he didn't complain as I massaged it into his hair, my fingers pressing into his scalp to try to ease some of the tension he had to be feeling.

"That feels incredible," he groaned, the words slurred as though he were drunk on pleasure. I couldn't wait to feel the combination of massage and the mate sparks for myself, but it would have to wait. For the time being, this was all about him.

With the loofah and some body wash, I scrubbed the dirt from his skin, drawing more sighs and happy groans as I made sure to leave no inch untouched. When I got to his ass, I couldn't resist running my hands over his taut muscles, and Jasper shuddered beneath my touch.

"You okay there?" I teased, moving lower down the back of his legs.

"Wait until I get my turn to do this," he warned. "You won't be laughing then."

A shiver of excitement went down my spine at his threat, which sounded much more like a promise to me. It took a couple of minutes of hard scrubbing, kneeling behind him, to get the soles of his feet clean, but finally, I'd done pretty much everywhere except his stiff cock that had only gotten harder with each passing minute.

Tossing the loofah to the side and getting back to my feet, I lathered the body wash in my hands and moved around to his front, reaching down to gently cup his balls from underneath.

"Oh, fuck." He hadn't expected that, or maybe he hadn't expected what the sparks would feel like there. His head fell back as I rolled his balls gently between my fingers before moving up, wrapping my hand firmly around the base of his shaft.

The sound that came out of him, I'd never heard before, but it turned me on as much as anything ever had. He was completely at my mercy and I loved it, almost as much as I loved the idea of being under his control later.

With the steady drumming between my legs growing stronger all the time, I stroked Jasper's cock slowly and firmly, savouring the feel of every inch beneath my fingers. Every vein, every ridge, every bump, I wanted to memorize. I wanted to know him by touch alone. I wanted to be able to imagine it when he had it inside me.

"I...I think... that's... clean... enough," he breathed between groans, as if I would actually leave him hanging like that.

"It is clean," I agreed, lifting his cock up and down to examine it carefully. "But I better make sure it works properly if I'm considering a long-term investment."

He didn't argue with that. He didn't seem capable of it. Instead, he lifted his cuffed arms over my head, embracing me as well as he could, and leaned down to kiss me while I stroked him harder and faster, one hand running along his cock and the other on his balls, multiplying the sensations and the flow of sparks between us.

"Fuck, Sav, yes," he groaned one more time into my mouth, his balls tightening in my grip before he came. Warm cum shot onto my stomach, his cock pumping in my hand as he shuddered under the force of his orgasm.

Yes, that definitely worked just fine, and satisfaction swelled in my chest as I glanced down at our two bodies. Even though I hadn't personally received any physical satisfaction from that encounter, it felt wonderful to know what an effect I had on him.

Jasper rested his forehead against mine as he tried to catch his breath. "That was amazing," he assured me, but his voice held a hint of frustration. "I wish I could do the same for you."

"You will," I promised. "As soon as we clear your name and get Kyle where he belongs, we're going to have all the time in the world for that. Right now, though, we should get dressed and go talk to Felix, Vaughan and Calista. I want to know as much as I can about what happened last night before we go speak to Alpha Warren."

Taking one more deep breath, Jasper refocused himself too. "Alright. Let's go see what we can find out."

Chapter Forty-Three

~Jasper~

I thought I'd been motivated before, but after getting a taste of what life with Savannah would be like, my determination to stop Kyle and clear my name reached new heights. I wasn't a virgin, and neither was she, clearly. No one could be that good without some practice. Even so, my previous experiences had been nowhere near that good, and she only used her hand. What would it be like when we could actually be together properly? The mere thought of it made me light-headed.

Or maybe that was the silver in the cuffs. It was hard to tell for sure.

After drying me off since I was still helpless to do anything for myself, Savannah wrapped a towel around my waist and put her own clothes on. Watching her dress was easily one of the sexiest, most entertaining things I'd ever seen, and it left me almost disappointed when she finished. She must have sent a message by mind-link to Felix because he showed up almost immediately after she'd finished getting ready with some fresh, clean clothes for me. After shooing him away, Savannah helped me get dressed, brushed my teeth and combed my hair, looking after me in a practical, unsentimental way that meant the world to me.

She'd be an incredible mom, I saw that already, and *that* was a thought I'd never had about a woman before.

At last, we were both presentable, and she once again linked to the others from her pack, asking them to join us. The guest room filled up with people, all dressed and ready for the day. I sat back on the chair where I'd spent the night, Savannah and Calista sat on the bed together, and Felix stood by the window, keeping an eye on any activity outside while Vaughan paced the room restlessly.

"You really don't remember anything else?" Vaughan asked after Savannah finished giving her account of what she *did* remember from the night before. She described the conversation she'd had with Kyle beneath the window, the one Felix had heard that led him to come and find me, but after that, she didn't remember anything until waking up that morning.

"I know a bit more than that," Felix told us. "In the lab, before you passed out, Sav, you told me that Kyle wanted your genes."

"My genes?" Her pretty face scrunched up tight as she tried to remember. "What for?"

"I'm not sure," the Beta admitted. "You said he abducted the kids to experiment on them, and that he wanted you for the same thing, and for your genes. You said the Alpha didn't know about that, and then you started to say something about the rogues and something being fatal, but you faded out. That's all I got."

The word 'fatal' struck fear into my heart. Hopefully, she hadn't been talking about whatever injection he gave her. Although, I couldn't think of a much better alternative for what it could mean. Anything involving fatality would be bad.

"It's not much to go on," Vaughan pointed out, his whole body coiled with repressed frustration. "If I were in the Alpha's shoes, I'd want more before I made any big decisions."

"Maybe there's a way we can get it," Calista suggested in a soft but firm voice, and everyone immediately turned to her.

"What do you mean?" Savannah asked on behalf of us all.

"Well, my family used to question people as part of our hunting," she explained, stumbling almost guiltily over the final word. "Sometimes, we'd use hypnosis to try to get information they didn't want to give us willingly. I'm not an expert, by any means, but I do have some experience, and it'll be a lot easier with a willing subject."

"Hunting?" I repeated, looking around the room to see if I was the only one who found that strange.

Felix shot me a wry smile. "Yeah, Calista used to hunt supernatural beings like us. That's how she and Vaughan met. Looks like falling for the outlaws runs in the family."

Vaughan gave his Beta an unimpressed look, but Felix didn't seem to take it to heart, and the Alpha's expression softened considerably when he turned to his mate. "It won't hurt her, will it?"

"Of course not," Calista assured him. "Her conscious mind will go into a dreamlike state, letting me speak to her subconscious. Depending on what he did to her, the memories might still be there. Or, they might not. There are no guarantees."

"I'll do it," Savannah quickly agreed, without any hesitation. "If I was trying to tell Felix what I knew, I must have gotten some good information. Let's try and find it."

Since we didn't know how much time we'd have before Alpha Warren summoned us, we got straight to work. Calista instructed Savannah to lie down on the bed, as comfortably as possible, and she suggested that I hold Savannah's hand.

"Having her mate nearby will help her feel secure," the pretty Luna told me, glancing over at her own mate with a sweet, almost shy smile.

Doing my best to keep the silver-filled handcuffs away from her, I did as Calista suggested, holding Savannah's warm, soft hand in mine as Calista began to speak to her in a low, calm, soothing voice.

"Close your eyes and roll them up into your head," she advised while I squeezed Savannah's hand, reminding her I would be right beside her the whole time. "You're safe here. Nothing can hurt you."

She counted out some breathing rhythms for Savannah to follow, and when she'd done them, Calista carried on.

"You're going deeper into relaxation. Every sound that you hear takes you deeper."

To my surprise, it actually seemed to be working. Savannah's hand went limper in mine as her breathing became deeper.

"Imagine that you're in Kyle's lab," Calista instructed next, her voice still smooth and almost melodic, like a lullaby. "Look around. What do you see?"

Savannah answered her in a monotone, far from her usual exuberance. "I see petri dishes on the table. He's showing them to me."

That didn't sound right, and I looked around at the others for confirmation.

"That's the wrong time," Felix whispered. "She went to his lab a few times."

Calista nodded to indicate she understood before speaking again. "That's really good, Savannah. Think about another time you were there. What do you see now?"

That time, concern crossed Savannah's face, her brows tightening above her closed eyes. "I'm looking up from the floor. There are bars in front of me."

That sounded more promising, and we all nodded at Calista to encourage her to continue, even though she no doubt would have figured it out on her own.

"Is Kyle speaking to you?"

Savannah nodded, her face still tight. "He says my genes are good, and he'll have the compound ready soon."

Fury flashed through me but I did my best to keep it under control. I needed to keep calm for Savannah's sake, and so that the haze didn't come back.

"And?" Calista asked simply.

"He says my curiosity is annoying and that he'll work on editing it out later. He says he can change all kinds of things."

What the fuck? Sterling growled in my head as my jaw clenched. *She's perfect. Nothing needs to change.*

I know. Trust me, I know.

"And then?" Calista prompted, keeping as quiet as possible to let Savannah fill the empty space.

"He says he's been testing his treatments on the rogues. Erasing their memories. Changing their personalities. He says Jasper was a mistake, that the treatment wasn't quite ready yet and it went a bit wrong."

So, the haze was some kind of side effect from a failed treatment? *Fuck*. Did that mean he wouldn't know how to fix it, even if he wanted to?

"He tested it on another rogue, but that one died," Savannah continued on her own. "And he tested it on Lee. That outcome isn't certain yet."

Shit. Things were worse than I thought for Lee. Hopefully, whatever had been done to him could be undone. Hopefully, it all could be.

What Savannah said next chilled me even more. "He wants my blood to use in his experiments. That's why the Alpha brought me here. Amanda won't have Vaughan's baby so they need mine. He tried using other kids from the pack, but Alpha blood will be better."

The utter depravity of it made me sick, and when I glanced over at Vaughan, he appeared equally livid. In fact, Felix had gone over to put a hand on his shoulder, no doubt to keep him from going to confront the Alpha immediately.

"Amanda doesn't know. The Alpha knows some of it, but not all. He doesn't know Jasper was framed. He wants to give me the compound. It will erase my memories and make me fall in love with him. He's going to give it to me. No!"

She began to struggle in the bed, her eyes still closed, pulling her hand from my grasp and pushing me away.

Calista immediately reached out to her. "You're safe, Savannah. You're in bed and you're safe. Open your eyes in three... two... one."

My mate's sweet brown eyes immediately popped open, her body relaxing in the same instant as she looked around at us all curiously. "Did it work?"

"It did," Vaughan confirmed grimly. "You still don't remember?"

Savannah shook her head, blinking her eyes a few times as if it might jog something in her mind, but finally she shrugged in resignation. "No, nothing. What did I say?"

The rest of us exchanged glances. We had the information we needed but the question remained: with Savannah unable to testify for herself, would the Alpha believe us? How could we convince him that Kyle needed to be stopped?

CHAPTER FORTY-FOUR

~**Savannah**~

It frustrated me that I couldn't remember what I told everyone, but at least the information hadn't been completely wiped from my mind. Maybe I couldn't consciously remember, but Kyle hadn't succeeded in destroying all the evidence. Somewhere deep in my subconscious, those memories survived.

And that gave me another idea.

"Calista, do you think you could hypnotize Jasper? Maybe you could help him remember exactly what happened when he found Kyle. Maybe the other rogues have suppressed memories too. The more information we have, the better." When I looked over at my mate in excitement, I realized he no longer held my hand. "Why did you let me go?"

"Because you pushed me away," he teased me gently. His green eyes looked even more striking now that his hair had been washed and brushed back away from his face. He would probably want a haircut and a shave when things calmed down, but I didn't hate the rugged mountain-man look he had going on. "I'm not going to force you to do anything you don't want to do."

The allusion to his haze and how close I came to being marked by it made me shiver. There had been too many close calls in the last few days.

"But I'm game to try to get at any memories that might be lurking in my head," he continued. "I dreamed about it yesterday, I think, so they might still be there."

Eagerly, I turned back to Calista, who gave me a smile as she replied. "I'm happy to try, but maybe we should bring in some Ravenstone pack members to witness it? They might be more willing to believe it if they heard it directly from him."

She looked to Vaughan for confirmation, and my brother nodded. "I know I would want to hear it for myself. Even then, I might not trust it, though. I'd have to wonder if he was faking the whole thing."

It annoyed me that Vaughan suggested Jasper would lie at all, but rationally, I understood his point. The Alpha would be defensive. He obviously had a lot of faith in Kyle and he wouldn't like hearing he'd been tricked.

Thinking out loud, I tried to come up with a compromise. "What if we went to someone else in the pack first before going to the Alpha? Someone who has influence but who might be a little more open to what Jasper has to say."

Felix immediately caught my drift. "Amanda."

My head bobbed in a nod of confirmation. "She confronted her father about the rogues when we asked about them, so unless she's in on it too, she should be willing to listen."

"I don't think she's involved," Calista said. "You told us that Kyle said she didn't know anything."

That had always been my gut feeling, and I was glad to know my memories backed it up. "If we can convince *her* we're telling the truth, the Alpha will have a harder time ignoring it."

We all looked to Vaughan for his opinion, and he reluctantly agreed. "I don't love the idea of having to ask her for a favour after... everything, but she hasn't done anything to make me think she can't be trusted."

"Everything?" Jasper whispered to me in confusion.

"I'll tell you later." We had more pressing things to worry about than my brother's complicated mating story. Looking over at Felix, I gestured towards the door with my head. "Is Heather outside?"

"As usual."

For the first time, her constant presence pleased me. Standing up, I strode over to the door and opened it, and sure enough, my shadow immediately appeared. "Do you need something, Lota Savannah?"

"Yes. Could you ask Lota Amanda to come and see me? Immediately."

A look of pain flashed across her face. "I'm sorry, I can't do that. The Luna took a turn for the worse during the night. The Lota is with her."

Damn it. As important as our reason to see her might be, family always came first. I couldn't really argue with that. "Alright, thank you."

Without giving her a chance to say anything else, I stepped back into my room and closed the door behind me. "You all heard that?"

Everyone nodded, but Vaughan wanted more information. "What's wrong with the Luna?"

"I'm not sure, exactly, but we haven't seen her at all yet. She's sick, that's all I know."

"She's been sick for a while," Jasper added. "It started when I was still in the pack. I heard that something happened that almost killed her but that our scientists were able to stabilize her with a new, experimental treatment. I guess it still hasn't fully cured her, unfortunately."

As the words 'new, experimental treatment' sunk into my consciousness, some other words echoed in my head, spoken in Kyle's detached, clinical tone. *He knows that I'm the only one who can give him what he wants most. He trusts me.*

I couldn't remember the context in which he said them, but I heard them so clearly, it had to be a memory, and the pieces began to slot into place in my head as I spoke my thoughts aloud once more.

"What if...hold on, hear me out, okay?" My fingers went to my temples, trying to force my thoughts into some kind of order. "What if Kyle's the one treating the Luna? What if the Alpha wants the treatment so badly that he authorized Kyle's experiments, gave him power, took his word about the situation with the rogues? What if it's all connected?"

No one answered me right away, all of them taking a minute to think that over before responding.

Felix came to his conclusion first. "I think you might be onto something, Sav. It always seemed strange that he would put so much stock in Kyle's work that he was willing to exile people in the first place."

Vaughan and Calista nodded, and when I looked over at Jasper, pride filled his eyes. "You could be a detective too."

"You agree with me?" I really hadn't been sure if I'd taken things a step too far.

"I think it's definitely worth asking some more questions about. The problem is that Amanda's with her mother and they won't let us anywhere near the Luna's room right now."

That *was* a problem, but from his tone of voice, I had a feeling he had an idea. "How do we get around it?"

His smile showed his pleasure that I picked up on his hint. "There's a back staircase that goes into the Luna's suite, in case she needs to be evacuated in an emergency. There were several of us in internal security who were trained on the protocol. I know how to get in."

It sounded good to me, and I looked once more at the others from my pack.

"If we're wrong, the Alpha and Amanda will be furious with us," Vaughan pointed out in his usual cautious, stern tone.

"But if we're right..."

He didn't let me finish. "I didn't say no. I'm saying we need to be prepared that things could get ugly. Luckily, I've already got my allies on standby outside the territory, just in case."

Sometimes, my brother's overprotectiveness could come in handy.

With determination, I turned back to the others. "So, what are we waiting for?"

Chapter Forty-Five

~Jasper~

Getting to the Luna's room didn't pose much of a challenge. Most people didn't know about the hidden service corridor that ran through the house, but as luck would have it, Savannah's room lay directly on the route. A secret door in her closet gave us access to the Luna's room without anyone in the house being any the wiser.

Finally, something seemed to be going our way.

"This was here the whole time?" Savannah asked in dismay when I instructed Felix on how to open the sliding door on the back wall of her closet and the passageway appeared in front of us. "What if someone used it to break in while I was sleeping?"

That was part of why I'd been so insistent on keeping watch over her during the night, but I didn't tell her that. Scaring her any further wouldn't have been helpful, but when I glanced back at Vaughan, I could tell by the nod he gave me that he understood.

He would have done the same. He wanted to protect her just like I did.

With my hands still cuffed, I had to let Felix take the lead but I followed immediately behind him through the narrow hall with Savannah and Calista behind me and Vaughan bringing up the rear. A tight spiral staircase led up the two floors to the top floor where the Alpha's family lived.

"The Luna's door is the second-last one on the left," I whispered to him as we got close. "The last one is the Alpha's room and we don't want to go in there."

"Definitely not," he agreed, looking back at the rest of us when he reached the right door. "Everyone ready?"

We all gave our agreement, and he slid the door open to reveal the inside of the Luna's walk-in closet, much bigger than the one in Savannah's room. The smell of disinfectant hung in the air, similar to a hospital, confirming the severity of the Luna's illness. Silently, Felix opened the opposite door, the one leading into her bedroom, and we all peered curiously inside, bending down or craning our necks to see better.

The large double bed sat in the middle of a room twice as big as the generously-sized one Savannah had been using. Machines were set up next to it, obscuring our view of the face of the woman who lay beneath the crisp white sheets. Amanda sat at the bedside, her back to us, but it didn't take long for the foreign scent of my companions to reach her nose, or maybe my own rogue scent, and she got to her feet, spinning around in surprise. Puffy red circles surrounded her eyes, making them look smaller than usual on her pale, unhappy face.

"What are you all doing here?" she asked in a whisper, her expression growing more confused and less friendly with each passing second. "How did you get in? You don't belong here! I'm calling security."

"Wait! Don't, please." Savannah stepped forward from our group, her eyes fixed on Amanda to try to keep her attention. She kept the volume of her voice low, not wanting to disturb the woman in the bed, but her tone was firm. "We're here because we think your pack is in danger. Not from any external enemy, but from within."

"What are you talking about?" Amanda's wary eyes moved from Savannah to look at the rest of us in turn. "You and Felix have only been here a couple of days. Vaughan, you just got here, and Jasper's a rogue. None of you know what's going on in the pack."

She didn't mention Calista, I noticed.

Vaughan responded to her. "I may have just got here, but Sav and Felix have updated me about what they've learned. Jasper filled in some blanks too." He gave me a nod, including me in the group in a way that warmed my heart. "Amanda, you pitched in when my pack needed help. Let me return the favour. Let us tell you what we know."

Glancing back at her mother, whose face I could finally see, hooked up to an oxygen mask while an IV flowed into her arm, Amanda took a deep breath. "You have ten minutes before my father gets back. Make it count."

Vaughan took the lead, explaining to her everything Savannah said under hypnosis. When he got to the part about Kyle wanting Savannah's baby's genes because he couldn't have Amanda and Vaughan's, she turned even more pale.

"If this is true, my father doesn't know anything about it. I'm sure of that."

"Sav had a theory about that," Vaughan explained gently. "She thought your father might have agreed to Kyle's requests because Kyle could help your mother. Or at least, he promised to."

Amanda's lips pressed together, clearly not read to make that leap yet. "He cares about my mother, obviously, but I don't believe he'd put her wellbeing ahead of the whole pack."

"There's a way we might be able to find out more," Savannah spoke up. "It seems likely that Jasper spoke to Kyle before being exiled. If we hypnotize him the same way Calista did to me, we might be able to find out more about what his plan is. We wanted you to witness it so that you could hear it from Jasper himself, rather than secondhand."

Amanda's eyes moved to me. "You think you were set up?"

"I do." After what Savannah told me, I could say those words with more conviction than ever. "I'm willing to let Calista poke around in my subconscious to find out."

Amanda shook her head, keeping her eyes on me. "Not her. I'll do it."

"You?" Savannah asked, voicing the surprise we all shared. "You know how to hypnotize people?"

"My mother was a healer before she got sick," the Alpha's daughter explained, throwing a tender, wistful look over her shoulder at the unconscious woman. "Sometimes, wounds caused by trauma need psychological healing as well as physical. She taught me to use hypnosis to encourage that healing."

I'd known about the Luna's gift for healing, but the rest of what Amanda said came as a surprise. Still, I had no reason to refuse. Presumably, she'd be able to tell if I faked the hypnosis or not if she did it herself, and since we were all interested in the truth, it didn't matter to me who put me under.

"Do we have time before the Alpha gets here?" I wondered. She said we only had ten minutes, and at least five minutes had passed since then.

"We'll have to be very quick," Amanda admitted. "But we can start right now if you're ready."

I'd never been more ready for anything. The sooner we could get the whole truth out, the better. "Let's find out what I know."

Chapter Forty-Six

~Savannah~

Amanda and Jasper wasted no time, and we all felt the urgency. With the Alpha's level of investment in Kyle's success becoming clearer, it seemed less likely than ever that he would be willing to believe us about all the evil things Kyle had done without some kind of further proof. Jasper might have that proof inside his head, and if we could get Amanda on our side, she might be able to make her father see reason.

That was a lot of 'might's, but at that point, we had to take the chance. Hopefully, they'd be able to get something useful before the Alpha returned. Amanda hadn't said where he went, but with everything that took place the night before, he must have had a lot of things to do. Maybe he would get held up along the way, or maybe he'd walk in the door in the next minute. Either way, we had to make every second count.

Leading us to the furthest corner of the room from her mother's bed, Amanda set up two chairs facing each other and she sat in one while Jasper took the other. *Is Calista upset that Amanda doesn't trust her to do the hypnosis?* I asked my brother through our link.

She understands why Amanda isn't her biggest fan, he answered me candidly. *She's not taking it personally.*

Amanda's method for inducing a hypnotic state involved a ticking metronome sound that she produced with her phone and some of the authority she naturally carried due to her Alpha parentage. It differed from Calista's more gentle approach, but it seemed to work just the same as Jasper's eyes closed and his body relaxed, his weighted hands hanging heavily between his legs.

When she confirmed that the right mental state had been achieved, Amanda began asking questions.

"You investigated a kidnapping a few months ago and you found something. Go back to that time. Tell us about it."

Jasper's voice sounded so unlike himself that at first, I thought the haze might have taken over. However, he spoke calmly and thoughtfully, and no one else seemed surprised by it, so maybe I had sounded that way too when I was under.

Weird.

"The children's mother said they liked to play in the woods, near the bay in the lake. We already searched that area when they first went missing, but with no other leads, I decided to search it again."

"On your own?" Amanda asked.

"Yes. The others were busy with their own inquiries."

"And you found something?"

"Yes," he repeated in the same monotone. "My wolf did."

At the mention of his wolf, Tala stirred in my head, but I quickly shut her down. *Not now. We still need to get him free first. You can spend time with him when this is over.*

"It was easy to see how we missed it the first time. Little rocks, blending in with the surroundings, but not naturally occurring. My wolf thought he picked up a scent on them."

Amanda glanced over at the rest of us. "I think I know what he means. Those rocks were all the rage among the kids in the pack a few months ago. It's a game, they have to build different shapes with them."

"So, the kids were playing with them when they were taken?" I guessed.

Jasper answered me, although whether he'd actually heard me or was just continuing with his story, I couldn't be sure. "After the first one, we found another one, a little further away, and another one. It seemed to be a trail, an unintentional one, most likely, so I followed it."

Though I knew the events were all the past, my heart beat faster anyway as I listened to Jasper's story, appreciating how brave and smart he was, and how he'd put himself in danger to try to find the children.

"The last one stopped almost a mile away from where they'd last been seen, further away from the pack house. Their mother told us that they weren't supposed to go past the bay on their own, so it seemed likely they'd been taken to get to that point. But there, the trail went cold. I was about to give up when I noticed an odd indentation in the ground."

"What was it?" Amanda asked.

"A trap door. In the middle of the forest. Buried under a bit of dirt to camouflage it. It didn't take long for me to brush it away."

"Did you communicate with anyone on your team? Ask for help?"

"No. I probably should have, but it seemed more important to get inside in case the kids were in there."

"And they were?" she prompted.

"Yes. The door led to a hole with a ladder inside. I had my weapon with me so I climbed down. At the bottom, I found a laboratory."

I had a pretty good idea who the lab belonged to, and if Kyle had a secret lair somewhere in the woods that nobody knew about, there was a good chance he went there after escaping the night before. When I looked over at Vaughan, he nodded back at me, already having reached the same conclusion.

"What was in this lab?" Amanda kept her questions slow and measured, though she must have been as eager as the rest of us to find out the answer.

"Machines. Medical equipment. And the kids, inside a cage."

Just like I had been, apparently. Kyle certainly had a pattern.

"Was there anyone else there?"

"Not at first. I was trying to figure out how to get the cage open when he came in from another room."

"Who?" Amanda asked, even though we all knew the answer.

"I didn't know him but he was tall, wore a lab coat, and had very pale blue eyes."

That couldn't describe anyone else in the pack and Amanda knew it as well as I did.

"I tried to mind-link for backup but I didn't get any reply. Perhaps being underground blocked it somehow."

Or perhaps Kyle had the same kind of dampening field in his forest lab that he did in his main one.

"I asked him what he'd done to the kids, and he said he was making them better. He said they were contributing to his research, that it would improve the entire pack and save lives but that he needed their younger cells. He said it shouldn't have any long-term effect on them."

Shouldn't. No wonder he hadn't asked for permission from the children's parents. It didn't sound very reassuring.

"I told him he'd gone too far and that I'd be telling the Alpha. He jabbed me with a needle, and... that's the last thing I remember."

Although I'd held my tongue up to that point, I couldn't hold back any longer. "If that doesn't clear Jasper, I don't know what would. Not only that, he's given us a possible location to find Kyle, or at least an area to start looking. We need to get the Alpha here immediately and tell him..."

At exactly that moment, as if it had been planned, the door opened and the man in question walked in, glowering at the small group of us in his wife's bedroom, obviously having heard at least the very last thing I'd said. "Tell the Alpha what?"

CHAPTER FORTY-SEVEN

Amanda's voice woke me from my subconscious state, sounding far less relaxed than before. "Jasper, you can open your eyes now. We're finished."

Raising my heavy lids, I did as she said. Unlike coming out of the haze, where I felt groggy and disoriented, my mind felt refreshed, like I'd had a long sleep even though it couldn't have been more than a few minutes that she'd had me under.

As the room came back into focus, I realized we had one additional person with us, one who definitely hadn't been there when my eyes first closed.

"What the fuck is going on?" Alpha Warren growled at all of us, keeping his voice low so he wouldn't disturb his mate who still lay motionless in the bed on the other side of the room. "What are you doing in here?"

Normally, the anger in his tone would have caused me to bow before him, but he was no longer my Alpha, not after casting me out, so I had no physical reaction to it at all.

Savannah stepped to the front of the group, putting herself directly in the Alpha's line of vision. "Alpha, we're very sorry to hear about your mate, but what we have to tell you could be important for her treatment, among other things."

His eyes narrowed suspiciously as he looked over the whole group before his gaze returned to Savannah. "You don't know anything about her treatment. You don't know anything about any of it, and all you've done is stick your nose in everything since you got here."

"Dad!" Amanda sounded shocked at the Alpha's tone, but I recognized the desperation in it. It had the sound of a man on the verge of losing what he cared about most in the world. "None of this is Savannah's fault. It might, however, be Kyle's."

The Alpha turned his blazing anger on his daughter. "Stay out of this, Amanda. Stay with your mother. Alpha Vaughan, you can take your Beta and your Luna and get off my land. I let you in yesterday as a courtesy, but after breaking into *my sick mate's bedroom*, you're no longer welcome here."

Clearly, the Alpha wasn't in the mood to listen, but I noticed he'd missed one important person when he ordered the visitors to leave. Did he forget, or did it have another meaning? I couldn't stop myself from asking. "What about Savannah?"

His jaw couldn't have been more firmly set as he glared over at me. "Savannah stays here, as per our agreement. You, on the other hand, have forfeited your life by disrespecting our borders and your banishment. You were warned and you still didn't stop."

"No!" Savannah cried out, and though the Alpha may have thought her protest was over her own fate, I knew better. Panic filled the sweet brown eyes that looked over at me in desperation as the Alpha's personal guard filed into the room. He obviously had them on standby, and they quickly surrounded all of us, cutting Savannah off from her brother and the others.

"This is crazy!" Amanda declared in frustration, speaking for all of us as two pairs of strong hands grabbed me. With the silver cuffs still on, I couldn't have fought them off no matter how hard I tried. "Dad, they're trying to help us. You haven't even heard what they have to say."

"I don't need to hear any more lies. I spoke with Kyle this morning and he made everything perfectly clear to me."

"Whatever he told you is the lie," I argued even as the men gripped me tighter, warning me to keep my mouth shut. "He experimented on people. On children, the very children I was accused of abducting. He wants Savannah's child so he can do goddess-knows-what to it. He's evil, Alpha. He has to be stopped."

Alpha Warren stepped closer to me, making his height and width even more intimidating, and his nostrils flared as he glared down at me. "I am not your Alpha, and I don't have any reason to believe a thing you say."

"You don't deserve to be anyone's Alpha, behaving like this," Vaughan interjected, his own furious expression making it clear he didn't take very kindly to being kicked out or to his sister being held hostage.

His anger made little impression on the man in front of me. "You have no jurisdiction here, Alpha Vaughan, and if you don't leave now, I'll have you imprisoned too. You're officially trespassing on my land."

The two Alphas started talking over each other, making it difficult to make out any individual words, but in the midst of all the chaos, with me and Savannah being held by the Alpha's men, Amanda and Calista trying to get between the two arguing men and Felix pulling a knife out of somewhere to keep the other men who were trying to surround them at bay, a small, frail voice somehow sounded out above the din.

"Warren."

In chagrined silence, everyone turned in unison to the Luna's bed. In the heat of the moment, we'd all forgotten about being quiet, and the noise must have woken her. She still lay back, her head against the pillows, her blonde hair looking straggly and thinner than the last time I saw her, but her eyes were open and fixed on her mate who immediately forgot about everything else as he hurried to her side, picking up her limp hand from the mattress.

"Carla? Can you hear me?"

"Yes." Each word sounded like a struggle, but she kept speaking anyway. "You're... loud."

A reflexive smile broke across his face, only for a second. "I'm sorry." Glancing back towards the rest of us, he instructed his men to proceed. "Take them all out of here. You have your orders."

That set off another round of protests as the guards began to drag me and Savannah towards the door and Felix refused to put down his knife.

"Wait."

Once again, the Luna's voice stopped everyone in their tracks.

"You're... also... wrong."

Confusion spread across the Alpha's face, and just about everyone else's in the room. "Wrong? About what?"

With an amount of effort I could barely fathom, she managed to get out one more sentence: "Let... them... speak."

Chapter Forty-Eight

~**Savannah**~

Every eye in the room remained fixed on Alpha Warren, waiting to see what he would do after his mate asked him to hear us out.

Why is she on our side? I asked Vaughan in my head. *Don't get me wrong: I'm glad she is, but why?*

I'm not sure, came his reply, though he never looked at me. *Maybe she heard us talking? Or maybe she knows something we don't.*

That certainly seemed possible. I had a feeling we'd only really scratched the surface of all the shady shit Kyle had been up to.

The Alpha's lips pressed together firmly, his need to keep his mate happy obviously in conflict with his own inclinations in the situation, but eventually, love won out. "Leave us," he ordered his own men gruffly. "Stay outside the door."

Apparently, he didn't want an audience for the conversation, but at least he seemed willing to have it, if not for our sakes, then for his Luna's. As soon as the men let me go, I wanted to go to Jasper's side and make sure he was okay but that would have aroused suspicion. Alpha Warren still didn't know that Jasper was my mate, and if he remained determined to mate me off to one of his men instead, that fact might put Jasper in more danger than ever. Reluctantly, I stayed where I was and kept my mouth shut.

"I don't need all of you talking at me," he grumbled when we were alone. "Amanda, say what you have to say."

What made her the designated spokesperson, I couldn't say, but as long as he would actually listen to her, we wouldn't complain.

Succinctly, she summed up everything we told her and what we learned from Jasper under her hypnosis. Jasper looked surprised when she mentioned him finding Kyle's secret underground lab, probably not consciously remembering it any more than I remembered the things I'd told the others. Kyle told me his compound would wipe my memories, but it seemed to only suppress them instead. Perhaps he thought it made no difference, but we were going to prove him wrong.

When Amanda had laid out the basics as clearly as possible, she stepped forward, going to the opposite side of her mother's bed and picking up the Luna's other hand. The woman in the bed had closed her eyes again, leaving me clueless about whether she could still hear us or not.

"I understand why you took him at his word," Amanda said softly, sounding far more sympathetic than either I or Vaughan would have. Perhaps it was for the best that she'd been nominated to speak after all. "He fooled all of us. I certainly had no idea, but now that we know, we can make it right."

"No."

The Alpha's refusal was so quiet, I almost missed it. Looking down at his mate's hand, his face was hidden from us, muffling his words, and Amanda frowned as if she didn't believe her ears. "No, what?"

"Nothing can be changed." When he looked up, the anger had vanished from his face, replaced with regret and sadness. "It's the only way to save her. He... he'll stop treating her if I don't agree."

Vaughan's eyes closed in disappointment while Amanda stared at her father in shock. "You're going to let him blackmail you? What about the innocent wolves who were exiled? Did you know all along that they did nothing but get in Kyle's way?"

"She'll die!"

My chest tightened at the anguish in his voice and the painful certainty it held. It must have been terrible for him to watch his mate fading away and being completely helpless to stop it, but it didn't excuse what he was suggesting: letting Jasper and the others pay for crimes they hadn't committed, all to appease the sociopath who used the Luna's treatment as bait.

Calista obviously agreed with me. "Alpha, forgive me for intruding, but my own father went through something very similar. My adoptive, human father, I mean."

Alpha Warren's broken expression hardened as he looked over at my brother's mate. "I can't believe it was all that similar."

"I understand your skepticism, but there are substantial parallels. He made a deal with an evil spirit in order to save his wife's life. Because of it, my entire pack was wiped out, and several humans besides. Once unleashed, he couldn't control it, and you can't control Kyle either. Once you start to feed evil, it will never be satisfied. Where will it end? Would you really have turned over your own grandchild to him for his experiments?"

He didn't answer her, his jaw clenching tight again, and Amanda gave her father an incredulous look, as if she didn't entirely recognize him. "Dad! You wouldn't have."

Rather than giving in, the Alpha doubled down. "He says getting the genes of a child with Alpha blood will make the treatment strong enough to cure her, not just sustain her as he's been doing so far. It's the only way."

So, the Alpha *did* know about the children. He knew, and he was willing to let it slide, to let Jasper take the blame, all to save his mate's life. Bile rose in my throat at the thought of the other wolf who died as a result of Kyle's 'treatment'.

It reminded me of what Jasper's haze had said about burning down the world for me. I didn't want that, and I suspected the Alpha's mate wouldn't want it either. Maybe she knew what he'd already done, and that was why she insisted he speak to us? Maybe she hoped we could talk some sense into him, but I didn't know if that would be possible. He'd gone so far down the road already, could he even see the way back?

"What are you saying, Alpha Warren?" Vaughan asked, his voice deceptively calm. I knew my brother; when he ranted, he was frustrated or exasperated, but when he got quiet, a line had been crossed. "That you're going to put this man to death to appease your mad scientist?"

As he gestured at Jasper, I realized how right Vaughan was: the Alpha told Jasper he'd forfeited his life and all the while, he *knew* that Jasper had done nothing wrong.

"Are you really willing to sacrifice your pack for the sake of your mate?" Vaughan continued. "To keep my sister here against her will to breed experiment subjects?"

"No."

That word came not from the Alpha, but from the Luna. Her sunken eyes opened again, looking over at her mate with a mix of affection and disappointment.

"You... have... to... stop."

The Alpha's face tightened in agony. "You'll die. As long as you're my mate, I will do anything to protect you. *Anything.*"

The Luna's eyes closed again, and from the corner of my eye, I noticed Amanda's eyes glazing over, obviously communicating with someone. I didn't have to wonder who for long, for the Luna's eyes opened again as she poured all her strength into her next words.

"Then... I... reject you... and... our bond."

A gasp echoed around the room, coming not only from the Alpha but from all of us. No one anticipated that; no one but Amanda, who sprang into action as her father keeled over in agony.

"Felix, your knife!"

The Beta didn't hesitate, reacting on instinct as he tossed the weapon, handle first, towards Amanda who grabbed it in mid-air. In the next second, she rounded the bed and come up behind her father, forcing him to his knees and bringing the knife to his throat.

"As Lota of this pack, I declare you unfit to rule. By my authority, my blood, and with the endorsement of the Luna, I am now Alpha of this pack."

CHAPTER FORTY-NINE

~Jasper~

As Vaughan and Felix rushed to Amanda's side to help her restrain her father, Savannah looked over at me, her eyes full of the same shock and confusion I felt. "Can she... do that?"

'That' was Amanda declaring herself Alpha, and honestly, I had no idea. The mysteries of the pack hierarchy were beyond a regular wolf like me, but it made some sense. The Alpha could strip others of their position if they stepped too far out of line, so there must have been *some* provision to overthrow the Alpha himself if he stopped acting in the pack's best interest. Amanda was next in line and her mother had joint responsibility for the pack with her mate, so combined, their power might just be enough.

It helped that his mate's rejection seemed to have weakened the Alpha, at least temporarily. I didn't know if their bond had been fully severed with those words, but they had certainly hurt the Alpha, there couldn't be any doubt of that. Amanda seemed determined to make the most of it.

The door to the room burst open a few seconds later, the men outside being summoned not by Alpha Warren but by his usurper, and they stopped short in confusion at the sight that greeted them: the man they had always served on his knees, restrained by a foreign Alpha and Beta, with his daughter holding a knife to his throat.

"Take the cuffs off Jasper and put them on my father," Amanda ordered, her tone leaving no room for anyone to doubt her seriousness. "Quickly."

Despite her command to move fast, the men hesitated, their uncertainty at the idea of restraining their Alpha clear as day.

In the end, the Luna made the difference yet again. "Do it," she gasped from her bed, looking even weaker and paler than before. The strain of the rejection had taken its toll on her too, and she didn't have a great deal of strength to begin with.

Outranked, and with the Alpha saying nothing in his own defense, the men gave in. My cuffs were removed, the high-tech restraints requiring only a code to unlock them, and as soon as they left my wrists, a surge of power ran through me, so strong I nearly lost my balance. At first, I thought the haze might be responsible, but that didn't seem to be it; it simply signified my repressed strength returning.

As soon as they had the Alpha cuffed instead, Amanda took a step back and began issuing orders. "Felix, go with these men to take my father to the prison. Stay with him and make sure no one goes against my orders and tries to let him out."

Technically, Felix didn't answer to her, so he glanced over at Vaughan for confirmation, who gave him a nod. "I'm on it," he assured Amanda, and he and the other men half-dragged the weakened Alpha out of the room.

"Vaughan, Savannah, Jasper," she addressed each of us in turn next. "We need to find Kyle immediately. I'm guessing he's hiding in the same place Jasper found him before."

"We'll come," Savannah confirmed before Amanda even had to ask, and Amanda gave her a quick, tight smile of acknowledgement.

Lastly, the new Alpha turned to Calista, Vaughan's mate. "Would you... stay here with my mother?"

Surprise registered on Calista's face at being entrusted with such an important task by her former rival, but she nodded immediately. "Of course. I'll let Vaughan know if there's any change."

"Thank you." Amanda's lips pressed together again as she took one more look at her mother's prone form on the bed. Bending down, she placed a soft kiss on her mother's forehead, whispering something to her before standing back up and taking a deep breath. "Alright. Let's go."

Outside, a small group had already gathered to accompany us, many of them my former colleagues who looked rather surprised to see me. However, there wasn't any time for pleasantries as Amanda laid out our objective.

"Jasper found this hideout once before," she told the group after explaining what we were looking for. "But his memory was tampered with and he doesn't remember the exact location. We'll have to try to find it as he did."

I didn't remember *any* of that, so I listened as carefully as the others while Amanda described the type of rocks that led me to the door in the forest floor. Once everyone understood, we began to shift, some of the wolves wearing their special weapon belts on their wolf forms so they'd be armed when we arrived.

Savannah should stay here where it's safe, Sterling suggested, but I knew instinctively that telling her that wouldn't go over very well.

She can make her own decisions, and so far, she's managed to get us freed and earned us the trust of the new Alpha. Besides, she deserves her revenge on Kyle as much as anyone.

As soon as that thought crossed my mind, I had another one, and I quickly walked over to Amanda who was making her final preparations. "The other rogues should come too. You want people motivated to find this asshole? They've got more reason than anyone to see him brought in. Other than me, I mean."

She only hesitated a moment before giving the order. "Get the three others in the holding cell up here. Now!"

Myra, Dan and Brent walked blinking into the sunlight a couple of minutes later. "Jasper?" Myra asked in bewilderment when she saw me. "What's going on?"

"We're going to get all the answers, for all of us, right now."

As quickly as I could, I gave them the same briefing Amanda had given us and we all shifted, joining the other wolves as we set off after Amanda, with Vaughan bringing up the rear as protection.

In our wolf forms, Savannah and I could be a little more obvious, knowing that no one would be paying attention to us. She ran right beside me, her body occasionally rubbing against mine, sending the mate sparks dancing across our skin and driving Sterling crazy. It seemed like her wolf was a bit of a tease, and he loved it.

Once we reached the bay, though, flirting took an immediate back seat. Spreading out over the area beyond the bay, since I said his hideout lay in the opposite direction from the pack house, we began searching the ground for any rocks that didn't quite belong. Sterling let me take control again, but as I sniffed my way along the ground, he suddenly spoke up.

Hold on. The scent is familiar. I think I remember being in this spot.

Scent was often tied to memory, so maybe even if he couldn't consciously remember, his sense of smell might.

Take over, I encouraged him. *Follow your nose.*

He did, and in less than a minute, he found a smooth, flat white rock that looked exactly like the ones we were looking for.

A short, sharp bark alerted the rest of the team, and Sterling nudged the rock with his nose to show Amanda. With a nod, she gestured further into the forest, and to me, indicating the rest of the team should follow my lead.

It felt natural after that. Each rock led to another, as if our feet knew exactly where they'd be, and soon, we located the dip in the ground that concealed the entrance to Kyle's secret lab.

We all shifted back to our human forms to dig the dirt away from the hole, and sure enough, a hatched opening appeared, exactly as I described it under the hypnosis. Amanda immediately gave the orders, addressing the internal security team first: "You three, stay up here and keep an eye out. The rest of you, come with us. Jasper, do you want the honours?"

I certainly fucking did. With grim determination, I opened the hatch and began to climb down the ladder into the darkness below.

CHAPTER FIFTY

~Jasper~

With each step, I kept my ears trained on the space below me, listening for any sound that might indicate Kyle was aware of my presence or that he'd set up a trap for anyone who might track him down. Nothing but silence greeted me, and I made it all the way to the bottom without being stopped, finding myself in a small alcove at the bottom of the circular tube that the ladder came down, with a closed door to one side which must lead into the main part of the lab. How Kyle managed to build all of this without anyone knowing, I couldn't begin to imagine. How many people had he blackmailed or cajoled?

Sometimes, though, people could be too smart for their own good. If you assumed you were the smartest person in the room, you began to think you were untouchable, and Kyle was about to find out the hard way that he wasn't.

Savannah was right behind me, or above me in this case, and I reached up to help her down the last few steps. "Stay behind me," I whispered to her. "If he has firepower, it's not hitting you before me."

She gave me a look equal parts affection and exasperation. "I'd rather it not hit either of us, but we're in this together. I'm at your side, Jasper, not in front of you or behind you."

That sounded pretty fantastic, actually.

Vaughan and Amanda were next down the ladder, and the space in the small entrance room grew pretty tight. For the others to have room to join us, we'd have to go through the door.

"Here we go," I whispered to all of them, reaching for the handle.

Any fears I might have had that it would be locked proved to be unfounded. Though heavy, it opened easily, and I swung the door forward cautiously, having no idea what would be on the other side.

Gradually, the room came into view, a room not unlike the lab where we found Savannah, with the lighting dimmed. Computer screens shone in the darkness, tracking something, though I couldn't guess what, and refrigerated units along one wall were also lit up. Any ceiling lights were switched off, but floor lighting let us see well enough with our sharper werewolf vision.

I couldn't see any sign of Kyle.

Fuck.

"There's another door somewhere," Savannah whispered to me as we stepped side-by-side into the room. "You mentioned it when you told us about this place. You said Kyle came in from somewhere else."

So, he might still be there, and for all we knew, he might have eyes on us at that moment. We'd have to proceed very carefully.

In one corner of the room, a cage sat empty. Was that the cage where I found the children, where he held them before arranging them to be found in my basement instead, setting me up to take the fall once he realized they couldn't give him exactly what he wanted?

The other wolves joined us in the room, their weapons drawn as they looked around in disbelief. How many times had we run over this spot, not knowing what lay beneath our feet?

"There has to be another door in here," I announced to the room. "Maybe behind one of the machines. Everyone spread out and..."

I didn't even get to finish before the door we entered through slammed shut, the sound making us all jump as we spun around. I pulled Savannah closer to me, just in case, but no one was there. The door seemed to have moved on its own, but while we were all distracted, metal poles descended from the ceiling, locking into place on the floor, effectively creating one giant cage out of the half of the room we were standing in.

Even before Dan tried the door and found it locked, I could see the situation clearly: we were trapped.

Kyle's voice echoed through the room a moment later, carried over a speaker system. "Throw the guns through the bars. If you don't, I'll pump the whole room full of carbon monoxide and you'll all die."

It didn't sound like a bluff, and Amanda clearly agreed. "I don't think it's an idle threat," she whispered to me, Savannah and Vaughan. "But he also wouldn't give us the option if he didn't want some of us alive. That's an advantage, so for now, I think we should go along with what he says."

"Have you been in touch with the team above ground?" Vaughan murmured back.

Amanda grimaced. "I can't reach them. My links seem to be blocked."

Fuck. We should have anticipated that.

"Before we came down, though, I gave them instructions about what to do if they don't hear from me in five minutes. They'll have the whole pack here in a matter of minutes. There's no way Kyle can get out of this unscathed, and I just need to convince him of that."

When we all indicated that we understood, she addressed Kyle, speaking into the empty air.

"We'll do it if you come out here to speak with us," she negotiated.

"I will, once you're unarmed."

With a nod, Amanda gave her approval, and the armed wolves reluctantly slid their weapons through the bars to the empty side of the room. A moment later, one of the cabinets slid to the side, as I guessed it might, and Kyle entered, wearing some kind of transparent mask over his face, slightly distorting his features but letting us still see his mouth clearly.

Every hair on my body stood on end at the sight of him. Now that I knew exactly what he'd done and what he was capable of, I wished I'd killed him back at his lab the night before when I had my hands on him. Whatever happened in the next few minutes, one of us wasn't making it out of there a free man.

He gave me a condescending smirk as he caught sight of me. "I've made a few upgrades since the last time you visited me here. Do you like them?"

Apparently, we weren't going to be playing any games or hiding behind lies, so I didn't hold back either.

"I found you then and we found you again now. You're finished, Kyle. Your luck has run out..."

A loud growl from behind me interrupted my threat, and everyone turned in surprise to Myra, who stood a few feet back from the bars.

"It's you," she snarled at Kyle, her eyes burning with hatred. "*You're* my mate. That's why you had me banished. I can smell you, you fucking bastard."

Kyle was Myra's mate? I hadn't even considered it before but it made sense. Finding Myra must have interfered with whatever ambitions he had.

"Wait, you had a mate and you were trying to seduce me anyway?" Savannah chimed in, stepping away from me to supportively link her arm through Myra's.

"And you were falling for it," Kyle reminded her coldly. "But not to worry: I'll still have you. I assume because you're all here that the Alpha has betrayed me."

"No," Amanda corrected him with a grimace. "He betrayed the pack, as you did, and he's been relieved of duty. I'm the Alpha now, and you can't blackmail me like you did my father. You have nothing that I want. All I want is for you to repair the lives you've damaged."

While she spoke, I surreptitiously examined the bars of the cage, trying to determine if and how they could be opened. They looked like the same kind we used in the prison. Kyle would have been able to use the same suppliers who installed those ones, and from my security training, I knew that in the event of a power failure, there would be an override mechanism. The lock would release and the bars could be manually raised if the prisoners needed to be evacuated.

I had a strong feeling that would be the case in the lab too. We needed to find a way to cut the power.

Meanwhile, the others around me kept talking. "What's your plan here?" Amanda asked, staring down Kyle with all the authority and disapproval of an angry Alpha. "You kill all of us? You keep killing people until there's no pack left?"

"I don't need to kill anyone," Kyle disagreed, his pale blue eyes completely emotionless despite the chilling smile on his face. "I'll wipe all this from your memories. While we've been talking, a mild anesthetic gas is being pumped into this room. It'll knock you all out, and while you're unconscious, I can give you an injection. You all forget about this, the Alpha reclaims his place, and we go back to the way things should be. Gaslighting people is remarkably easy. Just ask the rogues in here, and all their families who never went looking for them."

Myra growled again, her anger bubbling right at the surface. Kyle truly was delusional, but I didn't bother adding anything to that conversation. My thoughts were still focused on the power, especially now that I knew we were working on borrowed time.

In one corner of the room, on our side of the cage, I could see a large electronic device, similar to a computer server, and I suspected it would be the power generator. He had to be getting power from somewhere, and though he might have been able to build this underground lab without being noticed, I doubted he would have been able to lay power cables back to the pack house. It must be running off its own generator, and it seemed he'd foolishly left it on our side.

Taking a step back, I fell into line with Dan and Brent. "Can you guys cover me for a few seconds?" I muttered under my breath.

They didn't even ask why. Together, we moved slowly towards the back corner where the generator was, and some of the other pack wolves helped to shield us too, understanding without words that we had a plan in mind.

"Can you even cure the Luna?" I heard Savannah ask as I opened one of the panels on the generator as quietly as I could. "Or did you make her sick in the first place?"

"I didn't make her sick, but I love that you think I'm that creative." He did sound genuinely pleased at the accusation, but I did my best to concentrate on the task in front of me. Wires ran from port to port, and I had no idea what did what.

Unfortunately, I didn't have any further time to figure it out as Kyle noticed my absence.

"Where's... hey! What are you doing back there?"

With no more time to waste, I simply grabbed a handful of wires and pulled as hard as I could. Sparks flew from the broken connections, sending a shock of electricity through my body that knocked me clear off my feet as the room went dark around me.

Chapter Fifty-One

~Savannah~

It all happened so fast.

I'd been so focused on Kyle and the insanity spewing from his mouth that I didn't notice Jasper's disappearance until Kyle called him out. As the bastard shouted at my mate, all of us turned around to see what caught his attention, just in time to see Jasper pull a bunch of wires out of a machine, causing a burst of electricity that threw him back onto the floor and plunged the room around us into darkness.

"Jasper!" My body felt numb in the darkness, my heart stuck in my throat as I groped blindly at the floor, trying to find him.

He didn't answer, but a moment later, light appeared from above us, courtesy of back-up emergency lighting. The computers remained off, though, and Kyle swore angrily as he pulled a phone from his pocket.

"Idiots! Do you have any idea how delicate this work is? I need to get the fridges back online!"

None of us cared about his fridges, me least of all. The dim lights allowed me to find my mate, sprawled on his back on the floor, his eyes closed, and in a second, I was at his side.

"Jasper? Are you alright?"

My hand reached for his wrist, and I could feel his pulse, steady if a little fast. *Thank the goddess.* A second later, he groaned. "The bars... tell Vaughan... lift them."

I didn't need to tell him. My brother heard it himself, having come over almost as quickly as I did to check on Jasper, and he seemed to understand exactly what my mate meant.

"You two," Vaughan ordered, pointing at the other two male rogues. "Help me. We don't have much time."

I could feel it too. The sedative gas Kyle warned us about was already starting to make me feel a little light-headed. If we didn't get to him soon, we might all fall asleep, leaving him free to make good on his threats to erase our memories yet again.

Kyle's eyes were still glued to his phone as he tapped on the screen, muttering under his breath, but he looked up when the three men approached the bars separating us from Kyle. Squatting down, they wrapped their hands around the metal cylinders and began to pull them upwards. At first, nothing happened, but they didn't stop, and with a creak, a gap appeared between the bars and the floor, much to Kyle's dismay.

"No! You can't... that shouldn't happen..."

He glanced back towards the door he'd entered through, clearly torn between heading to safety and staying put to try to save his work. That moment's hesitation was enough. As soon as the bars were raised high enough for us to squeeze through, Amanda, Myra and I all slid beneath them on our stomachs, intent on trapping the asshole before he got away.

"Block the door," Amanda ordered, and I headed straight for it, cutting off Kyle's only possible escape path while Amanda and Myra cornered him. He tried to fight them off, but as a scientist, not a warrior, he only managed to throw wild punches that didn't land. Up against two highly motivated, angry women, he didn't have a chance. With impressive skill and strength, Amanda landed a hard punch to his gut, slammed her elbow down on his back when he bent over in pain, and brought him to his knees.

Once he hit the ground, Myra kicked Kyle in the groin for good measure. "That's for having me exiled, you piece of shit. And in case there's any doubt, I reject you as my mate."

The pain of her rejection made Kyle double over even more than the well-placed kick had. Amanda tore the mask from his face as the others shimmied beneath the bars, picking up the weapons that they'd surrendered earlier.

With the situation well in hand on that side of the room, I crawled back to the other side, to my mate who still lay on the ground. "How do you feel? Can you get up?"

"I feel... the haze..."

He grimaced as the words came out, and I hated that I couldn't do anything to help him. I hated that he had to go through the struggle at all. "It's taking over again?"

Jasper shook his head. "No. It's back inside me. Combined, I mean. I think the shock forced us back together somehow. I can't even explain how I know, but I feel it. I feel whole again."

I didn't know that integrating both sides of himself again would be possible, and clearly, Jasper hadn't either. "Is that a good thing?"

"I think so." With a wince, he sat up, rubbing his head as he did. "It means he can't take over anymore. I'll have to control him from the inside, like we all do with our darker sides."

"Like the way I'm keeping myself from tearing Kyle limb-from-limb right now?" I asked, only half-joking.

Jasper smiled back at me, understanding my humour perfectly, the way I always imagined my mate would. "Even better, my memories came back with him. All of them. Before the exile and after. I remember it all, and there's one thing I know for sure: we have to end this here. We can't give him any more chances to get away."

With my help, he got back to his feet as one of the wolves on the other side of the bars passed out, the sedative obviously working faster on him than the rest of it, and making Jasper's point for him. Kyle had too many tricks up his sleeve. Keeping him alive would be too risky.

"Let's get out of here," Amanda ordered as Vaughan and the other rogue men dragged Kyle under the half-raised bars. "Myra, get the door."

Jasper let Myra go by, but he stepped in front of Kyle as my brother and the others pulled him along. "You're not leaving here alive."

"I understand your anger," Amanda assured Jasper. "And you don't have to worry. He'll be punished accordingly and everyone exiled because of him will be welcomed back to the pack."

Jasper shook his head, his eyes, normally so warm, looking hard and cold as they stared at the man who caused us all so much trouble. His eyes looked like the haze's, and I supposed, in a way, they were. All of it made up the man he was. "I'm sorry, Alpha. I'm not letting him go."

Kyle still hadn't learned to keep his mouth shut. "If you kill me, the Luna dies too. I'm the only one who knows how to treat her."

"I know," Jasper replied. "I know because you told me how she got sick in the first place."

Kyle's eyes went wide with surprise, and for once, he seemed too stunned to speak.

"What do you mean?" Amanda asked my mate, her gaze darting between him and Kyle.

Jasper's eyes never left Kyle as he answered her. "He told me all about it the last time I was here, before he erased my memory. He was struggling with getting the Alpha's approval for his research, so he invited your mother to his lab. While there, he convinced her to let him inject her with one of his milder treatments, a beauty treatment meant to make the skin look younger by literally altering the speed at which the skin cells reproduced. However, he didn't know she had a minor genetic mutation which would react with that treatment, and it made it so that the rate of acceleration became *too* fast. Her body couldn't get enough oxygen into the cells because they would die off too fast. When he realized what he'd done, he wiped her memory, since that's his favourite move, and moved her to the woods where the Alpha's team came across her. Ever since, he's been the only one to know how to treat her because he's the only one who knew exactly what was wrong with her."

Based on the anger that surged through me as I listened to the horrific story, I could only imagine how Amanda felt. "You told me you didn't cause her illness!" I reminded Kyle, though lying ranked pretty low on the list of awful things he'd done.

"I didn't do it on purpose," he replied sullenly. "I made a mistake. I don't like making mistakes, but it doesn't change the fact that I'm still the only one who can treat her."

"Can she ever be cured?" Amanda asked. Her pretty face had gone ghostly pale.

"A cure doesn't exist," Kyle admitted. "Not yet. But if I get the blood of an Alpha child, I can..."

He never finished that sentence. Extending her claws, Amanda slashed him across the throat, delivering a perfectly-placed slice to silence him forever. His pale blue eyes looked over at me in surprise as blood gushed from his neck. *This is all your fault*, those eyes seemed to say, and if me coming there had brought an end to the madness in the pack, I would gladly take the blame.

As Kyle collapsed, his body held upright only by my brother and the others, Jasper's knees gave way beside me, as if he couldn't hold himself up anymore now that he'd finally, after his months of exile, solved his case and seen justice done.

"Jasper?" I tried to hold him up, but he proved too heavy and we both stumbled to the ground as my mate went unresponsive.

"It's the sedative, Sav," my brother assured me as gently as possible, passing off Kyle's body to the others so he could usher me towards the door. "He'll be fine, but let's get out of here before we all pass out too. I'll send one of the men outside down to bring him out."

With no other choice, I left my mate there on the ground as I began climbing the ladder back up to the fresh air and the fresh start that awaited us all.

Chapter Fifty-Two

~Jasper~

I had the most wonderful dream. Something warm and soft lay beneath me, cocooning my body in warmth and comfort. The temperature was perfect, not like the cold, damp dew I'd woken up to almost every morning for the past few months. And best of all, the most incredible smell filled my nose, making each breath satisfying and perfect.

Waking up should have been a disappointment, except when I opened my eyes, I realized none of it had been a dream after all.

The softness beneath me came from a mattress, in a real bed, and the blankets on top of me accounted for the warm and cozy feeling. And the scent... well, that came from my gorgeous mate, sitting in a chair next to the bed, who looked up from her phone with a smile when I stirred.

"We really have to stop meeting this way," she teased me gently, putting her phone down to give me her full attention. "How do you feel?"

"I'd be perfectly happy if neither of us got knocked out again for a long time," I teased her right back, pulling myself up to sitting so that I could get a better gauge on how I felt. My chest remained bare but someone must have put sweatpants on me at some point. Physically, I seemed to be fine, and mentally, I felt more at peace than I had in a long time. "I feel okay. That really happened, right? Kyle's dead?"

"He is," Savannah confirmed. "And that answers my next question about whether you remember everything that happened."

"I think so. Everything today, and everything before that too. It's all in there."

I tapped on the side of my head for emphasis, making her smile. Sterling seemed relaxed too, maybe because we no longer had the threat of the haze hanging over us, or maybe just because we knew that our mate was safe from that psychopath. They were both great reasons to feel at peace.

"The only thing I don't remember is how I got back here. What happened?"

"You passed out from the gas Kyle pumped into the air. Not just you; four people did. Vaughan brought you back."

"Is everyone else okay?"

Her lips twitched mischievously. "Other than Kyle? Yeah, everyone's fine."

Fuck, I loved her sarcastic side already. "What about the Luna?"

The humour fled from Savannah's face as she sighed. "It's not looking good. Amanda's with her now, along with Vaughan and Calista. I said we'd join them when you woke up, but they don't necessarily need to know that you're awake yet, if you catch my drift."

Her eyes moved confidently over the exposed part of my body, making it impossible to misunderstand her meaning even if my mind hadn't already been on its way there. For the first time since we met, we were alone, with no one chasing us, no handcuffs, no threat hanging over us.

Just two wolves who, against the odds, had found their other half.

"How about we start with a proper introduction? My name's Jasper. I grew up here in the Ravenstone pack and I joined the internal security service after my compulsory training. I've been working as a detective for the last two years until I recently took an unplanned leave of absence."

Her beautiful smile made my heart sing as she leaned forward, her brown hair falling over her shoulders enticingly, begging to be touched. "Hi, Jasper. My name's Savannah, but most people call me Sav. I'm from the Crimsontooth pack where my brother's the Alpha. I help out around the pack where I'm needed, but we recently got a new Luna so I haven't figured out exactly what my new role's going to be yet."

I'd heard of the Crimsontooth pack. They were one of the biggest packs around, several hundred miles south of us, across the border. "What brings you to the Ravenstone, Sav?"

"Ironically, I came to find a mate. My brother agreed to take your Alpha's daughter as his mate. They signed a treaty and everything, but before the ceremony could take place, he met his fated mate, and you know how that is. It's hard to stay away from the one meant for you."

I certainly did know that, and I loved the way she teased me. "So, when that fell through, you were willing to take a chosen mate for the sake of your pack?"

"I thought it couldn't hurt to take a look. Now, I know it *could* have hurt. A lot. Luckily, you were here to keep me safe."

The trust in her eyes made me feel both weak and strong at the same time. "I think you're equally as responsible for keeping me alive, and for helping to get to the truth. You're incredible, Savannah, and if I haven't already made it abundantly clear, I'm fucking thrilled that you're my mate. Over the moon. If you accept me, I'll dedicate myself to making every day of your life as perfect as I possibly can."

Her sweet brown eyes shone with happiness, reflecting my own feelings right back to me. "Will you burn down the world for me?" she teased, reminding me that the haze had promised her that very thing.

Part of me wanted to say yes, the part of him that still lived inside me, but I offered a compromise instead. "I'll make you burn for me whenever you want, how about that?"

Her lips pulled upwards as she cocked an eyebrow at me. "I think it's time for you to put your money where your mouth is. Or in this case, to put your mouth there too."

I had absolutely no problem with that. With a growl of anticipation, I threw the covers back and leaned forward far enough that I could grab her out of the chair and pull her back onto the bed with me. Savannah shrieked in surprised laughter, but the laughter didn't last long. As soon as my lips found hers, the sparks of our bond flowed through us both, and laughing became the last thing on our minds.

Unlike that morning when I'd been restrained, my hands were free to explore her, to touch and claim every part of her and show her exactly how I wanted to worship her.

She wore only the loose shifting clothing the pack provided, not having left my side even long enough to get her own clothes back on again, but at that moment, I was grateful for it. It only took a matter of seconds for me to pull the shirt off her and the pants down, leaving her naked on the bed as I took a moment to admire her. That morning, she'd been naked with me in the shower and she looked incredible then, but seeing her on the bed, flushed and aroused and ready for me, made every single moment of the last few months worthwhile. Fuck, I would have gone through a thousand exiles if I got to wind up in that bed with her at the end of it.

She reached for me when I took too long in my admiration, but I caught her wrists before her hands could make contact. "You already had your turn, remember? This is my chance. Are you going to be a good girl and let me make you come?"

Those irresistible eyes sparkled at me from beneath her raised brows. "One thing you need to know about me, Jasper, is that I rarely do what I'm told."

"Not even when it feels like this?"

Still holding her wrists in one of my hands, I reached down with the other, reaching between her legs to let my finger slide across her clit. When her hand connected with my cock earlier, the sparks nearly bowled me over, and it worked the same way for her, her whole body jolting in response to the intensity. "Oh, fuck!"

I thought so. "Is that a yes?" I teased, my finger circling her clit but not touching it again. "Are you going to be good for me?"

Her lips pressed together, her body warring with her rebellious spirit, but finally, she couldn't hold out any longer. "I'll be good."

"That's my girl. Now, grab onto the headboard for me."

The bed had a slatted headboard, and she obediently slid her hands between the beams, gripping onto the bottom of one of them. As soon as she did, I kissed her lips once more before moving lower, letting my mouth take the place of my hand.

The strong smell of her arousal literally had me drooling as I settled between her legs. "Fuck, you smell so sweet."

Her hands tightened on the headboard, my words turning her on. "It's the only thing about me that is."

"I don't believe that for a second." Slowly, my tongue moved along her slit, grazing over her clit before moving back down again. "But it is definitely the tastiest."

Hooking her legs up over my shoulders, I dove in fully, burying myself in her warm, wet pussy. My nose rubbed against her clit while my tongue plunged inside her, making my cock twitch as it longed to join the fun. That would have to wait, though; first, I intended to take my time and enjoy myself.

Every movement of Savannah's body, every clench and wriggle as I hit a good spot, felt like the greatest victory I'd ever achieved. Her whimper of pleasure meant more to me than any award I'd ever won. She was it for me: the ultimate prize, and making her happy made me happy. Nothing more to it than that.

"Stop teasing me," she finally moaned as my tongue flicked across her clit again, my lips and chin damp with her wetness. "Show me what you've got, Jasper. Let me know why you should be my mate."

I couldn't resist that challenge. Immediately, I dialled up the intensity, my fingers joining my mouth so I could get her g-spot and her clit at the same time. It took me a moment to find the perfect spot on her inner walls, but I knew the second I did. Her body contracted around me, her thighs squeezing together on either side of my head.

With the end in sight, I stroked her there again, and again, while my mouth closed around her clit, sucking on it firmly, and she cried out my name as her body trembled. "Jasper!"

Fuck, yes. Her orgasm hit her hard, as gloriously as I imagined it.

As her trembling subsided, I lifted my head to see her eyes closed, her lips parted, and her hands still clutching onto the headboard. "Have I proven myself, or do you need a further demonstration?"

Her eyes half-opened, looking down at me with a sinful, satisfied smile. "What else have you got?"

Chapter Fifty-Three

~Savannah~

A sexy smirk spread across Jasper's face. "You really want to know what else I can offer? Let me show you."

Getting to his feet, he quickly discarded his pants, giving me a fantastic view of his cock, already hard and ready for me. I always wanted a mate who couldn't get enough of me, who wanted me for *me*, and Jasper was certainly stepping up. In the few days we'd known each other, he'd proven himself to be everything I always imagined in a mate. Sexy? Absolutely. Smart? In so many ways. Decent and honourable at heart, but willing to take charge and get his hands dirty when necessary? Oh, fucking yes.

As he climbed back onto the bed, his hard body hovering above me, I couldn't resist teasing him again. "Do I still need to hang on?"

He always seemed to take things in exactly the way I meant them, smiling down at me with both affection and desire. "Not to the bed. Hold on to me, Sav. Let me make you forget where you are, other than attached to me."

He couldn't have stated what I wanted any more plainly. As he leaned down to kiss me, I wrapped my arms around him, pulling his body against mine as he pressed his cock against my entrance. Right as he thrust into me, slowly and firmly, I wrapped my legs around his waist, taking him as deep as I could, and he groaned in satisfaction.

"Fuck, how does that feel so good?"

I had no idea, but I couldn't argue that it did. I'd had sex a few times before, casually, when I could get out from under Vaughan's protective eye on the 'girls' nights' he'd rightfully been suspicious of, but as much as I enjoyed it then, it never felt the way it did with Jasper inside me. The sparks of our mate bond echoed deep within me and along the surface of my skin at the same time, and I clung onto him not only because I wanted more but because I wanted to hold onto that moment for as long as I could.

We would only have one first time that we made love.

The first of very many times to come, if I had any say in the matter.

Jasper didn't seem to be in any hurry either. He moved slowly, drawing out each motion as his hard cock slid through my wetness, pulling out and pushing in with equal attention and rolling his hips against mine so that my clit got the friction it wanted. He seemed almost overwhelmed, the same as I did, with how utterly perfect it felt and how we fit together in the most natural way, without any awkwardness or hesitation. I never fully understood what it meant to be made for another person, but at that moment, I thought I did.

He'd been made for me. No one else would have ever made me feel like that

Thank the goddess we found each other when we did. Fate must have been at play to put him at the border when I arrived, to give him that glimpse of me when I was on my way to choose a man I hoped would satisfy me. What if I'd never come there? What if he'd never been exiled? What if I'd chosen someone else, not knowing my mate was right there in that pack but not allowed to meet me because of his rank? What if I'd somehow found him among the pack and we *were* mated, producing the Alpha child Kyle wanted, and Kyle took our child to experiment on? There were so many ways things could have gone wrong, so many possible pitfalls, and somehow, we managed to skirt around them and end up in each other's arms.

"I'm not hurting you, am I?" Jasper's voice, filled with concern, pulled me out of my thoughts, and I realized that my cheeks were damp, my eyes watering with the weight of everything that might have been.

"No," I quickly assured him. "Trust me, I'm a lot tougher than that. You don't have to be gentle with me."

He smiled, as I knew he would, but his concern remained. "What's wrong, then?"

"I'm just... happy. So happy I found you."

Fuck, I sounded like as much of a sap as my brother, but every word was true.

Jasper's look of concern melted away, replaced by a deep affection and pride. "I'm happy too, Sav. So fucking happy. Don't you feel it?"

He thrust into me harder, his hand slipping between us to tease my clit, and I laughed even as my body trembled. "I think so. Maybe do it one more time so I can be sure."

With a grin, he pumped into me again, and again, his fingers rubbing against my clit at the same time as I moaned. "How about now?"

"Almost... a little more..."

With that encouragement, he thrust harder and faster, the tenderness of his earlier movements forgotten, until my pleasure broke again and I shuddered around him and he released inside me. When I opened my eyes, he stared down at me, his eyes clouded with lust and hunger, and I knew exactly what he was hungry for.

"You want to mark me, don't you?"

His haze tried a couple of times, but Jasper would never do it without asking. I knew that as surely as I'd ever known anything.

"I do," he admitted, his voice low and filled with need. "But if you want to wait, we can wait."

We could wait, but what would be the point? In the past few days, I'd learned so much about him by seeing him under pressure and in the most challenging circumstances. I couldn't imagine that anything I would learn about him over the next few days would change my opinion of him, so why wait?

I knew what I wanted, and Jasper seemed to have no problem with me stating it outright.

"I don't want to wait. Mark me, Jasper. Claim me as yours."

The growl that came out of him sent a shiver through my body, his wolf right there beneath the surface as his canine teeth extended and he bent down to my neck, nuzzling it and licking the spot. Pleasure began to build inside me again as his teeth pierced my skin, leaving the mark that would tell all the world that I had found my other half.

When he licked the wound clean, the lapping of his tongue sending more little shudders through me, he offered me his neck too. "This only works if I'm yours too. Claim me, Sav."

Tala howled in delight as I let my teeth sink into his neck and felt his cock hardening inside me, the experience as erotic for him as it had been for me.

"Feels like you might be ready for another round," I teased after I made sure his wound had healed and inspected my mark on him. It looked damn good, and I loved the idea that everyone would know he belonged to me.

"With you? I don't know if I'll ever *not* be ready."

He leaned down to kiss me again, but before we could get much farther, someone knocked at the door.

"If that's Heather, I'm going to..."

I didn't get to finish my threat before Felix's voice called out.

"Sav? Is Jasper up yet?"

My mate's eyes met mine in amusement, finding the question as funny as I did given our current position. "Yes, he's definitely up," I called back as Jasper snickered.

"Good. Come to the Luna's room as soon as you're ready. Vaughan just linked me. It's not looking good."

His footsteps faded away down the hall as Jasper and I exchanged worried looks, our euphoria fading as the rest of the world came crashing back in. "I guess we better go and deal with the aftermath of everything," Jasper sighed, and he gave me one more gentle kiss before we both pulled our clothes back on and headed upstairs.

Chapter Fifty-Four

~Jasper~

I held Savannah's hand as we climbed the stairs back to the Luna's room; the main stairs that time, not the secret ones. With the sparks of our bond flowing between us and the marks on our necks, I wanted to shout the news out to the whole forest that this incredible woman had agreed to be mine.

Unfortunately, no one in the Luna's room looked to be in a celebratory mood, so sharing our good fortune would have to wait. Vaughan stood next to Amanda at her mother's side, a comforting hand on her shoulder, while Calista hunched over her phone in the corner of the room, speaking quietly into it.

"What's going on?" Savannah asked, going to her brother as soon as we entered while I hung back next to Felix by the door, not wanting to intrude.

"Calista's on the phone with someone she knows from her hunting days," Vaughan told her, keeping his voice low. "Based on what Jasper told us about what happened to the Luna, she's trying to find a treatment, but I don't know if it's going to be in time. Her vital signs are getting worse."

"They're going to bring the Alpha up here to say his goodbyes, just in case," Felix added quietly. "We wanted Jasper here since a pair of extra hands could come in handy if the Alpha tries anything out of desperation. If I'd known what I was interrupting, though, I would have found someone else."

He gave a pointed look to the mark on my neck, and when Vaughan followed his gaze, my brother's eyes widened in surprise. "Really? That was fast."

I supposed it had been naive to think people wouldn't notice. "Really," Savannah told him, shooting me a smile before giving her brother a critical look. "And you're one to talk. Exactly how long did you know Calista before you marked her?"

He didn't seem to be able to argue with that, and he didn't get a chance to say anything anyway as Calista ended her call and returned to the group.

"Good news or bad news first?" Calista asked, directing the question to Amanda.

Taking a deep breath, Amanda tried to brace herself. "The bad news."

Calista didn't sugarcoat it. "The only person I've found who might be able to help is in Idaho and based on your mother's current condition, it might not be possible to move her at all, let alone in time to make a difference."

That *did* sound pretty bad. Hopefully, her other information offered some glimmer of hope.

Amanda nodded stoically even as her jaw clenched. "What's the good news?"

"The good news is that she understood the situation very quickly when I explained it to her, and she already has some ideas about how she might treat her *if* we can get the Luna to her lab."

"So, we need to buy some time?" I summarized, thinking out loud as everyone turned towards me. "Kyle was treating her, right? It would make sense that he had some additional doses of that treatment stored up somewhere. Probably his lab in the medical centre, where he could access it easily?"

Vaughan immediately understood me. "If we can find it and administer it to her, maybe it will be enough to get her to Calista's friend's lab."

"There is so much stuff in that lab," Savannah reminded us both. "We don't know what you're looking for, or how it works."

"We don't, but working with the other rogues, I might be able to figure it out. Dan worked in requisitions, so he'd be able to check what kind of materials Kyle started ordering around the time that the Luna got sick. Brent was an intern there so he has a basic understanding of the science. Myra used to clean the medical centre, so she would know of any instructions around cleaning the lab. I'm guessing if Kyle wanted to keep this all a secret, he didn't let anyone else near it."

"And you'll put all the pieces together to locate the treatment," Savannah finished for me, her eyes shining with pride.

I couldn't make any promises, but I hoped so. "I'll certainly try."

"Go," Amanda ordered. "I'll link the team to give you access. We can handle my father without you."

Back downstairs, I met my fellow rogues, all dressed in real clothes for the first time since their exiles and looking far more relaxed than I'd ever seen them before. We might not have been officially welcomed back to the pack yet, but we were no longer being actively chased off the land either. It felt like a big step up.

As soon as I explained the situation to them, they were all as eager to help as I was, and soon, we were back in Kyle's lab. I took charge to streamline our efforts. "Dan, you can use the computer to look up Kyle's requisition requests. Brent, help him figure out what those might have been used for. Myra, show me your routine when you used to clean in here."

The two men got to work at the computer while Myra explained her workflow in the lab. "There were quite a few things we weren't supposed to touch," she told me. "I'm not sure how much it'll help to narrow things down."

"That's alright. Any information is better than none. What was the first one?"

Together, we examined the first refrigerated unit she'd been told to avoid, but it appeared to be mostly specimen dishes. To my untrained eye, nothing looked like a potential treatment.

Next, we moved on to another unit, this one much less deep, even though it came out from the wall as far as the first one did. Looking at the two units, I couldn't help thinking it looked like something might be behind the second one, especially when I remembered how Kyle had a secret room concealed behind one of the units in his underground lab.

"Help me look for some kind of latch or connecting mechanism," I requested, showing Myra where I thought it would be most likely to be. She began searching one side of the unit while I looked over the other side, inch by inch so we didn't miss anything.

She came up as empty as I did. "It looks solidly attached."

It did, but I still had a gut feeling something lay behind it. If the latch wasn't on the outside, maybe it had been built into the inside, so I opened the doors of the unit and began grabbing some of the dishes inside. "Help me take these out of here."

Working together, we had the unit empty in no time, and I began reaching along the back wall of it, looking for anything out of the ordinary. Sure enough, beneath one of the shelves, hidden away, my fingers stumbled over a small switch, and when I flipped it, the whole unit moved forward a tiny bit. When I went back to the side, a small space sat behind the front unit and the block behind it which hadn't been there before.

"Grab the other side," I instructed, working my fingers into the tiny opening on my side. "Slide it forward with me."

Together, we got it separated, and once the front had been removed, we found a second refrigerated unit, hidden in the dark and filled with several vials of a prepared liquid. *That* looked a lot more promising.

"We've got something here, Jasper," Dan called out from the other side of the room. "It looks like he ordered a bunch of syringes and equipment consistent with ASO development."

"With what?" The acronym went over my head, but Brent quickly explained.

"Antisense oligonucleotide. It alters RNA and protein production in the body and it's usually administered via a spinal tap. We'd be looking for some kind of liquid, probably in vials..."

"Like this?" Myra asked before he could finish, and the two men hurried over to check out what we'd found.

"Exactly like this," Brent confirmed, and Dan nodded.

"And you know how to give someone this kind of treatment?" I pressed.

"I'm not sure of the dosage and how long it lasts, but if we assume one vial is one dose, I can give it to her."

That would have to be good enough. Our choices were that or letting her die, so working together, we located a cooler that could be used to transport some of the vials along with the equipment Brent would need to administer the treatment. We returned to the Luna's room to find the Alpha on his knees at his mate's bedside as her raspy breathing filled the room. Blotchy red spots surrounded Amanda's eyes, as if the worst had already happened, but we weren't defeated yet.

"Roll her onto her side, quickly," Brent instructed, sounding so confident that no one argued with him. "Keep her steady, it's important that she doesn't move."

Alpha Warren and Alpha Vaughan worked together to get her into position, following Brent's instruction, and he filled a syringe with the liquid from one of the vials. Everyone seemed to be holding their breath as he injected the liquid directly into the Luna's spinal fluid. She didn't react at all, too weak to even whimper in pain.

"She can go onto her back but she shouldn't sit up for a while," Brent advised once he'd removed the syringe from her back. It didn't look like she'd be capable of it for a while anyway, but as we all watched and waited, nobody uttering a word, the red numbers on the monitoring equipment slowly began to creep down.

"She's stabilizing," Calista breathed after a tense few minutes had passed. The Luna's breathing, though still shallow, had lost the hollow sound it had when we came in.

"I've got a helicopter on the way here," Vaughan announced. "It can take the Alpha and Luna to the treatment site."

"I'll go too," Brent offered in case any further temporary measures would be needed, and Calista volunteered to go to ensure a smooth introduction between the parties. Vaughan didn't look thrilled about that, no doubt worried about her being away from him, but he didn't contradict her either. It seemed he'd found a mate as sure of her own mind as I had.

"Thank you. All of you." Finally raising his eyes from his mate, Alpha Warren looked around the room, his gaze resting on each of us in turn. "After everything I did... everything I let him do... you didn't have to help us."

"That's what the pack is for, Dad," Amanda reminded him softly. "And our allies too."

She gave Vaughan and Calista a nod of acknowledgement which Vaughan returned, his arm around his mate.

"If you asked for help in the first place, we might have avoided all of this."

"You're right." The Alpha looked more humbled than I'd ever seen him. "Before we leave, I'd like to transfer my authority to you officially, Amanda. You're the Alpha this pack needs right now."

Though she didn't need his approval, I could see how much it meant to her anyway, and the elders were quickly called to complete the ceremony, right there at the Luna's bedside. The Alpha relinquished his authority over the pack, bestowing it on his daughter and heir, and soon afterwards, the helicopter arrived, ready to take the small group to the clinic.

With the Luna loaded on board on a stretcher to keep her back flat, Alpha Amanda called Brent over. "Before you leave, I'd like to officially return you to the pack, assuming you still want to be a part of it."

"I do," he confirmed gratefully. "Thank you, Alpha."

Quickly, she cut into her palm and his, mixing their blood to restore his pack bond, and he seemed to almost transform before our eyes, looking happier and stronger than he had a moment earlier.

"I'll do the same for the rest of you," she told me, Myra and Dan once the helicopter had taken off on its journey. "But first, there's one more person I need to take care of."

CHAPTER FIFTY-FIVE

When the Ravenstone men brought their Alpha back to the Luna's room, it quickly became apparent that we wouldn't need to restrain him. I'd never seen a more broken-looking man as he fell to his knees at his former mate's bedside. Now that I'd experienced the power of the mate bond myself, even for a little while, I had a better idea of how much pain he must have been going through, and Vaughan, Calista and I backed off to give the family some privacy.

"Congratulations," Calista whispered to me once we couldn't be overheard. "I'm looking forward to getting to know Jasper. He seems like a good man."

"He does," my brother agreed, which, coming from him, was high praise indeed. I hadn't been sure any man would ever measure up to his standards for my mate. "You're going to have to tell us the whole story about exactly how you two met."

"The *whole* story?" I teased him, giving Calista a wink that had her trying not to smile.

"The version of it that's appropriate for your brother and Alpha," Vaughan replied in a deadpan, sarcastic tone. Calista really was loosening him up for the better. "But will I be your Alpha much longer? Are you two going to stay here?"

"I honestly don't know. With everything else that's been happening, we haven't talked about it yet. We'll have to make a decision together."

There were pros and cons to both options. With the change in leadership, Amanda would need people she could trust to help run the pack.

This was Jasper's home and he might want to stay. On the other hand, after what he'd gone through in the past few months, he might relish a fresh start instead, and as pretty as the Ravenstone territory was, I would miss my home, my friends, and yes, even my overprotective brother.

"You did good work here," Vaughan told me, the sarcasm completely vanishing from his voice. "I'm proud of you, Sav."

"Thanks." Since I knew he meant it sincerely, I didn't give him a hard time about being sappy. Sappiness seemed to be going around that day.

When Jasper returned with the others and they were able to get the Luna stabilized enough to be moved, my mate stayed close to me but we didn't have a free minute to talk about much of anything. Even when the helicopter took off and I thought we might finally be able to relax, Amanda announced she had something else to do.

"What now?" I whispered to Jasper as we followed Amanda back into the house, my hand held tightly in his.

"I'm not sure," he admitted. "I want to get a minute of Amanda's time, though, as soon as possible. I need to find out what happened to Lee."

Of course he was still thinking about everyone else. I would haven't expected anything else.

Amanda headed down a set of stairs beneath the main staircase that led into the ground and it didn't take long to realize we were going to the pack house's prison. Once there, Amanda strode over to one of the cells which housed an angry, pacing wolf.

"Lee?" Jasper asked, his surprise evident in his voice. He hadn't expected Amanda to be taking us to the very person he wanted to discuss.

She nodded. "He won't shift. We can't get through to him at all."

A shiver ran down my spine as I looked at the wolf's snarling mouth and fierce eyes. He didn't look like a werewolf at all. The creature in front of me was all wolf.

What did that mean for Lee?

Jasper offered his opinion. "Under her hypnosis, Savannah told us that Kyle wanted to separate the wolf and human side. It's what he tried to do to me but it didn't work. I'm not sure why he wanted to do that, but it seems he succeeded with Lee. His human side must be buried somehow, lost beneath his version of the haze."

Amanda's brow furrowed at the word, but I knew exactly what he meant. I also had a theory about why Kyle had been working on that. "He was allowed to experiment on animals, right? So, if he could separate the wolf and human and convince everyone the person in question was a regular wolf, he'd be able to carry out his experiments on werewolf genes without it being unethical, at least in his mind."

"You might be right," Amanda agreed grimly. "But how do we reverse it?"

I had an idea about that too. "Jasper's haze reintegrated when he touched the electrical wires. Maybe some kind of controlled shock therapy would do the same to Lee?"

All of us turned to look at the feral, angry wolf, and I had no idea how anyone would get close enough to give him any kind of treatment, let alone hook him up to an electrical current.

Amanda seemed determined to try, though. "Get me some doctors and the necessary equipment," she ordered the prison guards, who hurried to obey their new Alpha. Since the official transfer had been completed, the power emanating off her had increased a great deal, to the point that I could feel it too despite being a member of a different pack. "While we're waiting for that, why don't we..."

Whatever she planned to suggest, she didn't get to finish as loud footsteps came rushing down the stairs towards us. "Amanda?"

I recognized the man as he appeared, though I couldn't remember his name. I met him the night I arrived, at the same reception where I met Kyle. This man had ignored me in favour of Amanda, and his attention remained focused entirely on her at our second meeting.

"Troy," Amanda greeted him, straightening her back in a way that made her look even more imposing. "Do you need something?"

"You know I do." He seemed to have forgotten anyone else existed as he stepped towards her, his intense gaze never wavering. "I heard that you're the Alpha."

She held her ground just as strongly. "Yes. And?"

"And?" he repeated in disbelief. "What do you mean 'and'? You make the rules now! You can restore the emphasis on fated mates. You can accept our bond, at last."

'Their bond?' I mouthed at Jasper who shrugged back, equally clueless. It felt like we'd walked into some TV drama partway, missing half the context, but I was hooked anyway.

When Amanda didn't say anything, Troy tried again. "All these years, I never rejected you because I hoped some kind of miracle would happen to let us be together. And now, it has. We don't have to hide anymore."

Man, I wished I had some popcorn. This was the juiciest thing I'd seen in a long time.

Amanda's reply, when it came, couldn't have been what Troy hoped for. "You didn't reject me because you were too weak to claim me and too selfish to let me go. You kept me dangling all this time, trying to scare off anyone else who might be interested in me, and now, you expect me to fall at your feet? Do you really think I have so little self-respect?"

She glanced over at me and Jasper, aware of her audience even if Troy wasn't.

"Over the last two weeks, I've seen Vaughan fight for his fated mate and risk rupturing the alliance with my father to do so. I've seen Jasper risk his life, time and again, to protect Savannah and help the pack. *That* is what a fated mate should do. All *you've* done is glare at people from the sidelines and whisper in the shadows about things being unfair. If you were ever worthy of me, you're not anymore."

"Don't say that." Troy looked so devastated that I almost felt sorry for him, despite agreeing 100% with everything Amanda said. "I didn't claim you because your father would have disowned you. We'd have been rogues."

His nose wrinkled in distaste at the word before he seemed to remember he was in the presence of some of them.

"No offense," he tried to claim, giving Jasper a sheepish smile, but my mate's expression didn't alter. He obviously took Amanda's side on this too.

"A sacrifice you wouldn't make for me," Amanda summarized bluntly.

Troy winced at her conclusion. "It's a sacrifice I couldn't ask *you* to make, not for me."

Amanda still looked unconvinced, but the conversation was interrupted by the arrival of the doctors and equipment Amanda had requested, and she turned away from Troy, blocking him out of her mind to deal with the matters concerning her pack.

Had they really known they were mates for years and done nothing about it? I couldn't imagine. Jasper consumed my thoughts since the moment I met him, and without either claiming or rejecting him, it truly might have driven me mad.

How did Amanda survive all this time? She really was tough, far more than I'd given her credit for when I first met her.

The doctors had to give Lee's wolf a sedative, administered by blow dart, to get him to calm down enough that they could get into the cage with him. Working as quickly as possible, they attached the electrodes to his head. It all looked much more scientific than the shock Jasper got when he pulled those wires out, but hopefully, it would have the same effect.

Jasper and I watched as the doctors sent currents through the wolf's body, speaking to him between each one, trying to determine if the human side had resurfaced.

"Nothing's happening at this voltage," one of the doctors told Amanda. "We could try a higher one, if you think it's necessary."

If I were in Lee's shoes, I would be willing to take the risk, and it seemed Amanda agreed as she gave her permission.

The next round caused the wolf's whole body to convulse, but still, nothing seemed to change.

"Try once more," Amanda ordered.

That time, after the convulsion, the wolf began to tremble, and Amanda stepped right over to him, putting her hands on him so he would feel her strength.

"You're safe now, Lee. You're home. Please, show yourself."

It took a few false starts, but eventually, the wolf in front of us shifted into a large, bearded man, and the tension in Jasper's frame relaxed, a smile of relief spreading across his face.

"Now, it's over," he whispered to me, and though I certainly hoped that was true, I also knew that in so many ways, all the ways that really counted, we were still at the very beginning.

Chapter Fifty-Six

~Jasper~

In the pack prison, Dan, Myra and I watched as Amanda slit her palm again and welcomed Lee back to the pack. Having the pack bond would make him stronger and help him heal faster, and I felt more relief than I could put into words that he would be okay. My fellow rogues all put their trust in me, and somehow, we all made it through.

When she finished, Amanda turned to the three of us who still remained packless. "Are you ready to come back home?"

Myra and Dan stepped forward eagerly, receiving Amanda's Alpha blood to bond themselves to the Ravenstone pack once again, but I hung back next to Savannah. We hadn't had a chance to talk about our future yet and I didn't want to make any big decisions without consulting her first.

"Jasper?" Amanda called me over once the other two were finished, both of them beaming at me in satisfaction. Though we might have proven there could be honour among rogues, it didn't compare to the feeling of belonging to a pack.

"Can I get back to you later? Finding my mate has changed a few of my priorities."

My hand squeezed Savannah's and she returned the pressure while Amanda nodded in understanding. "Of course. Whenever you're ready."

Pressing down on her palm to heal the cut, and with a side-eyed glance at her own mate, Amanda cleared her throat.

"I'm sure you're all eager to get back to your families and friends, and I have a lot of work to do. Jasper, you can find me in my office for the rest of the day."

"Amanda, wait, we still need to talk…" Troy tried to stop her but she ignored him, heading back upstairs while the doctors continued to care for Lee.

After shaking hands with Dan and Myra, Savannah and I also retraced our steps back up the stairs and back to her room where we could have a bit of privacy. Vaughan and Felix were preparing to leave and they'd want an answer about whether Sav and I would be going with them, just as Amanda was waiting to find out if we would stay.

I had no idea what my mate wanted to do, so I asked her straight out as soon as we were alone. "Where do you want to live?"

I really meant 'what kind of future do you see for us?', and I knew she understood that unspoken question as well as she intuitively understood everything about me.

"I was going to ask you the same thing." She gave me a teasing smile before going over to the window and looking out over the land as if it might give her the answer. "Do you have family here?"

"I have some cousins, a few aunts and uncles, but no immediate family. I'm an only child and my parents moved away a few years ago. They didn't like the direction the pack seemed to be heading, but I was in the middle of my training so I stayed. At the time, I thought they were being stubborn and set in their ways, but maybe they were onto something." I tried to keep the mood light, and it seemed to work as Sav smiled. "I definitely don't have anyone as close as you and your brother seem to be. Do you have more family?"

She shook her head. "My father died a few years ago, which is when Vaughan took over as Alpha. Our mother moved south. Vaughan's been my only family for a while, but now, he has Calista, so I think he'd be more willing to let me go than he would have been before. It shocked me that he even let me come up here in the first place."

Everything she said fascinated me, since I wanted to know everything about her, but it didn't get us any closer to a decision. "You must have a pretty good life there as the Alpha's sister," I guessed. "Living in the pack house? Helping to run things?"

The alternative, I left unsaid: mated to an unranked wolf like me, she'd be just another member of the pack if we stayed at the Ravenstone. Any special privileges she had at home would no longer exist.

"I told you that Calista will take over a lot of my work," she reminded me. "And yes, I have a good life there, but I wouldn't mind a new challenge."

"What do you want, Sav?" I asked her bluntly, since we still weren't getting anywhere.

She answered me equally plainly. "I want to be with you. I don't really care where we are, as long as we're happy. I'll find some way to make myself useful. The two packs are close enough that we could visit regularly. So, what do *you* want, Jasper? You're the one who had everything taken from you and lost months of your life. Now that you're back in the driver's seat again, where do you want to go?"

As she said, it had been a while since I had full control over things, and the more I thought about it and truly pictured our lives in both packs, the clearer it became to me. "Amanda's going to need some help to keep the pack in line. There will be some who won't be thrilled about reporting to a female Alpha."

Sav rolled her eyes. "They're going to have to fucking get used to it."

As usual, her bluntness made me smile. "That's the kind of attitude she could use as backup. If you really have no preference one way or the other, I think I'd rather stay here, at least for now. If we change our minds, I assume your brother would always welcome us back?"

"He would," she assured me. "And that sounds fine with me. I guess we made our first big decision as mates."

With the talking out of the way, she walked back over to me, her arms wrapping around my neck to pull my body close to hers. Instantly, the sparks of our bond lit up my skin, making my desire for her flare back to life yet again. With our lips only millimetres apart, someone knocked on the door and Savannah groaned.

"My first condition of living in this pack is no more interruptions!"

Grinning at her, I snuck a quick kiss before heading to the door where I found Vaughan and Felix on the other side.

"I want to get home as soon as possible, to be there when Callie gets back," Vaughan told us both as Savannah joined me in the doorway. "Have you made a decision?"

"We have," Sav answered for us both. "We're going to stay here."

His quick blink of surprise made it clear he hadn't expected that, but he nodded slowly anyway. "If that's what you want, then of course I support you. I'll miss you, Sav."

"No, you won't," she scoffed, giving his arm a nudge to stop either of them from getting emotional. "You'll be glad to have me out of your hair."

Vaughan neither confirmed nor denied that. "Well, you're welcome to visit anytime. Once you're all settled, I'd like to get to know you better, Jasper."

"Ditto." He and I shook hands, and Felix offered me his hand as well before both men gave Savannah a hug. When she pulled back from her brother's embrace, I could have almost sworn that moisture filled her eyes, but she blinked and the tears were gone.

"We're going to head out now," Felix confirmed. "Sav, we'll have the rest of your things sent to you. If you need anything else, let us know. Congratulations, both of you."

With their good wishes still ringing in our ears, we headed down to Amanda's office to share the news with her. The Beta walked out as we approached, a dark scowl on his face, and Sav and I exchanged curious looks before we walked in the open door.

"Is this a bad time?" I asked in greeting. After spending most of my life never seeing the inside of the Alpha's office, it felt strange to walk in like I belonged there. The severe lines of the room seemed at odds with the young woman who now occupied it and I wondered if she would redecorate it now that it belonged to her.

"Yes, but there's not going to be a better one." Amanda sighed from behind her desk. "I shared my initial plans for changes within the pack with Beta Chad and he gave his resignation. He's set in his ways, like my father, and not interested in disrupting the status quo. Looks like I'm in need of a new Beta."

"What about Jasper?" my mate immediately suggested, giving me an encouraging smile as I turned to her in alarm.

"What? I don't have any kind of training for that."

"What kind of training do you really need?" Sav argued. "You're smart, loyal, and devoted to the pack. You're as good a man as Felix is, and he's a great Beta."

"Who probably trained his whole life for that job," I countered.

"Do I get a say here?" Amanda interjected, and Sav and I both turned back to her sheepishly.

"Sorry, Alpha," I apologized. "It seems my mate likes to say whatever's on her mind."

I fucking loved that about her, but I could see how it might get us into trouble every now and then.

Amanda, however, didn't seem upset. "I've had the same impression from Savannah in the time we've known each other, and I think it's wonderful."

She gave the woman at my side a warm smile, and I beamed with pride at hearing my Alpha praising my mate. I couldn't help myself.

*You **should** be proud,* Sterling agreed with me. *And you shouldn't talk yourself out of a job either. I would be a great Beta wolf.*

Of course he would think that. *You're half the size of the Deltas.*

Size isn't everything. You of all people should know that.

Really? Dick jokes? That's what you're resorting to?

Even though my wolf mocked me, it felt incredible to be joking around with him again, not just trying to survive as we'd done for so long.

Meanwhile, Amanda kept talking. "As great as Jasper is, and as much as I want him to remain here if that's your decision, the pack would never accept an unranked wolf as Beta. In a lot of ways, we're still a traditional pack, and they're already going to need to adjust to having a female Alpha. Jasper as Beta would be a step too far."

I nodded in acceptance of that fact. Honestly, it had never really felt like a possibility.

Amanda hadn't finished yet. "They couldn't, on the other hand, argue with having the daughter of an Alpha as their new Beta."

Immediately, I caught on to what she meant, my heart soaring with even more pride than before, but it took Savannah a moment longer to put the pieces together. "But... you're already the Alpha," she pointed out.

"Right." Amanda tried not to smile. "If only I knew another Alpha's daughter."

At last, the penny dropped, as did Savannah's jaw. "Wait. Hold up. Are you saying you want *me* to be your Beta?"

"If you're interested, and assuming that you came to tell me that you decided to stay here."

We had, but we never anticipated the rest of it. When I looked down at Sav, her eyes were full of wonder. "What do you think?" I asked, leaving the decision entirely in her hands.

"I... I don't know." It might have been the first time I'd ever seen her speechless, but it didn't last for long as her excitement over the idea began to grow. "I did say I would find a way to make myself useful."

"You did, and there could hardly be a more important job than Beta. Except for the Alpha herself."

My eyes darted to Amanda for a second, who sat quietly watching us with an almost wistful smile, waiting for us to make a decision but not interfering in any way.

"I think you'd be incredible," I added truthfully.

"This is a lot of change all at once." Sav looked overwhelmed for a second before her jaw set in determination, her expression firming into the headstrong, fierce look I'd seen on her so many times already, every time she set her mind to something. So far, I had never seen her fail. "The pack could use some change though, and I could too. I'm ready for this."

She absolutely was. I had no doubt of it.

"In that case, we'll have a ceremony tomorrow to welcome you both to the pack, and to appoint you as Beta. Jasper will get a promotion in recognition for his work in stopping Kyle and exposing what happened to the other rogues." Amanda looked considerably more relaxed than she had when we walked in, as if knowing Sav would have her back made her burden lighter. I felt the same way. "In the meantime, why don't you two have some time to yourselves? I'm sure you'd appreciate some."

She could say that again. After thanking her, and with our heads still swimming with all the new possibilities opening in front of us, Sav and I headed back upstairs.

Chapter Fifty-Seven

~Savannah~

As soon as we were back in my room, I tried to pull Jasper close to me, craving the feel of his hands on me, but he held me at arm's length. "You should link to your brother and tell him what happened. He's probably still on pack territory, so he should be within range."

Part of me thought it would be kind of funny to wait for Vaughan to find out on his own when Amanda casually name dropped me as her Beta, but equally, I wanted to hear his reaction to the news. My desire to brag won out, so I stepped away from Jasper and opened the link to my brother. *Vaughan? Can you hear me?*

I'm here, his answer quickly came back. *Did you change your mind?*

The hopefulness underpinning the question made my heart melt. We both tried to play it pretty cool when we said goodbye earlier, but I knew when Vaughan said he'd miss me that he meant it. I teased him so I wouldn't think about how much I'd miss him too, but when he hugged me, I almost got a little teary anyway. As annoying and overprotective as he could be at times, he'd always been a great brother. I loved him and I loved my pack but the time had come for me to find my own path, and I knew he understood that.

No. We're staying here, but Amanda asked me to be her Beta.

Really? He sounded so surprised, I almost took offense, but he quickly amended his response. *I mean, of course she did. She needs someone she can trust, someone without entrenched interests in the pack other than hers, someone who will give it to her straight. You're perfect for it.*

Thanks. I'd never imagined holding that kind of position on my own before. As the male and the older one between us, Vaughan was always going to be Alpha. At most, I thought I might have been a Luna if I ended up mated to another pack's Alpha, but it seemed far more likely I wouldn't hold any official position at all. The idea that I'd been offered one on my own merits made it even sweeter. *There's going to be a ceremony tomorrow.*

We're coming back then, Vaughan immediately suggested, but I knew in his heart he'd be worried about his mate the whole time, not to mention that his own pack didn't have their Alpha or Beta at the moment. He'd already put everything on hold to come and look after me, and he didn't need to do that anymore. I could stand on my own, and he would have to get used to that. Just the fact that he would offer meant enough to me without him actually following through.

No, don't. You need to get home. I'll make sure someone takes some pictures and I'll send them to you later.

Are you sure?

I'm sure. Go home and see your mate. Oh, and tell Felix that he doesn't outrank me anymore.

Vaughan's warm laugh filled my head. *I will. Congratulations, Sav. I'm so proud of you.*

Those pesky tears threatened to come again as we closed the link, but one look at my mate managed to chase them away. Even though it hadn't been much more than an hour since we marked each other, I wanted him again, desperately, and from the way he looked at me, I could guess he felt the same.

"What did he say?" Jasper asked, sensing that the conversation had ended.

"He's proud of me. He offered to come back for the ceremony but I told him not to. He's got his own things to do and I'd rather not have to worry about him interrupting anything when he returns."

Jasper's eyes immediately darkened, his wolf close to the surface along with his own desire. "What did you have in mind?"

"I think that's pretty obvious," I teased, walking back over to him and reaching for him, but once again, he stopped me.

"I want to make this night something you'll never forget. What's your fantasy, Sav? Something you always wanted to do but never have?"

My heart beat faster as I stared into his determined green eyes. He absolutely meant it. Whatever I asked for, he would agree, and there *had* been something I'd been thinking about ever since the first time we met in person when he chased me through the woods and pinned me beneath him by the lake.

Some women might have been too demure to state those kinds of thoughts out loud, but nobody had ever accused me of being shy. "I'd like to play a game."

Curiosity joined the desire written across Jasper's face. "What kind of game?"

"An outdoors one. We both shift. I run, you try to catch me. If you do, you can do whatever you want with me."

Jasper's body grew tenser as I outlined my idea, anticipation coiling within him the same as it did inside me. "I think you mean *when* I catch you."

"I guess we'll see about that."

My whole body tingled with excitement as Jasper pulled the door open without another word and we headed back down the stairs and to the back door of the pack house. Most people were inside as evening set in, so no one was around to see us both shed our clothes and shift.

Tala felt almost as giddy as I did. *I'm not going to make this easy on him,* she warned me.

I don't want you to. Make him work for it.

Howling in joy, she took off into the trees. Jasper's wolf gave her a few seconds head start, but soon, the thundering of his paws on the forest floor came up behind her. Jasper's wolf knew the territory better than she did, but that only made her more unpredictable. Tala constantly changed direction, adjusting her course fluidly as adrenaline coursed through our body, the thrill of the chase combined with the anticipation of what would happen when we were caught. We didn't *want* to be caught, but at the same time, we most definitely did.

The fresh air of the Canadian Rockies filled my lungs with each breath, the scent of the trees and the soil beneath my feet, and the sweet marshmallow scent of my mate on my heels spurring me on. My heart pounded in exertion and excitement as we approached the lake and Tala tried to decide if she should go forward, running along the water, or try to turn back.

The moment of hesitation proved to be our downfall. Jasper's wolf must have sensed her indecision and in that split second, he sprinted forward, leaping and pulling down her hind end so that her feet lost their traction and she hit the ground beneath him.

Still, she fought. He wouldn't win that easily.

She slipped away beneath him, wriggling back to my feet as he scrambled after her.

The next time, he pinned her harder, his claws digging into her skin just enough, a warning and a sign of possession. Laughing in my head, Tala twisted back and licked him across the face, startling him so much that he let go and she got away again.

At the base of the mountains, he caught her again. That time, he got her on my back as he pinned her down with his whole weight, his bared teeth just above her, growling at her as he demanded her submission.

Luckily for him, we both wanted to give it. My need for him had been driven higher and higher through the chase, and when I shifted back to my human form, naked on the mossy ground, Jasper immediately shifted too. Hard, greedy hands grabbed my thighs, spreading them around him as he kissed me hard. In that kiss, I could feel the lust of his haze that had been absorbed back into him, the animal side of him, mingled with his natural sweetness. He was all those things, a mixture of all of them, the same as I was.

"You're mine," he growled down at me as he thrust his hard cock into me without any further foreplay, claiming his prize. "Body and soul, Savannah, you belong to me."

With each thrust, I arched towards him, wanting every inch of him, wanting to possess him as he possessed me. "You think you can tame me?"

"I don't fucking want to. I want you to make me chase you, to make me prove myself to you over and over again. I'll do it every time, because as much as you're mine, I belong to you too."

He leaned down to suck on my mark as his hips pumped faster against me, and for a moment, it felt like I'd left my body. Joy and satisfaction and desire and hope and every good feeling in the world seemed to gather within me, growing stronger and bigger until I couldn't contain it anymore. With a cry of pleasure, it burst. I came harder than I ever had before, my spirit lingering somewhere between heaven and earth while my body lay on the hard ground, my mate shuddering deep within me.

Somehow, though nothing about coming to the Ravenstone went the way I expected, in the end, I got exactly what I wanted.

Chapter Fifty-Eight

~Jasper~

The last time I wore a suit must have been years earlier, probably at another pack ceremony where I earned a service award. Thankfully, the one in my closet still fit.

Thankfully, I still had a closet at all.

My house had been locked up when I got exiled, sealed off as a crime scene and abandoned, so although dust sat on every surface and an unpleasant odour lingered in the air, especially when I make the mistake of opening the fridge, all my things were still there where I left them, as if someone had simply pressed pause on my life while I'd been away.

While I began opening windows to air the place out and spraying air freshener into every corner, Savannah curiously explored her new temporary home. Beta Chad and his wife would be moving out of the Beta's suite in the pack house and we would move in, but it would take them a few days to make the arrangements. When we checked in with her that morning, Amanda told us we could stay in a guest suite until our new apartment was ready, but Savannah wrinkled her nose before turning to me.

"I'd rather have a little more privacy until things are settled. Where did you live before?"

That was how we ended up at my old house on the day of Savannah's Beta ceremony, after Amanda had the key located among the evidence storage, and I couldn't help feeling inadequate as Sav examined the small, two-bedroom log house. "I know it's not in the best shape."

"That's not your fault," she quickly assured me. "And I love it. I especially love the quiet."

She had that right. The house sat at the end of a long trail in the forest. We couldn't see our nearest neighbours and people rarely came down that way unless they were looking for me specifically. It made quite a contrast to the busy pack house.

"Maybe we could keep this place as a weekend house," Savannah suggested. "A getaway. A retreat. When we need a break, it would be nice to have a place to go."

"If that's what you want, absolutely. There are some downsides to the remoteness, though. When we get a blizzard in the winter, the snow gets so high, I can't open the door for days until someone comes and digs me out."

"An excuse to stay inside for days, huh? That doesn't sound like a bad thing to me."

Her teasing smile instantly had my blood pumping. It didn't seem fair that she could do that to me with a single look. No matter how hard I tried to keep my thoughts clean, she had a way of dragging them right back into the gutter.

Half an hour later, we were pulling our clothes back on when Savannah's phone rang. She grabbed it while I finished doing up my pants.

"Hey, Vaughan. Did you get home alright?" He barely had a chance to get a word out before she interrupted him. "Wait, let me put you on speaker. Jasper's here too."

She placed the phone down between us on the couch where we'd just been naked, and Vaughan's voice rang out from the little speaker.

"I'm calling to let you know that Calista got home this morning. The flight went fine."

His relief practically bled through the phone. Would I feel that kind of fear every time Savannah was away from me? It certainly seemed possible.

"How's the former Luna?" Sav asked.

"She's stable. She regained consciousness and was able to speak a little bit. Brent explained the whole situation to the doctor, and they're working together to find a long-term solution."

That all sounded like great news, and I could see how much it pleased Savannah too.

She still had more questions, though. "How's the Alpha doing? Does he regret what he did? Will the Luna forgive him? Is there a way for their bond to be restored?"

Vaughan laughed at the rapid-fire interrogation. "Hold on, let me get Callie and she can answer."

A moment later, he put us on speaker too so that his mate could join the conversation. "Hi, Savannah. Congratulations, first of all."

"Yeah, thanks." Savannah obviously cared more about getting her questions answered than bragging about her new position. "Do you know what's going to happen with Amanda's parents' mate bond?"

"Well, I've actually been reading up on werewolf mate bonds since you left. I figured it would be good to know more about them, now that I have one. For ranked wolves, the rejection has to be accepted to fully break the bond. Since the Alpha didn't accept it, the Luna can rescind the rejection and restore their bond. She hasn't done that yet, but if she wanted to, she could."

I never knew that, but then, it had never really been relevant to my life before.

As if she could read my mind, Calista addressed me. "Keep that in mind, Jasper. Once your mate has her new Beta rank, you're stuck with her."

"Hey!" Savannah's outrage made us all laugh, and I quickly leaned over the phone to kiss her.

"I wouldn't have it any other way."

Amanda found a dress for Sav to wear for the ceremony, a pretty, elegant, red one that looked both feminine and professional at the same time. Giving me a wink, the Alpha handed me a red tie to match. The ceremony took place on the large terrace on the front of the pack house, overlooking the lake, with the entire pack gathered below us.

Glancing out at the assembled crowd, I could see many faces I recognized, the faces of my past and my future. My colleagues, who I'd soon be working with again. My cousins and extended family. Near the front, Dan stood with a woman I assumed must be his mate, and he gave me a satisfied smile. Myra was there too, and even Lee made it, though temporarily in a wheelchair. I visited him earlier that afternoon and they expected him to make a full recovery in a matter of days.

Another figure also caught my attention: Troy stood on the edge of the crowd, his eyes fixed on Amanda in a way that made me slightly uneasy. Sav would have to find out the whole story of what happened between them and what Amanda intended to do about him so we could make sure she had all the support she needed.

That would be a problem for another day, though. First, my mate needed to have her chance to shine.

One of the pack elders, a studious-looking grey-haired man with thin-framed glasses atop a thin, narrow nose, recited the official words, reminding Savannah and everyone of what we were there to witness.

"By accepting the position of Beta of the Ravenstone pack, you are pledging to protect and defend this pack with your life. Your loyalty is to the pack first, your Alpha second, and your mate third. Do you agree with these conditions?"

Those were the very rules by which Amanda had been able to depose her father. He broke that oath by placing his mate above the pack, and when Savannah's eyes met mine, I knew that she understood that and took it seriously. I also knew that giving her agreement didn't mean that she would care for me any less. Her heart was big and fierce enough for all of us, and I couldn't feel luckier that I got to be the one to call her mine.

"I agree. From now on, my loyalty is to this pack and all its members." Her strong, firm voice carried easily over the assembled crowd, and Amanda stepped forward to make it official. The elders symbolically tied their wrists together, demonstrating the bond between Alpha and Beta, before slicing through their palms. Confidently, the two women shook hands, mingling their blood between them, and Savannah's eyes widened, looking almost overwhelmed as her old pack link severed and the new one took hold. The gathered wolves let out a cheer as Amanda held their joined hands aloft.

After all that, my own return felt like a bit of a letdown, but Amanda took it seriously as she held out her hand to me once my palm had also been cut. After months of silence in my head, cut off from everyone but Sterling and my uncontrollable haze, my pack link was restored. A rush of belonging flooded my body, like a warm embrace from thousands of people at once, and along with the proud smile my mate gave me, my new Alpha's voice echoed in my head.

Welcome home, Jasper.

THE STORY CONTINUES...

If you enjoyed the book, please take a moment to leave a review. Thank you!

See what happens when Felix returns to the Crimsontooth pack in the third book of the *Rocky Mountain Wolves* series, Hidden in Plain Sight. Coming in January of 2025!

Keep In Touch

For more about my other books and to keep up-to-date with new releases, find all the links here:
https://linktr.ee/melodytyden

www.ingramcontent.com/pod-product-compliance
Lightning Source LLC
Chambersburg PA
CBHW071130180726
48291CB00007B/2124